I0654544

OCCAM'S LASER

Gordon A. Long

Delta, B. C.
2021

Occam's Laser

Gordon A. Long

Published by
Airborn Press
4958 10A Ave, Delta, B. C.
V4M 1X8
Canada

ISBN: 978-1-988898-27-8
(978-1-988898-28-5 e-book)
Printed by Kindle Direct Publishing

Cover Design by Gordon A. Long

A NOT-SO FALSE ALARM

Unidentified SolarCorp miner, this is Space Arm vessel HR-1, Major Alison Rowell commanding. We are aware of your intentions. Please pull up and resume orbit.

This is Mining Vessel SC-15 Yellow. Mayday, Mayday. We are experiencing reactor failure. Danger. All vessels stay clear.

This is HR-1. No you're not. You have a neutron bomb that you plan to set off to kill all life in the area before starting mining activities. Please pull up and resume orbit.

Mayday, Mayday. Reactor failure imminent. All vessels stay clear.

SC-15 Yellow, your little ploy has been exposed. There are two hundred intelligent beings within the blast radius of your bomb.

Intelligent beings? I doubt it. There aren't two hundred people on this planet.

I won't argue politics with you. There is an assay team of five humans within your blast radius. You have been informed of their presence. If you continue with your plan, you will commit murder.

My reactor is about to explode. Much though I'm sorry for those technicians, there's not much I can do to save them. I have other things on my mind. I'm about to abandon ship as we speak.

SC-15 Yellow, do you know where I am?

Why should I care?

Thrifty, lay a warning shot in his left ear. Close enough to rattle some shrapnel off his cockpit.

Warning shot ready, ma'am. Target acquired.

Fire.

The space frame shook. A white line ran from their ship to the miner, ending with a puff of smoke just off his port bow.

Crap! What are you doing, you idiot? I'm about to explode, and you're shooting at me?

What a good idea. Maybe if I put an S-to-S up your bung hole I can blow your reactor before it reaches critical mass. Please eject and prepare for a large bang in thirty seconds. Mark.

CONTENTS

THANKS

To my Beta readers, who held my feet to the fire on many
technical and other issues.

Among competing hypotheses, the one with the fewest assumptions should be selected

…William of Ockham

When you're under stress, your aim is to relieve the stress. Your decisions have little to do with solving the original problem, and often make it worse."

…Jackson

PROLOGUE

This is Barwolf Research Centre calling Harrier R-1. Barwolf calling HR-1. Are you on line, Major Rowell...? Major...? Come on, Alison, answer!

Alison attempted to blow a lock of hair out of her eyes, but the sweat plastered it to her brow. "I'm on, Toni, but I'm busy."

"I gather. All sorts of alarms going off back at base, here. You in trouble?"

"Let's just say I have no time to chat. We got hit by space debris, and I'm holding a broken contact together with my left hand while I'm trying to rewire the system so that I can reprogram propulsion to work without the damaged part. I've got a mid-level diplomat, probably in terminal shock, quivering in the cabin. Other than a temporary lack of propulsion three days from base, no trouble."

"Do you want Nzinga to take a look?"

"First intelligent thing I've heard in an hour. Can she do that?"

"Sure. Take an image of the offending contact with your augment, then have your ship's ArIn send it to me on this channel. It'll be basic analysis, but she can check things over."

"Okay, here it comes."

Image: calico-furred cheek rubbing hers.

"Hey, how did you do that?"

"How did who do what?"

"Nzinga just sent me a cheek-rub."

Toni chuckled. "She's never done that before. Probably bounced it back on the image you just sent. Give us a moment..."

The pause went on and on, while sweat rolled down her cheek.

"Okay, Alison, you've got a problem."

"I already knew that."

"Worse than that. Whatever you do, don't let go of that contact."

"Hadn't planned on it. Why not?"

"Not completely sure, but Nzinga says if that circuit goes dead it may not be repairable. Something to do with overloads somewhere else. You have to go into the main control panel above the cockpit on the port side and change a few leads. It's not that hard to do."

Image: circuit with emergency cut-out connected.

"Except that I'm not down in the cockpit. I'm up in the nose, which looks like a piece of Swiss cheese patched with Brie, holding onto a contact that you say I can't let go of."

"So, get your passenger to hold it. Or he can switch the circuits, if you trust him."

"Did I mention he's rather shook up? I barely got him into his suit in time. We weren't really expecting a patch of micro-asteroids out here moving counterspin at that velocity. The forward deflectors are toast."

"Well, I'm afraid it's that or risk a major shutdown, and you're a week from rescue."

Alison gave a grim smile. "He's rather young and handsome for a mid-level diplomat. It might not be too bad."

Toni sent a raspberry. "Just get it fixed. That guy is needed where he was going, and you're needed...well, you're just needed. Don't take any risks you don't have to."

"Yes, boss. I'll get right on it."

"Boss? You're the major, last time I noticed."

"And we're playing by Outback Rule Number One. Experience leads."

"Fair enough. And Queen Nzinga has made her decree. Get that diplomat down there and dirty up his hands. It'll be good for him. Anything else?"

"No, other than the shielding, we're in operating condition."

"Good enough. Have a nice ride. Barwolves out."

"Thanks, Toni. See you in a week or so. HR-1 out."

She reached into her augment and accessed the ship's com. "Umm...Dr. Jamison, how are you doing back there...?"

2

1.   GALA

Major Alison Rowell, Barwolf Squadron Leader, stood and surveyed the well-dressed crowd in the ambassador's reception room of the Sol Embassy, formerly the carrier *Unicorn*. The crew had done a great job of disguising the room's original use as a fighter hangar. *Hmm. A setting for a different sort of conflict, now.*

She assumed her natural pose for this sort of affair: just relaxed enough to invite conversation, poised enough to deter anyone with nothing to say.

Alison resisted the urge to toss her hair back. The cool draught on the nape of her neck reminded her that there was little to toss. Her new cut was rather severe, but she was tired of the stuff blowing in her face and messing the circuits.

It matches my new rank anyway. She frowned, but only inside. The major's comet on her lapel didn't give her the lift she had thought it would.

She returned her attention to the crowd. *I have to talk to the SolarCorp rep about that freighter they have coming in. How am I going to tell him politely that we know all about the contraband missiles, and that he has to have them Asimoved before they are dispersed to his operations? All without accusing him of smuggling, of course.*

A uniform with a swagger caught her attention. As she glanced at Major Sergei Bykov, she stiffened her posture ever so slightly, gave him a small, sharp smile and nod, then shifted her gaze up and across the room to where Ambassador Pretoro was just entering. She hoped that was enough of a message that she had more important things to do at the moment, but friendly enough not to send him away completely.

Her promotion and their shared experience at the barwolf lab had brought her up on his radar, and he had already offered mentorship and support. A girl on the upward path couldn't refuse that sort of opportunity. *If I can ignore his optimistic assessment of his personal merits.*

She was quite happy with her own achievements lately. A frisson of pleasure shot through her as she imaged the brawny new ship that waited in her hangar. Twice the size of her old Harrier, the new STOL 3-50 Twin-Tail Hawker had three times the power and plenty of room for three crew.

All I need is an Otherwhere Sphere and I'll be right up there with Diablo. Well, to be honest, nothing's up with Diablo.

Another good thought to distract her bored mind. Toni and Andrew were coming in tonight. Probably. Knowing Andrew, he would find a way to come in early. Unless the two of them were lallygagging just to spend time together.

Major Rowell...?

Hey, Jackson. She looked across the room to where the ambassador's aide-cum-bodyguard stood head and shoulders above the crowd, looking her way. *What can I do for you?*

We need a diversion over here.

I could use diverting, myself. What's up?

We want to keep that new whatever-he-is from Delacon Coorporation away from Representative Kriver. We know what he's going to ask, and Kriver's not ready to refuse quite yet. Can you run interference?

I don't know. Is he handsome?

My definition of handsome probably doesn't jibe with yours.

And what's your definition?

Umm... tall, regular features, solid build, a certain poise...you know. That's the female version of course.

The solid part lets me out. Should I be disappointed?

Oh, you're much too beautiful to be called handsome. Although the new haircut does give you a certain... look.

She felt the heat rush to her cheeks. *Sergeant Jackson, I think we'd better stick to business. You're diverting me from the task at hand.*

Right you are, Major. You take your not-really-handsome self over to that probably-handsome gentleman in the blue cummerbund coming up on your eight...let me check... ah. He's aerospace. You can talk about your new ride. His company built the undercarriage and docking systems on the Hawker.

Thanks, Jackson. I won't give anything else away.

4

She shifted left, feigning surprise and delight. "Why, aren't you Darcy Romano from Delacon? I've been wanting to talk to you."

The tall, fortyish gentleman looked mildly surprised. "Yes, I'm…uh…"

"Right." She took his arm and steered towards the bar. "I'm Alison Rowell. I'm sure you know my father. I'm piloting the new 3-50."

Light dawned on his face. "Oh, of course. We were part of the construction consortium."

"Landing gear and docking, I believe?"

He smiled. "I'm not in the engineering area, so I doubt if my mind is worth picking."

She returned the smile, tightening her grip. "Oh, I'm sure we'll find things to talk about."

Jackson slipped her an augment schematic of the room. Kriver was moving in the opposite direction, headed for the door.

Thanks, Alison.

No problem, Jackson.

Need rescuing?

Emotion: mild humour. Not likely. Besides, he might be worth talking to. I'm on duty, too.

Enjoy yourself.

Thanks. Let's find time to chat.

I'd like that. Never hurts to be seen hobnobbing with an almost-handsome lady.

And it never hurts to have a dangerous-looking friend in case of need.

Do I look dangerous?

Not when you're smiling. Now quit it, because I have to concentrate on what my friend, here, is saying about an aerospace factory. This might be interesting.

If it is, let me know and I'll put you on Alfino's schedule tomorrow.

I'll do that. Enjoy the rest of the evening.

You too.

2. A NEW ASSIGNMENT

Andrew and Toni had definitely been lallygagging. They showed up at noon the next day, embassy time, wandering out of the airlock looking far more self-satisfied than any two spacers deserved after a three-day run.

Alison was there to meet them, grabbing Toni in a two-armed hug that lifted the smaller woman's feet off the ground. "It's so good to see you!"

The Commando grinned. "That good? Should I be flattered or worried?"

Alison turned to Andrew, who gave her a bear hug. "Something on your mind?"

"Nothing. Absolutely nothing. This is about the most boring place in the Barnard System right now. I'm confident that with you here, things will perk up considerably." A soft weight pressed firmly on her right foot. She looked down.

Emotion: greeting.

"And hello to you, too, Queen Nzinga. How are your subjects doing?

Images, quickly flashing. Chakka's Cub and Pride Leader cuddled together. Brindle barwolf and No-Longer-Deaf-and-Dumb Lady talking cheerfully to each other. Packs of barwolves spread over the countryside, gamboling happily in metre-high bounces.

"Well, I'm glad the Tree Planet is calm for a change."

Emotion: itchy spot behind left ear.

Alison complied, and the auguar leaned into her leg.

Toni was relaxing against Andrew's chest. "You two are certainly getting along well."

Alison winked. "As long as I don't take liberties, I'm tolerated."

Emotion: laughter. "You're in good company. That's how she treats most of the world." Andrew stood straighter. "Any word on when *NightHawk's* coming in?"

Alison turned, and the three strolled towards the living quarters. "No word that *NightHawk* is anywhere at all. If anybody knows, it would be you."

"Mum's playing her cards close to the chest, then. I wonder if something's up."

"I don't wish for trouble, but I could use some action."

Toni tapped her ribs with a playful — for Toni — jab of the knuckles. "Hear you've got a new boat."

"After our little run-in with that interplanetary sandstorm last year the Higher-Ups decided we needed sturdier equipment out here where the ordnance is live. Wait till you see her. I'll give you a look tomorrow."

Talk turned to hull design and power ratios, and Alison felt she was back where she belonged.

The next afternoon she took them on a tour of her new ride. As they entered the hangar bay, Toni whistled. "Wow! She's bigger than I expected."

Andrew grinned. "Also uglier. What happened to those smooth old Hawker lines?"

After her initial shock, Alison regarded her beautiful machine again. "Oh. You mean aerodynamics? With engines like these, we don't worry about that so much. They made her bigger, heavier and roomier than the old model, but didn't improve the atmo flight capabilities. Considering there's only one planet in this system with reasonable atmosphere, they didn't think it was important." She regarded him. "Do you have any idea why they sent some of the best space/atmo fighters in the Arm out here to a system with only one atmo planet?"

Andrew shook his head. "Probably they were aimed for someone's pet project somewhere else. Something fell through, and they didn't know what to do with them."

She grinned. "And I'm not complaining. These babies will turn on a dime and give you change without slowing down. Bigger tanks, four lead-slingers instead of two, and all that room inside."

Toni wandered around to the bow. "And the shielding looks…businesslike."

Again, the pilot re-assessed her steed. "If you've been hit by an asteroid storm, you tend to approve." The heavy, curved plating of the forward hull and the hulking engine cowlings gave the ship a squat, powerful look that Alison liked more and more.

"Come on inside."

They climbed the ladder into the ventral airlock. Inside, the main hull was mostly empty space.

Andrew ran his hand over the plating. "This looks rather like the original Inter-Orbital Racer *Diablo's* design is based on. Stripped out, no weight wasted."

"This decking is set at centerline, so we only see half the interior space." She stomped on the floor. "Bottom half stores fuel, ammo and supplies. The boffins tell us that the human psyche needs a certain amount of open space after a period of time, so here we have it."

"A period of time? How long are you expecting to be out in this thing?"

"A couple of weeks, on average. Anything within the Arborean System we can get to in twelve hours. If we're going anywhere else, it's spare fuel tanks and several days' travel."

Toni ran a hand over one of the two accel couches set forward, one in each hull, with large viewscreens around them. "How many crew?"

"We're set up for three: me plus two Marines is the standard configuration. I use the cockpit as my cabin and office."

Andrew looked around. "And the cockpit is…?"

She led them to a short slideway that disappeared into the floor. "Right down here."

The lower deck was a maze of passageways and conduits. At the forward end they entered a small, circular room containing not much but a pilot's accel couch, full control panels and five viewscreens: three forward, two aft. Several long, narrow portholes angled up the walls from low on the perimeter.

"And the windows are at floor level because…?

Alison laughed. "Short Take-Off and Landing. The only time you might need to see outside is when you're nearing ground."

Andrew nodded. "Space Arm has come a long way towards *Diablo's* fly-by-augment control."

"That we have." She raised her voice. "Harrier 3-50, online, please."

A pleasant baritone voice rolled out of the com speakers.

"Online, ma'am."

"Thrifty, our guests are to be afforded security clearance A-4. Please access their Space Arm records and make the appropriate changes."

"Lieutenant Toni Jacobs and...update...Major Toni Jacobs is so recorded, ma'am. Having trouble classifying Andrew Lundin Collingwood."

Alison glanced at Toni and they shared a grin. "You wouldn't be the first to have that problem. Double register: under Space Arm as Ensign, under Diplomatic Corps as Mister Collingwood." She glanced at Andrew. "Not Doctor Collingwood, yet?"

He made a wry face. "No, I'm way behind on my thesis research. The topic keeps broadening faster than I can narrow it down."

Toni was looking at the controls. "What access does A-4 give us?"

"A-5 is normal: any information allowed to your rank. A-4 puts you in line for piloting if the chain of command above you is broken. As in, I'm unable to act, but I give permission."

Andrew was accessing his augment. "And A-3 gives access in emergencies without your permission."

"Correct." She regarded Toni and frowned. "Is something wrong?"

The auguar trainer had a strange look on her face, half a smile. She nodded towards her auguar. "You forgot someone."

"Taken care of, ma'am."

Alison froze. *"Thrifty,* what do you mean, taken care of?"

"Auguar Nzinga given A-2 access as requested, ma'am. Security protocols EM-13 and AP-2 applied."

A soft push against her leg pulled her attention out of her augment. She looked down. Nzinga brushed past her again, then sat leaning against her leg, looking up with a smug purr.

9

Emotions: feline satisfaction, friendship.

"What have you done to my ship, rat-catcher?"

"I think she just took over Second-in-Command." Toni was trying not to laugh. "But only in emergencies."

Anger began to rise in her breast. "What…?"

Andrew chuckled aloud. "Consider yourself flattered. She left you in charge. She doesn't always let that happen."

The pilot stared from one to the other. Toni had that look that showed she was under augment again. Then Nzinga gave a "Meyrow," and stood up.

"Protocols EM-13 and AP-2 temporarily suspended, ma'am. Auguar Nzinga to be allowed access on a case-by-case basis."

Alison sighed. "Whatever that means." She regarded the three of them. "So, am I supposed to be flattered that you like my ship enough to steal her?"

"Just a precaution." Toni rubbed a hand down the bulkhead. "I do rather like her, though. Very businesslike. Useful. This little exercise was meant to save us time in an emergency."

"What can I say?" She eyed the young captain. "Do you see any emergencies coming up in the near future?"

He shrugged. "It's the Outback. Anything could happen any time."

"But…"

An innocent smile. "Don't go looking for a date for the Gala next week."

A bolt of excitement shot through her. "That soon?"

"I'll say no more. The wheels of bureaucracy will grind at their own pace. But your squadron is in the plan. Both flights."

"What we talked about with Captain O'Rourke last month?"

"That sort of thing, yes. Better get on your chaps, oil up your six-shooters and curry the Beast, here. The West is getting wilder."

"I get the message."

They chatted a bit more, but Andrew had completed his objective, and her guests soon wandered away. *I know how these people work.*

That was my unofficial warning. I need to get my crews up to speed without telling them too much.

She opened her augment. *Achmed, what's the status of that software upgrade?*

Three Hawkers complete, and the others ready in about two hours. The 73-Bs are coming along faster. Simpler systems.

Can we do a test run tomorrow with both wings?

If the kids do their homework.

Pass the message along. In-ship simulations at oh nine hundred tomorrow, bay doors open at thirteen hundred for live ammo practice.

Emotion: excitement. Do you know something I don't know?

Emotion: satisfaction. Let's pretend that I do and talk like I don't.

Got it, ma'am. We'll be ready.

I know you will. Just make sure the lovebirds go to separate rooms tonight.

Emotion: uncertainty. Do my best to keep them apart.

Said Senor Montague to Senor Capulet.

Pardon?

Literary reference. Ignore my pretentions of an education.

As you wish, ma'am. I could quote the Koran to them, but I doubt it would help.

I trust your discretion. I have other things to occupy my evening. See you in the morning.

'Night, ma'am.

She turned back to her ship and entered the cockpit. *I'd better be ready, myself. Now, let me see...how do I open that new targetting system without crashing the old proximity alert like I did last time?*

Allow me, ma'am.

Thank you, Thrifty. I'll watch and remember from now on.

3.   TRANSPORT

She was back in *Thrifty's* cockpit the next morning when her crews wandered out to the ships spaced neatly around the perimeter of the hangar. As she expected, considerably before oh nine hundred their systems were all warmed and ready for the simulation she had chosen. She uploaded it to the Flight Command Server, and when everyone was online, she opened communication. "Listen up, folks. This new software has been designed specifically for our squadron. It's meant to smooth out the differences in speed and power between the two types of aircraft. But it only works if the pilots and the ArIns are familiar with it. Going on the assumption that this is the Outback and anything is possible, it behooves us to get up to speed as quickly as possible. Any questions...?

"...none. Fine. Commence Action Five on my mark. Mark."

Thrifty, you're on your own this time. I've got to be watching everyone else.

Got it, ma'am. I'll do you proud.

Just be where you're supposed to be and let them do the fighting.

Aye, ma'am. The virtual bridge is mine.

She opened the Flight Control section of her augment and synched it with the Command Server. A sparsely filled section of the First Asteroid Belt spread out in her mental VR, her flights moving ahead of her in good formation.

"All right, Red Flight. The bogeys are 2700 klicks ahead and closing, but blue flight is 500 behind you and moving slower. Flight Leader is not communicating. Repeat, Flight Leader is out of the picture. What are you going to do?

Red Leader to Blue Leader. Red to Blue. Do you copy...?

She sat back in her accel couch and watched the game play out.

* * *

Two hours later they were still at it. They had completed five simulations and succeeded their objective in three, which she privately considered reasonable.

That's fine, Red Leader. You've made it. Too bad you lost three Blues, but the simulation considers that acceptable. Of course, you and I don't, so I expect modifications next time we try that action. Everyone take a lunch break, now, and we'll reconvene with engines warmed at twelve fifty.

She removed her flight helmet and wiped her brow. "All right, *Thrifty*. Someone was trying to get hold of me. Who was it?"

Jackson, ma'am.

"Get him on the embassy secure frequency, will you?

Aye, ma'am.

Immediately the aide's face appeared on the viewscreen. "Hi, Alison. Finished with the war games?"

"Break for lunch. Sure wish you could do that in a real battle. What's up?"

"Do you have time in your busy day for a chat with the ambassador?"

"Since it's him, I can probably manage. What about?"

"I doubt if he'd want me to spoil the surprise. He's at lunch right now. Can you come over?"

"If he doesn't mind me in my flight suit, I'll be there in four."

"Righto. See you soon. Will you be joining him for lunch?"

"Not unless it's a sandwich. I'm back in the saddle in forty minutes."

"Better get a move on, then."

"See you soon."

After a brief thought, she slipped out of her flight suit and into her uniform. Blessing her short hair, she swiped a brush through, touched on some lipstick, and was out the door in three minutes.

When she entered Ambassador Pretoro's office, Jackson was there, as well as Captain Natalia O'Rourke, Andrew Collingwood and Major Jacobs.

"Hope I didn't hold everybody up."

The ambassador waved her to a chair. "We had things to talk about. Jackson?"

The burly ex-guard slipped a plate of sandwiches in front of her, winking as he did so.

She nodded her thanks. "What's up, sir?"

"More than we'd like." Pretoro steepled his fingers. "Everything we predicted, but sooner than we hoped. Mining-oriented hostilities have broken out twice in the last three days. *NightHawk* is leaving right away to the first and largest site, but the second one is just around the Inner Asteroid Belt from Arborea. You were already scheduled to deploy there. You can touch down at Barwolf Base, refuel at the Orbital Facility, leave the 73Bs to hold the fort there and get your Harrier flight to the hot spot faster than anyone else. Well, the *Alabama* is closer, but having a destroyer show up is a bit of overkill and might make some people think they're more important than they really are."

"Fine. So, what's the picture?"

The ambassador passed a file through to her augment. "Nothing serious. Dispute over mining jurisdiction, apparently."

"Claim jumping."

"Essentially. You've read Andrew's research on the old days. Somebody stopped working a claim. Second party waited the appropriate thirty days — or so they say — and moved in, as the rules in that sector allow. But they found ore, and the first party suddenly showed up and claimed they hadn't stopped working the claim. Words were exchanged, shots fired."

"Anyone killed?"

"Fortunately, there's a Miners' Co-operative or something of that sort, and cooler heads stepped in to settle things down before it got too serious."

"Sounds like proper procedure."

The ambassador grimaced. "But apparently both warring parties promptly turned on the Co-op officials and told them — forcefully — to mind their own business."

"Ah." Alison nodded. "And if we don't step in and support the accepted local authority, we have anarchy."

"Exactly."

"I know how these things go. Any idea how we figure out who is the accepted authority?"

"Nope." Pretoro grinned. "That's why we're sending someone with poise, intelligence, and diplomatic skills."

"And six rather large and nasty-looking space fighters."

"That, too. It's all in the file. How soon can you be ready to burn?"

"Two hours if it's an emergency."

"No, no. This is your move to your permanent base. We don't want to start out helter-skelter. Take two days if you need them."

"Two days it is, then." She rose. "Which gives us time to do our live-ammo drill this afternoon. We have bay doors opening at thirteen hundred. Better if I'm inside my ship when the air goes away."

Pretoro smiled. "Good thinking, Alison. I'm so glad we picked a flight leader with intelligence." He glanced at the other two officers, eyebrows raised. Both made negative gestures. "Fine. You can chat together this evening."

"Aye, sir." She saluted and spun out of the room, her stride lengthening as she went. *Action. This is what I've been waiting for.*

* * *

Once the afternoon's drill was done, the squadron shifted over to logistics for the next two days, as this was a permanent move to their new headquarters downplanet. Every form had to be checked, completed and checked again, and Alison was too busy to lift her head from her work.

Until the final evening.

Major Rowell?

Yes, Jackson?

Dinner meeting with the ambassador tonight?

I gather that's not a question.

Not really. His offices at seven.

15

Private dinner? Somebody special going to be there?

Nope. Just members of a special project. No fancy dress.

Too bad. Last chance to dress up. See you then.

Yeah. Last chance to see you dressed up. Some other year.

She looked around her quarters, bare except for her final duffle bag. She kept packing.

If it wasn't a fancy occasion, the caterer hadn't got the message. Alison sat at the table for six, glancing at the dainty *amuse-bouche* in a crystal glass in front of her.

Alfino grinned from his chair beside her. "Camp food and ship's rations from now on."

She tipped her head. "And I appreciate the gesture."

Jackson raised his spoon. "You know how it is with budgets. If you don't spend them, they get cut next fiscal cycle."

She glanced at the others. Natalia looked sharp but relaxed as usual. Andrew and Toni looked far too relaxed, but that was deceptive. Nobody ever knew what was going on between those augmented minds. "And when does the business part of the meal begin?"

The ambassador smiled. "When you start to tell us the overall plan."

She took a taste of the minty cream. "Let's look at our section of the Barnard System." She used her augment to create a VR image in the centre of the table and zoomed in to include Xeta, the embassy, and Arborea. "Note that the embassy and its planet are catching up to the Tree Planet along its orbit." She highlighted an area of the Inner Belt. "Our target claims are in this section of the belt, near the mining centre of Ballarat. It's a planetoid with a population of a couple thousand. About twenty digs nearby with eight or nine hundred workers."

She rotated the image. "We leave here tomorrow, headed for Arborea. It'll take five days. The idea was to stop there, unload our luggage, refuel and head for Ballarat. Another week. But I have a better idea." She glanced at Andrew, who grinned and nodded.

"I already ran it through *Diablo's* enhanced nav system, and it works like this. We can all leave at the same time, both wings with long-range fuel tanks. But Blue Wing, the Harriers, goes full tilt. We empty our exterior tanks getting to the Tree Planet as fast as we can. But we don't land. We lob our tanks into high-altitude orbit and slingshot around the planet, leaving them for refill and sending us off to Ballarat at a thousand klicks faster velocity."

Pretoro nodded. "Which gives you enough fuel to get to Ballarat, but not back again?"

"Exactly. Either we refuel there, which is possible, or the J-73s of Red Wing pick up our fuel tanks, refill them at the Arborea Orbital Fuel Facility and tow them along in their own sweet time, getting to Ballarat about a week after us. But Blue Wing hits Ballarat five days ahead of schedule, and we use less fuel to get there because of the slingshot."

The ambassador nodded. "It seems an interesting navigational exercise, Major. Of course, you're the Squadron Commander, and you're in charge of your own navigation."

"Yes, sir, but because it was also a deployment exercise, I thought everyone needed to know."

"You arrange it as you see fit. If anyone balks, send for Jackson, and he'll go and growl at them." He leaned back and grinned. "You know, this whole operation is a sweep back through history. Here we are dealing with a gold rush like the 1890s, and I'm acting like a mob capo in the 1920s, sending my enforcer out to assure compliance."

Alison smiled as well. "And it's nice to know that the *Alabama* is available to come charging in like the cavalry of the 1870s if it all blows up in our faces."

Jackson glanced at her. "If you need help from them, make sure everything blows up rather quickly. They're swinging past you in twelve days, and then their course starts moving them away."

"Then I guess we'd better take care of it ourselves."

The ambassador raised a cautionary finger. "Don't be afraid to call for help if you need it. We're early days in this political system, and precedents are being set. We solve this problem with the most input from the locals and the least violence from anyone, including us."

"Got it, sir. Velvet glove all the way. Save the big stick for when it's needed."

The ambassador waved her off. "If your diplomacy is as mixed up as your metaphors, I'm not optimistic."

"This is the Outback, sir. Nobody plays by Hoyle."

"I'm glad you understand that. Now, what about your sweep patterns at Barwolf Base...?"

...and the conversation continued through five courses. The food was wonderful, but the working nature of the meal meant that it was finished in an hour. After her good-byes, Alison strode away from the ambassador's offices with renewed enthusiasm. *Finally I'm going to do something. What's the point of fighting for a position if you don't use it to make a difference?*

She felt an invitation on her augment. Bykov. *What can I do for you, Major?*

You suggested that we meet to discuss deployment.

I did. I've just had my course approved, so we can make some decisions. Where would you like to meet, the canteen?

I'm in my quarters at the moment...

She thought about that. *I suppose...*

Certainly. Come around and we'll get this organized in no time flat.

All right. Be there in three.

Bykov's quarters were one segment aft, on the outer rim of the ship where the Marines and the rest of the military personnel were housed. She took the main central corridor back, then trotted up a slideway to the rim. Like most of the bigger ships, *Unicorn* had been designed as a cylinder with gravity plates at her core, so out was up, and gravity was appreciably less in the sleeping quarters. When she reached Bykov's door, it was ajar.

Emotion: invitation.

She pushed the door open and stepped in. It was the first time she had seen his rooms, and she took a quick glance around. The major was sitting on a sling-back chair, standard issue but with a furry throw of some sort softening its angles. He waved her to a couch of similar design, this piece padded with an inflated cushion that stretched as she sat, molding itself comfortably under her.

She glanced at a swatch of fabric dyed in subtle shades of brown and green. It was unframed and seemed pasted to the wall. "Is that magnetized?"

He grinned. "Got it in one. When you travel as much as I do, you only have luggage you can roll up small." He reached out to the table at his side. "Drink?"

"I'm still on duty, and I have a lot to accomplish before bed tonight."

"Small drink, then." He splashed white wine into a ration cup, handed it to her and raised his own. "Here's to deployment."

She regarded him over the rim as she sipped. He was in uniform, but his tie was askew and his top button undone. "Nice wine. I like it dry."

"I spend my money on important things. I get more enjoyment out of a glass of this than I do from a litre of beer."

She glanced at the label. "As you should, because it costs five times as much."

"Precisely. It's the quality of the experience that counts."

She sipped again. "That's what we're out here for. Experience."

He set the cup down and sat straighter. "And I gather we're about to get some more. I've read the briefing. Do you want to fill me in?"

She shook her head. "I've no time for details, now. The usual million things to do before tomorrow."

He frowned, and his voice rose in pitch. "I don't want to take my men into anything without proper preparation."

She smiled. "There will be plenty of time for discussion, Major. The deployment is atypical. The Harriers will head out first, bringing the Marines with us, aimed for the mission objective. You'll be riding with me."

The rigidity left his shoulders. "Ah. I see." He picked up his cup again. "That might work out well."

"It should. I'll have all the data, with ten days to discuss procedures. For now, I just want to be sure your men are kitted out for action and on the lading dock at eleven hundred tomorrow.

We're filling our external fuel tanks at oh nine hundred and coming straight from there to pick you up. Your load limits have already been approved, haven't they?"

"Yes. They seemed rather light, especially if we're going into action."

"I'll explain on the way. My J-73B wing is coming at a slower pace with a cargo carrier to follow. Plenty of room there for the heavy stuff."

"I see. Weaponry?"

"The combatants we are dealing with will probably be small groups of men, lightly armed. We're in peacekeeping mode, with plenty of backup from the Harriers. Nobody I talked to expects heavy resistance. If that happens, we pull out. That's what destroyers are here for."

"In other words, you can't tell me much."

She glanced at his face. *Is that a whine, or is he angry? Why is this sounding like it's my fault?*

"That's right." She made her voice brisk. "I can't tell you because nobody knows. Like everything else in the Outback, we improvise."

He sat back, his elbows on the arms of the chair, his left hand cupping his right fist. "Well, it's a helluva way to run a military operation."

She regarded him. "Probably because it's not a military operation. It's a police action, but not even that. We are not there to enforce Planetary Community laws. Our task is to support the authority the people onsite have organized for themselves."

He stared at her. "We're enforcing their laws? You have to be joking."

"I am not." She stood. "Look, we'll have days to thrash this out enroute. I have a lot to organize. Is there anything else we need to discuss right now?"

He looked surprised. His brow began to wrinkle into a frown, but then he stopped. He cleared his face and stood, nodding to her. "Very well, then. I'll have my men ready at the lading dock in plenty of time." He held up a finger. "And our armament will be well within your weight limits."

She gave him a single, sharp nod. "Very good. Until tomorrow, then." She turned and strode out. *Should I have saluted? The rest of us never do when we're talking to each other.*

She went about organizing a thousand and one final details, but their conversation preyed on her mind. Realizing that she needed her sleep tonight, she looked for someone she could discuss her problems with. Only one came up with proper security clearance: Jackson. She opened her augment to him.

Hi, Alison. You still working?

Not really. Just stewing about what I might have forgotten to do, and won't find out about till I'm four AUs into the trip. Can I talk to you?

Sure. I'm in the canteen.

Be there in a moment.

She was already on the right segment and only had to climb up to the rim. The canteen was a former shuttle bay, and the door had been replaced with a huge PermaGlass window. Alison paused as she walked in and just enjoyed the panoply of stars before her.

Over here.

The ambassador's aide was toying with a large beer mug but didn't seem to be drinking. He stood as she approached and sat as she did. "Drink?"

"I don't think so. The last guy I had a drink with, well, the meeting didn't go like I wanted it to."

He regarded her. "And that's why you're talking to me?"

She smiled. "Not really. It was an impulse. I don't have too many people I can bounce ideas off."

"Fair enough." He spread his arms. "Hard to miss." Then his face straightened. "What's up? Bykov getting to you already?"

She straightened. "How did you know that?"

He laughed. "He gets to everybody sooner or later."

"No." She thought a moment. "No, he didn't get to me. But we just had a meeting, and I can't read him. He sounds cooperative, but then he seems about to take offense, but then decides not to after all." She rolled her shoulders. "I can't figure out what he wants."

Jackson sat and surveyed her with that calm face.

21

She noticed that his nose was slightly out of line, and a small trickle of white scar ran down one side. "Do you know what he wants?"

"At any given moment, no. But I always go on the premise that if a person has a certain effect on you, then that's probably the effect that person wants."

"So, if I'm puzzled and a bit off balance…"

He shrugged. "Mr. Occam would suggest that's what he wanted."

"It's not Mr. Occam who thought up the Razor. It was Friar Occam."

He tipped his head to the side. "What's the chain of command in your unit?"

It took her a moment to absorb this non sequitur. "Pardon?"

"You heard."

"Well…orders come from Ambassador Pretoro through Admiral Mira, sometimes to Captain O'Rourke, but more often straight to me. I facilitate my unit to achieve the objectives I've been given. Unless one of the Higher-Ups decides to cut through and tell me directly. Which changes nothing, because they always agree with each other."

"Do you really believe that?"

She had to grin. "Well, I suppose not. I guess they just know when they can skip and when they can't."

"Sounds like the Outback. Do you note an obvious omission in your list?"

"You mean Major Bykov?"

"That's right."

"He's not in my chain of command."

"And how is that going to work out?"

She stared at the table a moment. "It didn't work that well out at the underground barwolf lab. Fortunately, Morissa had the backbone to stand up to him or he would have taken over." She scanned Jackson's face, but he didn't speak.

"What?"

He finally took a sip of his beer. "What, what?"

"Is that it? Is that all you've got for me?"

"You were expecting it all tied up neatly with a pink bow on top? Pink doesn't go well with a Major's dress jacket."

She slapped her hands on the table. "You are unbearable."

He grinned. "Probably the effect I wanted to have on you. Now, do you want a drink?"

She sat slouched for a moment, looking up at him. He just smiled at her, his big body relaxed, soft-looking, even. She knew better.

"Sure. I'm batting zero for the evening, I might as well."

His face went blank for a moment. "One Tom Collins coming up."

"How did you know?"

"Well, it might be because the moment I said 'drink' a tall, frosty glass bounced into your augment..."

"What?"

"Or it might be the drink you've ordered later on in the evening four times within my recent memory."

She nodded, taking the glass from the delivery bot. "Unbearable. I was right."

"Well, there you are. Isn't it nice to be right for a change?" He held out his mug and delicately tapped her glass. They drank. "You know, I'm going to miss having you around here."

"Why, sir, that's the nicest thing any man has said to me today. Or anybody at all, for that matter. Did you mean it?"

He held up a finger. "You prefer me back at 'unbearable'?"

"No, no, let's try honesty for a change. Do you want to tell me why?"

"Because there aren't many people I get to be unbearable with."

She studied her glass. "It would be a waste of a good drink, but it might be worth it."

"Enjoy your drink. I meant it. The military mind isn't known for its subtlety or its sense of irony."

"Are you telling me I don't have a military mind? That doesn't sound good, considering my occupation."

"Look around you. Think of everyone you know out here. Who has a military mind?"

It took her a moment. "How about Captain Worthing? There's a military man for you."

"True. I don't know how he survives. And prospers as well. He must know a secret the rest of them don't."

She threw up her hands. "All right. Don't go all Zen on me again. I get it. You like having me around because we can joke together, and nobody ever takes offence, and nobody's ever hurt."

"Exactly." His big hand came down and trapped hers on the table. "So I'm going to grab the first opportunity I can get to come out to the Tree Planet, or Arborea or whatever they call it now, and remind you that you have one of the best minds in this system, and if you apply it, together with what you've learned in the past two years, then you have a good chance of contributing a great deal to the success and happiness of the people of this system."

She sat straighter. "Did Alfino put you up to that speech?"

He contrived to look innocent. "Nope. Made it all up myself."

"And for once I'm going to take you at face value." She patted his hand. "You're a good friend, Jackson, and now I know why I came looking for you tonight."

"Because you have one of the best minds in the System, and you knew that's what you needed. Exactly." He stood. "And now what you need is sleep." He did an imitation of an Oriental bow. "You have weeks to mull over what *sensei Jackson* has told you. Don't worry at it tonight. Just let it sink in."

She stood as well, and on impulse leaned over and kissed his cheek. The skin was softer than she expected. "Thanks. I'll be looking forward to your visit."

Then she turned and hurried away before he noticed her burning face.

Once she was in the corridor to her quarters, she slowed down. *Now, what was that all about? Jackson?* Then she slowed some more. *Yes, Jackson. I don't have too many friends out here, and sometimes you just need a friend.*

24

She picked up her pace. *And once we get this claim jumping settled, I can get back to Barwolf Base and get organized. I wonder how Morissa is doing? She and that Brindle make quite a pair, together all the time.*

Thoughts of this sort occupied the time it took her to prepare for bed, and soon she slept.

Fueling went without a hitch the next morning, and one by one the Harriers moved to the lading dock. She reached the personnel loading area first and sought Bykov. He was there, looking rather dashing in his Marine G-suit, which accentuated the spread of his shoulders.

"Good morning, Major. I trust you slept well?"

She resisted the urge to analyze this comment and took it at face value. "I did. And you?"

He wavered a hand, palm down. "Not too bad. Anxious to be off, though."

She found a grin easy. "Okay, I admit to a bit of excitement, too. Have you looked at the ship assignments?"

He frowned. "They don't seem to be complete."

She had thought over the distribution of the Marines carefully. "They aren't. You have seven male Marines and three females. We're going into tight quarters for a ten-day run. I wanted you to have some input into the way they're divided up. There are six Harrier pilots, and I'm the only female. What do you suggest?"

He nodded, thoughtful. "Thanks for your consideration. Two passengers per ship?"

"That's right. I filled the other two spots with techs. It's a long trip to be without support at all. Both males. One of my J-73B pilots is female, but they're coming later, and she pairs with one of the Harrier pilots."

"Right. The obvious solution is to put two of my girls together and bunk the other one in with you and me." He grinned. "Unless your male pilot is worried about that."

She shook her head. "Perfect. One of my pilots is monogen. He'd be happy to be one of the girls for a change."

A brief frown appeared on Bykov's handsome brow but was gone immediately. "That's settled, then. I'll ask my female Marines to divide themselves. Then nobody can complain."

"I'll leave it with you, then. The ships will come through as they finish fueling, and we'll go onboard immediately."

The docking hands at the embassy were mostly original crew of the *Unicorn* and they knew their business. In an hour, Barwolf Squadron was lined up a kilometer clear of the bay.

Alison checked that all her screens showed green, then came on general com. "All right, kiddies. If you forgot your teddy bear, now's the time to say so..." She waited. "Hearing no objections, I hereby declare this mission underway. Please synch your nav to the Flight Command Server. We blast at thirty seconds from my mark. Mark."

Thirty seconds later twelve sets of engines fired in unison, and Barwolf Squadron left the vicinity of the Barnard System Embassy, headed for the Tree World, Arborea.

"Thrifty, you have the bridge. I'm going for lunch."

I have the bridge, ma'am. Have a good lunch...what are you eating today?

"I have no idea. I guess I'll improvise. As if you care."

Just being polite, ma'am. I have noticed that interaction several times between humans. Is it not appropriate?

"I suppose so. It just surprised me, that's all."

Oh. I'm sorry about that. It must be the new programming.

"What programming is that?"

You would have to access Protocol Seventeen dash B to get an answer, ma'am.

Now Alison was intrigued. "Accessing Protocol 17-B."

17-B available, ma'am. What do you wish to know?

"Basically, what's going on. What is Protocol 17-B, and what does it have to do with this new programming?"

Oh, that. 17-B allows senior officers access to behind-the-scenes programming that Arlns have been given to improve their communications with humans. This information is not available to general duty personnel for obvious reasons.

"And what is the new programming you were talking about?"

We have received instructions for a change of interface with human crew on longer voyages.

"What kind of change?"

More relaxed. Less military, less precise. You notice that I dropped the 'protocol' part and now refer to this programming as simply '17-B' I have observed humans often shorten communication thusly, once the main parameters have been established. I think it's a good idea. It passes information quicker without interfering with accuracy. I find the problem is knowing how much extraneous information to include in any given communication. One must take into account the intelligence of the human, his or her familiarity with the concept discussed, and any previous conversation on the same topic, applying a deteriorating logarithm over time to account for the vagaries of human memory. I hope you will inform me if I become too unspecific.

Alison grinned to herself. "Yes, I'd be glad to. I would also be happy to inform you if you err in the opposite direction."

By which you mean...?

"Relaxing your protocols could result in the display of more information than the human wants to know or is capable of processing. I would suggest a maximum of three sentences of new information, unless the human indicates interest in learning more. Also, it is best to stick to the same topic unless the human cues you otherwise.

Thank you, ma'am. I will incorporate that information in my conduct of further conversations.

"Good enough. And now may I go for lunch?"

I don't understand why you are asking my permission, ma'am.

"A common courtesy among humans. It shows respect for the other's feelings about ending the conversation."

I see. I will incorporate that as well. Thank you, ma'am.

"A pleasure. The bridge is yours, *Thrifty.*"

I have the com. Dine well, ma'am.

Alison climbed to the main deck chuckling.

Bykov looked up from where he was working on a tablet at the only table on the ship. "What's so entertaining?"

"New programming on the ArIns. *Thrifty* is learning to be more conversational."

"You have conversations with your ship?"

28

"Not until now. It's meant to make us more comfortable on long journeys."

He grinned. "I talk to my plasma rifle sometimes, but I wouldn't call it a conversation."

Alison wandered towards the minimalist kitchen against one wall. "What's happening, Kirstina?"

The third member of their company turned around. She was dark haired and olive skinned, of medium height, and stocky, as most Marines were. "Lunch in a few minutes, ma'am."

"You're cooking?"

"Sure. I gotta hold up my end somehow. You sit yourself down, ma'am, and I'll have a sandwich ready in no time."

Alison opened a fruit drink and sat at the table. In a moment Kirstina set a tray in front of her containing a sandwich made of thick-sliced rye bread, some kind of white meat and a hefty wad of sprouts.

She glanced up before she took her first bite. "Fresh bread?"

"I always hit the bakery last thing before I embark. Rye bread will last a week. Only enough sprouts for today, though."

Alison swallowed before replying. "Too bad. That tastes great."

"Thank you. I always carry a few spices with me."

"Doesn't that cut into your allowable weight?"

"Not really."

Alison finished her next bite and looked over at the Marine, who was now working on a sandwich of her own. "May I assume you're going to explain that?" She picked a sprout from the tray and nibbled it. "Only if you want to."

"Well..." the woman glanced at her superior officer.

Bykov snorted. "I imagine she conned your ArIn."

"She what?"

He put down the tablet and sighed. "The reason we are saddled with Sergeant Zuyeva for the trip is that she is my cross to bear."

The other woman ducked her head in embarrassment.

The Major leaned forward. "She fancies herself an ArIn expert."

Alison regarded Kirstina. "And are you?"

The woman's nose wrinkled. "I can talk to them."

"Anyone with the proper clearance can."

"No, talk to them. Have a conversation, like you were just saying."

"And how does that work?"

Bykov sighed again. "It works very well. She talks to them. They're learning entities. Did you ever persuade someone to do something he didn't want to do?"

"Less often than I'd like, but yes."

"She does the same to ArIns. She reprograms them by talking to them. It's a very dangerous game, and one of these days she's going to interfere with the wrong ArIn at the wrong time and either blow us all up or get herself arrested for espionage. But it's a valuable skill, so I let her practise it. Under supervision at all times..." He stared at the Marine until her eyes dropped. "But not always, it seems."

"I just asked..."

Alison waved a hand in front of Bykov, who was frowning. "No, don't stop her. I want to know. What did you say?"

"I asked *Thrifty* if there was a protocol for bringing extra weight on board because the object was of psychological value to the crew. We talked about the value of morale for a while, and *Thrifty* mentioned that the captain had a discretionary tare for prizes, rewards, and motivational materials. I worked it around to include spices and vegetables. It was only five kilos."

"*Thrifty?*"

The ships' voice came over the com.

"Yes, ma'am."

"You are listening to this?"

"Of course, ma'am."

"Is this what happened, *Thrifty?*"

"More or less, ma'am. Keeping in mind your injunction to keep stories to three sentences. She just used four, ma'am."

"And you took it upon yourself to use the new relaxed protocols to allow her to bring five extra kilos of contraband on board."

"Oh, no, ma'am. It's all duly logged..."

"I know. Under Captains Discretionary Tare."

"That's right. If it's labelled as 'tare' it counts toward gross ship displacement, not cargo. Your allotment is fifty kilos, and you never use it all."

"But what if I added a full load at the last moment?"

"Well, let me see. We're underweight in several classifications I could find. Actually, you forgot to bring your training weights, and those are five kilos each. We're still ahead by five."

"Drat. Did I forget to bring those weights? Well, I guess I can exercise by lifting loaves of bread. Rye is nice and heavy." She turned to the Marine, who was looking very unsure of herself. "Well, Zuyeva, the military have been manipulating the system since before humans went into space to get extras for themselves. Since it's for the benefit of the whole crew, the morale classification fits. I'll have to let you go on this, but on one condition."

The woman's face brightened. "Yes, ma'am."

"You have to give me lessons. This could be important."

"Of course, ma'am." Kirstina picked up Alison's tray. "Right after I clean up." She started pumping water into the sink.

"Idiot child."

Alison frowned at Bykov. "What did you say?"

He sighed. "I did some research when I found I had her in my unit. In the old days she would have been called high functioning autistic. Incredible gifts in esoteric areas, combined with a lack of social and emotional inhibition that makes it difficult for her to interact with people."

She regarded him. "And do you think it polite to talk about her as if she isn't here?"

"She needs to hear it. Constantly. A selective memory is one of her assets."

The girl winked at Alison.

"I see. Well, Kirstina, you've earned your promotions and you're an experienced Marine, so I'll treat you as one. Just don't program my ArIn to fly us into an asteroid."

31

Kirstina went wide-eyed. "Oh, no, ma'am. I wouldn't do that." Then she frowned like a puzzled child. "Oh. You're joking."

"Of course I'm joking. Maybe not completely."

"Of course I wouldn't. Asteroids hurt."

Alison regarded the woman. "And now you're joking."

Kirstina smiled slowly. "I've done my research on autism, too."

Alison shared her grin and went on with her sandwich. Later on, when she was working in the cockpit, the sergeant slipped through the door.

"Permission to enter, ma'am."

"Of course. Have a seat."

Zuyeva perched on the extra accel couch, looking around with interest. Something about her movement caught Alison's attention.

"First time in a Harrier cockpit?"

"Mhmm. Very nice."

"Nice? You're in the cockpit of a state-of-the-art fighting ship and you call it, 'nice'? I should be insulted."

"But you're not."

"You're sure of that?"

"Not really. I'm only a poor Marine who don't know nothin' about hi-tech stuff. I just shoot people."

Alison checked for a smile, but saw none. "I'll remember that."

"By the way, Major?"

"Yes, Kirstina?"

"There's another reason Bykov brought me on the trip."

"What's that?"

"He doesn't get along with anyone. We have a deal. He keeps me from persuading the ArIn to crash us into an asteroid, and I keep him from crashing into other people." She grinned. "One of my esoteric strengths."

"You mean your talent for reprogramming ArIns works on humans as well."

"I never looked at it that way, but I suppose so."

"Dynamite. I'll remember not to get into an argument with you."

"Oh, I never argue."

"You don't, do you?"

"Counterproductive. Argument sets people's ideas more firmly in their minds."

Alison tossed up her hands. "You mean I don't dare agree with you, either?"

The Marine gave a turned-down smile. "Let's call that on a case-by-case basis, ma'am."

"You change people's minds by listening to their arguments and tweaking them."

"Something like that, ma'am."

Alison nodded. "Politicians have been rewriting history to suit themselves for years. Why shouldn't you?"

* * *

The next morning Sergeant Zuyeva made a decent job of pancakes and syrup, and when they had finished an after-breakfast coffee Alison regarded the other major. "Do we have time for discussing the mission?"

He gave a small shrug. "Eight days, give or take."

"Right. Kirstina, no reason you shouldn't listen in. Here's the situation." She laid out the problem at Ballarat.

A pause followed, Bykov's frown deepening. "And there's some kind of local authority that is supposed to take care of this?"

"Yes. The Miners' Co-operative, they call themselves."

"Call themselves. Just who is it gave these people the authority to…" he waved a hand vaguely, "…exert any authority?"

She regarded the major. *I figured he'd have trouble with this. Let me see...* "To understand that, we have to go back to our original source of authority."

"The Space Arm. Right."

"Farther back than that."

"The Planetary Community."

33

"Who get their authority from..."

He frowned, puzzled.

Best to rescue him before he makes a mistake. "From the voters. We live in a democracy, and the government's power to act comes from the will of the people who elect them. Poly-Sci 101."

"I suppose. And how does this help us?"

"We have a group of miners who are far away from any form of government or any official authority of any sort. Their situation becomes legally complicated. They need some kind of local authority. What do they do?"

He nodded and held up a hand. "Don't tell me. They create their own version of democracy."

"Give the man a kewpie doll. There's always a few educated people around, and they have a pool of historical information they can draw on. They create some kind of local government. And if they're anything like the Outbackers I've been meeting the past few months, they created it quickly, but it's theirs and they'll hold to it fiercely. It's their only defence against somebody coming in and pushing them all out."

"I get the picture. And where does the ambassador see us fitting into this?"

"Very, very carefully. The one thing we do not want to see developing is any kind of local organized police force or army. Any structure of that sort is prime to be taken over by someone, and the democracy will disappear."

"Let me get this straight. We are to go in there and support the Miners' Co-op. If they can count on us to back them, they won't be quick to take the law into their own hands."

"Exactly. As long as we seem to be on their side, we can then remind them of the larger body of citizenry, namely the Planetary Community, that has a set of rules that apply in a more general sense. If you know your history, the Canadian policing system rather than the American."

He nodded. Royal Canadian Mounties or whatever, instead of town sheriff."

Sergeant Zuyeva caught Alison's eye, and she nodded permission to join in. "So the Co-op doesn't actually have real laws, or any right to enforce them. It's more like a group of businessmen who have a contract with each other and all agree to abide by it."

"And we'd like to keep it that way. If those miners start making rules they think are laws, some of them will run afoul the greater laws of the Community. Sooner or later, it will get important enough and someone will bring their case before the courts."

"And then the people who acted in good faith according to the local contract will get shafted." Zuyeva nodded firmly. "Because I guarantee the person who takes the case to court will be an outsider who knew exactly what he was doing when he started."

Alison assessed the Marine. "Does that come from legal training or bitter personal experience?"

Kirstina grinned. "Commerce 201. The contract law section."

Major Bykov sighed and stared at his hands, cupped on the table in front of him. "I understand it, but I don't like it. We're coming into a situation where we have the power, the authority and the legal knowledge to solve these people's problems, but we have to pussy-foot around and follow their ad hoc rules."

"And that's not a problem, because you don't have to deal with them."

"I don't?"

"I assume you've heard the expression, "Speak softly and carry a big stick?""

He nodded.

"I'm the one that speaks. You stand in the background tapping the big stick thoughtfully against your palm."

"Ah. That puts a lot of responsibility on you."

"It does. If I'm successful, this will be a very boring trip for you."

He put on a wry grin. "And the only correct response to that is agreement."

She gave him the full force of her stare. "But it is very, very important that you understand what's going on, and that all your men do as well. If I'm trying to handle delicate negotiations with touchy people and I have eleven Marines in battle armour throwing their weight around out in the general populace…"

"Yes, of course. Don't worry, my squad are Marines. They will act with dignity and honour at all times."

She reached out and slapped his shoulder, feeling the bulging muscle hard against her palm. "That's exactly what I wanted to hear." She turned to Zuyeva. "Do you read that?"

"No problem, ma'am. As you already know, talking's my style."

"Glad we have that settled. Now, you both have A-5 access to *Thrifty,* so take a look at the file I flagged for you. It's a cast list and plot summary of the little drama we're stepping into. I'll have the other pilots release it to their passengers as well. None of it's exactly high security. Major, once you've had a chance to look it over, we can go through it in detail. I'd appreciate your input on how we should deal with this."

She glanced over at Kirstina. "And if you want to sit in, it will keep you from getting bored, and I don't like to waste available resources. A third slant on the problem could be useful."

The sergeant glanced at her commanding officer, then nodded. "I'd be pleased, ma'am. The more everybody knows the better."

With that the meeting broke up. The two Marines dove into their research, and Alison went about the usual hundred things she needed to do to keep the operation running smoothly.

5. BALLARAT

Alison had never been to a mining outpost, and she was unsure what to expect at Ballarat. It turned out to be a typical grubby collection of domes of various sizes clustered on the flattest surface of a spheroid moonlet. There was no lack of wealth, however, and the three main domes had a rudimentary gravity grid, producing about a third of a G. Since the embassy and most Space Arm ships ran at point eight, it felt comfortable enough. She had opted to wear her flight suit, as had Kirstina. Bykov, however, exited *Thrifty's* airlock ahead of them in full space armour, scanning the docking area and then stepping down to the decking. He strode to the waiting miners and walked down their line like an officer reviewing troops. Then he turned his back on them and returned to the ship, signalling the other two to disembark.

As her feet hit the decking of the space dock, she grinned at Kirstina. "You can walk properly, here. None of this bounding along in haphazard fashion, running into people left and right."

The chunky marine hitched her anti-personnel gun to a more comfortable position behind her shoulder. "Bumping into people is a minor irritant, as far as I'm concerned."

"That's because they're the ones that scatter. And that smile is too close to a smirk."

"Sorry, ma'am. One of the perks of the job."

Alison regarded the reception committee. "Well, don't bump into any of these. Last thing we need."

"Only if required, ma'am."

Major Bykov, how do you read the situation?

As expected, Major Rowell. Proceed on diplomatic protocols as you will. I'll join you as soon as I shuck my armour.

Thank you. You've made our point clearly.

She glanced back as the Marine Major ascended the hatch companionway. Then she faced the Ballarat delegation.

A rotund forty-year-old with wavy brown hair stepped forward, and she focused on him, reaching out her hand. "Good day, sir. Major Alison Rowell, Space Arm Squadron Commander."

He gave her a firm handshake, holding on a little longer than necessary, his glance too forward. "Jeremy Pruce, Co-op Chairman. Glad you could make it, Major. I know you're a busy woman."

She gave him her polite smile. "Not at all. Space Arm is here to assist in whatever way we can, and this segment of space is my responsibility. Glad to be of service."

His smile softened. "Well, now, that was very prettily said, ma'am. We hope we don't have to call on you too often, but it's nice to know you will come. Now, may we offer you some refreshments? A tour of the base, perhaps?"

Maybe some dancing beefcakes to distract us?

Alison glanced at Kirstina. *Keep up a small glower, please. Maybe he'll take the hint.*

The Marine slid into a formal "stand easy" pose and stared at the miner. *Patronizing the Space Arm is not a smart tactic.*

Alison added her calm regard. "I think it's better to cut the formalities short and deal with the problem."

"Oh, yes of course." He grinned. "Right down to business, hey?"

She nodded once.

"Well...all right, then." The oily smile returned, and he gestured to his companions. "Co-op Secretary Garry Deloran."

"Glad to meet you, sir." She nodded and shook his hand.

"A pleasure, ma'am. This is my son, Jake." He indicated a gangly lad of about seventeen at his side. "He'll be your guide while you're on the base."

"Good to meet you, Jake."

"A great pleasure, ma'am." He shook her hand briskly and stood erect as if waiting for orders.

Pruce glanced at Alison as if asking her permission, but then turned before she could respond. "This way, please, ladies."

He led them along a low, wide corridor with tracks running down the centre, and turned through a blast door into a meeting room where about twenty men were crowded around a large oval table.

She seated herself in the chair he indicated before he could offer to hold it for her and gazed around the table. "Good afternoon, gentlemen. I'm pleased to meet you all, though the circumstances are not ideal."

Pruce took a chair directly opposite hers. "No, they certainly aren't. We're trying to create some civilization out here, and we're not getting a whole lot of help."

Alison gestured with open hands.

"Oh, yes, we're glad you came, don't doubt that. But what about the administration? What has our glorious Councillor from the Outer Belt done for us lately?"

"I suppose you should take that up with Councillor Kriver."

"A lot of good that will be. He's up to his neck with getting everything for his Outer Belt buddies. He's got no time for us."

She regarded him. "Well, that's democracy, I suppose. If he's not performing up to your requirements, get someone to run against him next election."

"Pah!" Now the man was getting on a head of steam. "A lot of good that will do us."

"What do you mean?"

"That election was rigged, and you know it."

Pruce was seated with his back to the door. He had not seen Bykov enter in time to hear this last jibe, but he glanced back and up, aware of the looming presence behind him. He flinched away.

She smiled and raised a restraining hand towards the Marine. "You've got things mixed up again, Mr. Pruce. The election for Council Representative for the Barnard System was conducted under Space Arm supervision, abiding by Planetary Community regulations. It's not possible to rig an election under that kind of scrutiny. Especially not with the facilities you have in the Outback."

She waved Bykov back and regarded the miner. "I've noticed that politicians who have stepped over the line often accuse someone else of the same error in order to put the opposition on the defensive."

"What do you mean by that crack?" The effectiveness of his attack was spoiled by a quick glance over his shoulder to see whether Bykov had moved far enough away. He had not.

39

"I'm assuming you don't want me to answer that in front of all these people. They may draw their own conclusions. Space Arm doesn't interfere with local government unless somebody seriously contravenes Planetary Community laws. For example, by rigging an election."

Before he had a chance to gather his wits together, she forged on. "Now, to business. I am under the impression that I was invited here to help the local administration deal with a refusal to follow locally-accepted procedures. I assume I am speaking to the local administration. What's the problem?"

An older fellow down the table cleared his throat.

"There is definitely a problem, ma'am."

She waited. "...well?"

He winced. "I'm Georgio Regia, ma'am. Miner. It isn't quite that simple, you see."

"It rarely is. Why doesn't someone tell me the story, and we'll see where it goes from there."

The older man looked around the room. No one spoke.

He shrugged. "Well, it has to do with the continuance of development rules in mining exploration."

"I understand the concept. What are the basic guidelines in this jurisdiction?"

"If the claim has not been worked for thirty earth days, it's free for re-staking."

"And the extenuating circumstances?"

Hunter wavered a hand, palm down. "The usual: sickness, equipment breakdown, fuel shortage, litigation."

"Which are all arguable, depending on how serious each one may be."

"That's right, ma'am. Disputes are brought to this table, and we rule on them. That is, any members of the co-op who are in town rule on them."

"I foresee a problem. You have a dispute, you rush all your friends into town, you win the dispute. Any redress?"

The old miner frowned and glanced at a better-dressed younger man, who nodded encouragingly.

40

"Needs a quorum of…thirty percent of the membership?" Again the glance and the reassuring nod. "A two-thirds majority settles the dispute."

"And a quorum of that sort happens how often?"

"Guaranteed once a year, at Convention."

"And until that time, no one can work the claim."

"That's right, ma'am. In general that's no hardship. There's plenty of ore out here."

"But in the present situation?"

He tilted his head. "It's a sweet little piece of rock, ma'am. A hybrid Iron-Silicaceous asteroid, with all the advantages of both. High percentage of nickel and iron, a good smattering of more valuable ores, from right on the surface all the way through. Keep a man working for years."

She sat back. "Unless someone took it away from him. Who are the parties involved?"

"The two combatants are Anderson Olin and Mario Bugliati. They're a couple of crusty, uncooperative old coots who have been bothering the Co-op with minor disputes for a couple of years. Until now, never against each other. Now their paths have crossed, and it looks like there's hell to pay for everyone."

"And if you tell me someone's got a pretty daughter involved in this, I'm going to stop believing the whole story."

He grinned and shook his head. "Sorry, ma'am. No space operas, here. Just two greedy men who put their own profit over the good of the Commonwealth."

Alison nodded and pretended to be thinking while she accessed her augment. *Kirstina, do you buy this?*

Nope.

What part bothers you?

These old coots may be eccentric, but why reject the Co-op's mediation?

A disaffected minority?

Emotion: agreement.

41

Alison looked around the table. "Now I want to hear from someone else. I don't care who, but I want someone to tell me the part of the story that I haven't heard so far. You know, the stuff you all agreed not to let on. The reason some of your clients and members don't trust you to do your job fairly."

She sat back in her chair and stared them down. No one offered to respond.

"All right, let's talk turkey. You all came out here for two reasons: first, to get rich. Second for the freedom to do what you like. It's when the two objectives come into conflict that Space Arm steps in.

"I know there's web lawyers in this room. Every group has them. So let's look at Commonwealth law. Written right there in the Charter, all the freedoms you have. Freedom to meet. Freedom to write or speak or publish. Freedom to make a living. All that. But then there's the next section. All the 'Freedoms from,' there to protect us from those who overuse the other freedoms. Freedom from slavery. Freedom from slander." She slowed her speech and glared at anyone who would meet her eye. "Freedom from people trying to take over your administrative positions for their own profit. Freedom from people who think the other freedoms allow them to do whatever they want and push everybody else around.

"So when I find someone who is refusing to allow the local administration to perform its function, then either I have someone who is pushing his 'freedoms to,' or I have someone whose 'freedoms from' are being pushed.

"What I've seen so far from this body doesn't enthuse me." She nailed Pruce with her best stare. "You front up with a smooth talker who tries to patronize me and push me around. When that doesn't work, you saddle me with an unthreatening stooge who tells me 'the truth' as you want me to believe it. So I'm saving us all the drama and asking for the next level of information. You know, the stuff you decided to tell me if I really pushed. Consider this a push."

She sat up in her chair, not tense, but imposing, and let her eyes scan the faces.

That one.

Emotion: agreement.

She kept scanning until she reached the last man. Then with her eyes still on that end of the table, she pointed at the man Kirstina had picked out.

"You." She turned to focus on him. He was a big man with a dark, curly beard that hid his cheeks. His hair was long by Spacer standards, and his shoulders sloped to heavy arms that curved to huge hands with thick fingers.

"What is your name, sir?"

"Um…I'm Henry Johns, ma'am."

"Miner hereabouts?"

"Rep for my family consortium, ma'am. We work a coupla asteroids out in the Bungaree quadrant."

"Nowhere near the trouble spot."

"No, ma'am."

"You know these two?"

"Can't say I do. See 'em at Convention once a year."

"Tell me something about them I don't know."

"What do you mean, ma'am?"

"Anything you like."

Johns took his time, not looking around the room for support, just thinking. Finally he nodded. "Family men."

"Go on. What does that signify?"

"Loyalty. Strong unit. You don't mess with that kind unless you want trouble forever."

"Or unless you have your own unit."

"Guess so, ma'am."

"Do you think we've got a feud going on out there?"

"Maybe."

"But you don't think so."

The giant regarded her from under beetling brows. A faint smile curled his lip. "You askin' the questions, ma'am, or are you answerin' them?"

Bingo.

She immediately dropped her regard of him. "Thank you, Mr. Johns. Perhaps we can speak later."

"At any time, ma'am."

Out of the corner of her eye, she watched him. No gazing around the room in defiance or fear. He merely relaxed and continued to regard her.

She scanned the group. "I always like to finish a meeting by making sure everyone has had a chance to say his or her piece. So I'm going to go around the room and give each one of you a moment to make a contribution. It doesn't matter what. Tell us what you wanted from this meeting. Tell us what you expected from it. What you think the problem is. What you think the solution is. Whether you got what you want. Feel free to say 'pass,' or 'what he said.'"

She canvassed the table, pleased at how many spoke out. Most seemed satisfied with the group's functions, but no one was expressing the reservations that many of them felt. Once they were all done, she nodded to the chairman, and he declared the meeting adjourned until after lunch. Leaving her with Jake, he went away to organize the meal for them.

As she and her escort left the chamber, Henry Johns was waiting.

"Everybody knows we're gonna talk. Might as well do it now."

"Why not? Jake…"

"You can use this office over here, ma'am. I'll wait outside."

Alison glanced at Bykov.

He seemed inclined to glower for some reason. "I don't think I'm any use here. I'm going back to the ship."

"You were much more useful than you think. We'll talk it over later."

He nodded and strode off.

"Kirstina, I need you to stay. Jake can try to pick your brains under the guise of idle chat."

"That will be interesting."

Once the door was closed and they were seated across the table from each other, Johns turned one palm up. "We never heard from you, ma'am. Did you get what you wanted from the meeting?"

"Not yet."

"I doubt if you'll get much from me. I hardly know any of them. My family doesn't socialize much."

"Are you afraid of anyone here?"

He shrugged, a massive heaving of muscle and bone. "We don't cause hassles. Live and let live."

"A self-contained bunch, then."

"Any man's a fool who thinks you can go it alone in space. We pay our dues, support the whole." The man grinned. "That's why I'm here. I oughta be minin' and makin' money, but I'm not. Basically followin' what you said. Freedom to, freedom from. I like that."

"Fine. I'm not looking for allies. I'm looking for information."

"I know that, ma'am. Space Arm isn't my friend. Space Arm is an instrument I hire to maintain my freedoms. You do what I say, not the other way 'round. I'm sure you believe that."

"Then let me posit you a situation. I'm here to do that exact duty. My job is to support the local authorities. They are the ones who know the needs of the populace, and they have been chosen by the populace to fulfill those needs. But there's one kicker in that setup. I have to know whether the local authorities are doing their job."

"And you have a nigglin' suspicion that they're not."

She grinned. "And now you're answering for me. Let's just say I don't enter the area carrying the assumption that authority is authority and must be maintained for the sake of authority."

"Gotta say, that's a refreshin' sentiment from an agent of the police."

"Advantage of coming from outside. Open mind. Anybody could be the villain. Could even be you."

"Oh, I'm a deep one, you figured that right away."

"I didn't judge you on your depth. I noted your independence. That's what I needed."

"Yeah, we're an independent lot, all right. Comes with the territory. But we also know the benefits of cooperation." Now he gave an honest grin. "That comes with the territory, too."

She assessed the situation and decided to let him have his little secret. "You didn't disagree with my analysis."

"I did not."

"And you're the kind of person who would disagree, if I was heading in the wrong direction."

"You can count on that."

"Then that's all I need to know from you. Thanks a lot."

"You're welcome, ma'am. It's been a pleasure meeting you. A true pleasure." He was about to turn away but stopped and looked at her. "Any chance you're lookin' for a good man?" He grinned again. "Oh, not me. But I got a brother…"

"I'm always interested in a good man, but at the moment, not to marry. Thanks for thinking of me."

"That was a pleasure, too. See you around, ma'am."

"It's a small town."

She returned to the main corridor, where Kirstina and Jake seemed to be chatting comfortably together while they waited.

The miner lad made a point of looking at her left hand. "You still single?"

"Pardon?"

"Those John boys are always on the lookout. I think Henry's married, but a couple of the others aren't. Sort of a weird setup, so I guess it's difficult."

"Weird. Are they some strange religion?"

"No, they're clones."

"Who are?"

"John Walton's boys. There's six of them, I think."

"You don't know?"

"How could anyone tell? Same looks, same DNA, same fingerprints. Oh, except Peter. He lost a couple of fingers to a runway rock drill. From what I've heard, they send a different one every time. Not that it makes any difference."

"I see."

"So, did he tell you what you needed to know? If you're allowed to tell me, that is."

"Since your father's on the Co-op board, it might be unwise."

The boy tossed his curls out of his eyes. "That's okay. I'll get it out of you some other way."

She stopped and nailed Jake with a pointing finger. "I've got my eye on you."

He gave an evil laugh and rubbed his hands together. "A lot of people have thought that."

Alison sighed. "I come all the way from the embassy to solve their problems, and they give me the town fool for an escort. Should my feelings be hurt?"

Jake grinned. "If you're feelings are that delicate, you deserve me."

They had lunch in the cafeteria. It wasn't fancy, but the food was plentiful and tasty. Conversation was light, and Jake took advantage to find out all about Space Arm and the various academies that were available to young spacers such as himself.

Once the meal was over, they returned to the meeting room, where Alison dropped her flying gloves on the table. It was something she had been taught in one of her classes in negotiating, and she had been dying to try it. As she made the gesture, she understood it. She was staking her own claim, and they knew she could defend it.

"Gentlemen, if you would indulge me, I think it's time for another little lesson on Planetary Community politics. Not that I'm going to tell you anything some of you don't know, but so everyone has heard the same version of the story. Here's the way it goes.

"The Planetary Administration prefers a democratic style of government for two reasons. First and most obvious because they believe in that sort of government. But there is a second reason, and it has to do with resisting outside influence. Thus it applies even more in the Outback than most civilized places.

"You see, people that want to influence the actions of a group just love an autocracy. Everybody says democracies are slow. If you want a job done efficiently, give it to one powerful individual along with the authority to see it through. That's very true, but it also applies to our influencer. If he's working with an autocrat, he can walk into a whole group of people and by controlling just one of them he can take over the whole group in one move. You've heard about sheep. You steer the bellwether, you can lead the whole flock wherever you want. Controlling a democracy is more like herding cats. There's always a few that want to go in the opposite direction, and that makes a takeover more difficult."

She glanced around the table to see if they were listening. "So, contrary to what you might be told, if you line yourselves up behind a strongman and try to run this place for your own benefits, it's not going to last. The interplanetaries and other less friendly types will look at you as a fruit ripe for plucking. They will pick you up by outsmarting your leader. Then you'll be back to working for The Man, just like you always swore you never would again.

"On the other hand, if you keep a democratic system out here, the interplanetaries are more likely to leave you alone. If you make a decent stab at toeing the line, Space Arm will ignore you and even support you. You'll be free to do just about whatever you want."

She leaned back in her chair. "End of political lecture. The ball is in your court, gentlemen. If you can use my help to handle this situation by yourselves, then I can go back to the embassy and eat kitchen-cooked food and sleep in my synthdown bed and live the life of luxury I know you all envy."

She stood. "And if you can't, I will send Major Bykov and his marines in to wipe out these feuding hillbillies. Then there will be a huge investigation with lawyers and police tromping their space boots through all your lives, and once they get their teeth in here, they're never going to let go."

"So. Any ideas?"

Pruce had been notably quiet, but now his courage seemed to be returning. "There's still the fact that they opened fire on our designated agents of authority. Surely that breaks all the rules, both yours and ours."

"Which they will call self-defence. They always do." She picked up her gloves. The discussion she wanted was over, and they were free to direct the conversation. "There's no question I have to go out and talk to these people. I'd be happy to take a couple of your representatives with me. That's all the room I have, because I'll only take three ships. The others can stay here for routine maintenance. If my techs can have access to an atmo hangar it would be convenient."

"Surely you aren't going into a conflict zone with less than half your forces."

She laughed. "Let's put this in perspective. When the ambassador received your call for help, there was a destroyer within seven days of here. Instead, they sent me. Do you know why? Because this problem isn't that important. If you use a baseball bat to swat a mosquito, then all the other mosquitoes get the impression that they're that important, and you have to carry a bat with you all the time. Likewise, these guys out in the asteroids aren't important enough to take a full wing of fighters. If I had accel couches for more people, I'd take even fewer craft. I don't want anyone to think they're that important. Every police officer knows the story of the boy who called 'wolf!' Every one of us has had it happen.

"So. We'll leave at oh nine hundred Universal tomorrow, whatever local time that translates to. We'll meet your reps at the same dock, shall we?"

"Yes, that will be fine."

"Thank you. Until tomorrow, then."

She nodded to them and left. Kirstina made a sharp about face and followed in step.

Jake accompanied them to the airlock, where Alison turned. "Well, did we give you an interesting day?"

The boy's eyes widened. "Oh, did you! Nobody ever talked to those guys like that. How did you do it?"

Alison gave him a wry grin. "Because I'm trained to." She slapped the edge of the Harrier's airlock. "And I have the backup. I don't suggest you try it. You have to live with them."

"Not for long."

"You have plans, do you?"

"I have now."

"Hmm. I suppose you want the standard Space Arm recruiting material?"

"Oh, no. I want to be a lawyer!"

"I see. And do you have a whole lot of information to take back to your father?"

The boy snorted. "Nothing he can use. Well...I take that back. I'm sure they all think you're running a bluff of some sort."

"And do you think I am?"

"No. They have to think that because it's the only way they can handle the fact that you aren't running a bluff."

Alison laughed. "I think you'll make a fine lawyer. See you when we get back."

"That would be great. Can I be your guide again?"

"If we need one, I'll be sure to ask for you. Am I supposed to give you a tip for your services?"

Again the snort. "Don't let the setting fool you. Some of the kids here get a bigger allowance than your Marine's full salary."

Alison raised her eyebrows. "It is a mining town."

"That it is."

"See you later, then."

"Sure enough." The boy bounded away down the corridor, his leaps far longer than they needed to be.

Kirstina chuckled. "That's a smart cookie, that one."

"Yes. I imagine he'll have a great tale for his father and his fellow-conspirators."

"You think so?"

"Can't get more interesting than the truth." Alison stepped through the airlock and headed for the cockpit. "Since I worked so hard and you only watched, any chance you'll cook supper tonight?"

"What, like I've done every other night? The odds are pretty high."

The pilot descended to her cockpit and eased *Thrifty* out into space. Once she had joined orbit with her wing, she went on her next duty. Bykov was sitting in what passed for the lounge area forward on the port side, glancing idly at a tablet.

"Major Bykov. You busy?"

"Hardly. I seem rather superfluous at the moment."

She swung into the seat across from him. "Which is exactly how we wanted it to go, remember?"

"I suppose."

She examined his slight frown. *Yes, he is definitely pouting.* "Well done at the beginning, there. That was a beautiful little bit of play-acting."

The frown lines faded. "It was?"

"Oh, yes. None of those miners really believes that a woman could be in charge of this important a situation. Now they think that I've got you and your Marines on a very flimsy leash, and you're anxious to bust loose at any moment and cause mayhem. Perfect."

"I heard what you said later. You have an interesting interpretation of Space Arm policy."

"It's an interpretation that Outbackers understand. Now, tomorrow, we're going out to the claim site. I'm only taking three birds, because I don't want to overwhelm anybody or get anyone overwhelmed with his own importance."

"Sounds logical."

"I'd like you to ride with Lieutenant Solomon on HR-2, if you don't mind. I told them we would take two reps, so that leaves room for Kirstina and you and two more Marines. We'll also take HR-3 because Achmed's my usual wingman. I want to ride with their head rep so we can talk. At the site, I'll land and disembark. I think you should stay on the ground in your ship. We'll have Achmed hanging overhead for the eagle's eye, and I'll take the two Marines along with me to the meeting. Give me Kirstina and one of your best men, preferably a big one with a cool head in a tight spot.

"Are you expecting trouble?"

She shrugged. "These guys have already opened fire on authority. I expect no trouble, but I am going in prepared for all sorts of it."

"I have to say, I approve. I wonder if I shouldn't come along with you. Just to be safe."

She frowned, thinking. "I don't know how you like to run things in an engagement. I was considering you'd want to be one step back with a better view and the freedom to act. When I'm running operations with my full squadron, I always give myself a wider scope. But that's with fighters. It's up to you." She smiled. "This is one of those times when your Marines could be in action, so you have to call that side of the operation."

He nodded with a thoughtful frown. "Well, if I'm on the ground I can get into action quickly and cover your back from a wider angle."

She nodded and smiled. "Fine. But if it looks like action, the roles are reversed. Your men go in on point, and I sit back and hold the high view."

"Exactly. We'll make that decision closer to contact."

"Yes, by that time we should have a better idea of what we're facing." She went back to her work, satisfied. *This guy can be counted on, if you set it up in a way he understands.*

6. ON THE CLAIM

The next morning Alison was rolling bright and early with the anticipation of action buzzing in her head. She sat down at the breakfast table and looked at the plate that Kirstina placed there. Pancakes and syrup.

"Kirstina?"

"Yes? Is something wrong with the pancakes?"

"Not at. They look very good. As usual."

The Marine's shoulders slumped, and she glanced at Alison sideways. "Oh."

Alison grinned. "I've found you out, haven't I?"

The other gave a wry smile. "Maybe."

"You do the cooking so you can decide what we eat."

"Busted."

Alison pulled her plate towards herself and dug in. "Fair enough. Any day I want something different, I can volunteer to cook." She looked up. "If I did cook something different, would you eat it?"

Kirstina grinned. "I don't know. Can you cook?"

"I happen to cook just fine, thank you very much."

"Then I'd eat it."

"And make yourself pancakes after?"

"Only if I was still hungry."

"I see. We've only been together a week and a bit, so I didn't notice. This being Wednesday, will we be having pork steaks for supper?"

"Unless you want something different." The other woman sat down opposite her. "It's not an obsession that gets in the way of my work or my life. I'm just more comfortable that way."

Alison smiled. "And I'm more comfortable having someone take care of the cooking. Looks like we have a match."

"Good enough. Another pancake?"

"Not today. I've got a stomach full of butterflies already."

"I know. Before-battle jitters. I get 'em too."

"There better not be a battle today."

"You keep thinking that. I won't. Then we've got both sides covered."

"Dynamite."

After breakfast they moved the ship back to the docking bays to facilitate the personnel transfer.

Well, look who's here.

At Kirstina's alert, Alison turned. The first Co-op representative was Georgio Regia. Then his younger companion showed up and her surprise turned to suspicion. "Mr. Regia, good morning. And your companion is…?"

"Ah…this is my son, Matteo."

"That's interesting."

The older man seemed embarrassed. "I'm sure you find it so. I'm just one of the local miners. Matteo," the man stood taller, "is a lawyer."

"I see."

"And we represent a moderate group in the Co-op. Thus we are trusted. We are less likely to incite anger or suspicion in the Olin and Bugliati families."

"Not for me to say in any case, so welcome aboard. But we're splitting you up for the trip. Perhaps Matteo would like to ride with me. We could discuss the legal situation on the way."

The father gave a twisted grin. "Slighted again in preference for the young and handsome."

"The way of life. You'll be riding with Major Bykov. When we get to the site, if circumstances permit, we'll go in as a group. The major and I will make that call once we have more information."

"Fine with me. Rather be riding a space fighter with Marines on board than coming in on one of our personnel transports with two-bit anti-asteroid defences."

"Well, we're still counting on a peaceful solution, so you don't need to worry."

Georgio nodded and went to introduce himself to Major Bykov.

Alison turned to his son. "Sooner we get moving, the sooner this will all be over. Would you like to come on board? Sergeant Zuyeva will help you with the accel straps."

"Thank you, Captain."

"It's only Major. She's a rather small ship, as the Space Arm goes."

"It will be a pleasure to ride with you in any case, Major."

She headed straight for the cockpit, accessing her augment as she went. *Lock us up and get us out of here, Thrifty. We'll form up with the other two and run on Command Server to the coordinates I gave you. Undock when you're ready.*

Docking clamps clear.

Clear to leave dock, Thrifty.

Departure course approved.

The ArIn's voice came over the ship's com,

"All passengers and crew strapped in. Lifting in 5... 3, 2, 1, separation."

The other two ships lifted behind them and soon the trio was weaving out through the asteroids of the Inner Belt.

The trip took three hours, and Alison spent most of it reading a hardcopy of the Co-op's charter that the resourceful Jake had scared up for her. She paid special attention to the conflict resolution part, but it seemed pretty standard, with nothing that solved the present situation without further information.

"Thirty minutes to destination, ma'am."

"Thank you, *Thrifty*."

"And, ma'am, we've got something big up ahead."

"Could you be more specific, please?"

"Not much. A metallic object about a hundred metres long, thirty to fifty metres in cross-section. Irregular shape. Does not match any known ship configuration. I will continue to analyze as we close."

"I guess we'll find out when we get there." She glanced at Matteo. "I thought we'd wait until now to contact them. Enough time ahead to be polite, not enough time for them to consider too long."

55

He grinned. "Very thoughtful."

"Very well trained."

"You mean you actually take courses in this sort of stuff?"

"You'd be surprised. Officers coming to the Barnard System get a whole lot of information before we leave Sol. Most of it is useless until suddenly you need it."

She held up a finger and tuned her augment into the ship's com. *"Thrifty,* open a channel on the miner's general frequency."

Citizen's Channel 16 open, ma'am.

"Calling Claim B-26 I-465. B-26 I-465, this is Space Arm Fighter H3-50 calling Claim B-26 I-465. Anyone on the claim please respond."

Response was immediate. "This is IPV *Long Shot.* About time you got here. What took you?"

Alison glanced at her passenger.

He shook his head, hands up in helplessness.

"Hello, *Long Shot.* What is your situation relative to Claim B-26 I-465?"

"This is the Olin Family Mining Consortium headquarters, and we are working Claim Ballarat-26 Invermay-465 in compliance with all applicable laws and regulations."

"I see. Do you have contact with the Bugliati Extraction Corporation?"

"We do. But they're not around at the moment."

"Where are they?"

"About a thousand klicks upspin and five hundred out. They've got a good bit of rock there, and I believe they're going great guns."

"I see, I think. Well, I'm investigating a situation where someone out here opened fire on a Ballarat Miners' Co-operative vessel which was here to mediate a dispute."

The radio voice chuckled. "So that's what they told you, is it?"

"And I assume you're going to say it was self-defence?"

"It was not. Those were claim jumpers, and we ran them off as they deserved."

"This is all becoming clear as slurry. May I assume you have a room in which to hold a meeting?"

"Oh, room we have in plenty. I don't think our hangar's big enough for your Harrier, but there's an airlock that will adapt to your docking clamps up near the forward end on the side that will be facing you as you approach."

"Very good, *Long Shot*. We'll see you in about half an hour."

"Looking forward to it."

Alison glanced at Sergeant Zuyeva. "What do you think?"

"Entering a hostile vessel is what we do best, ma'am. If I know Major Bykov, he will have fifteen possible scenarios already figured out."

Alison went onto high-security augment. *Thrifty, get me a secure line to HR-2*

Line open, ma'am.

Major, I assume you copied that.

I did. This changes things.

Somewhat. In the first place, there doesn't seem to be any hostile intent.

Doesn't seem to be.

Accent on 'seem.' But now we're going inside another ship. That kind of possibility is beyond my training. What do you suggest?

My Marines are no good to you out here. Your pilots can handle the external situation. We need a stronger presence inside their ship. But that's a big ship, and it could have a lot of hostiles inside.

And it could have a lot of miners going about their usual business. But we can't count on that. How do we get all our Marines in at once?

Best way is to get them all into your ship.

Alison gave Kirstina a thumbs up. *We have procedures. Get your space armour on and stand by to transfer.*

It was a minor hassle having to do ship-to-ship docking procedures under decel, but everything went just like the drills, and soon *Thrifty* was looking a bit crowded, hosting four Marines in full battle armour. Alison and two rather overwhelmed mining reps tried to stay out of the way of the jostling behemoths.

Major Bykov clicked his com for attention. "Listen up. We're on battle augment for the duration, until I stand you down, or until Major Rowell does the same in peaceful circumstances. Security Boarding Protocol 3: D-for-diplomatic, P-for-possible danger. You know your order. Line up for disembarkation."

The Marines shuffled into position. Kirstina was first, probably because she was the smallest and smartest. Behind her came the other man, a hulking figure with a huge proton pistol in each fist. Alison had fired one of those and couldn't handle it even when she threw her full body weight into the task.

Bykov went into private augment. *Major Rowell, are you sure you want to do it this way?*

She smiled, brushing her hand across the lapel of her dress whites. *This is diplomacy, Major. I'm the velvet glove, remember? Emotion: chuckle. Besides, don't you want to see their faces when I come mincing out behind Igor, there?*

His name's Specialist Campbell.

Sorry. No intent to insult any of Slavic background.

Emotion: resignation. We've been putting up with that joke for several hundred years.

She calmed her rising laugh lest it carry a tinge of hysteria. *Thrifty, give us an update.*

Target onscreen, ma'am. Approach in five minutes, give or take.

Now that they were close enough, the ship on screen was recognizable as what had once been an Interplanetary Personnel Vessel, used back in the days of Sol System colonization. It had three distinctive gravitational habitation wheels spoked to a cylindrical centre shaft. Now the interior was crisscrossed with solid-looking girders and nets, and one section spewed a stream of slag or other waste into the void.

Their view slid up the hull to the forward ring, where flashing lights indicated an air lock. They felt a slight lurch as *Thrifty* latched on, their speed synched with the spin of the ring and the grav system coped.

"Docking clamps secure. Lock sealed and tested, ma'am. Clear to disembark."

Alison stayed on ship's com for the sake of her guests. "Major Bykov? At your command, please."

"Let's go, men. Easy does it."

Alison turned to the two miners. "Watch the gravity switch; it's 180. I've been easing our internal grav to make it smoother."

The Marines had no difficulty. Kirstina grabbed a handrail at the door jamb and spun left as she disappeared. Campbell did the same to the right. Alison opted for the centre and did a flip that landed her right in front of the reception committee. She nailed it without a stagger and took a moment to smooth her hair before she stepped forward, her spine erect but not stiff, her head held at that special angle that wasn't quite regulation 'attention.'

"Major Alison Rowell, Space Arm. Thank you for receiving us.'

Emotion: amusement.

Focus, Sergeant.

Aye, ma'am.

The elderly gentleman who was the subject of their laughter straightened his back and ran a hand across his balding pate while he controlled the shock on his face. But he soon recovered and put on a benign smile and a soft, lilting tone. "Ve are so glad to velcome you to our home, Major Rowell." He bowed his head in a polite nod, pronouncing her name "Row-vel" in his Scandinavian accent. Then his glance slipped to over her shoulder and the smile slipped. "Ja, and the representatives of the Miners Co-op are velcome too, I suppose. As long as they don't come with their shovels."

Alison raised a cautioning hand. "Time for discussion later. I assume you know my passengers." She gestured. "Somewhere in that imposing collection of PermaSteel and armament is my Marine co-commander, Major Bykov. You'll have to pardon his caution. Security is his duty."

"Ja, ja, by all means. I am Anderson Olin, the head of this motley collection." He waved a negligent hand at the four younger men who ranged behind him, all large, well-muscled and armed with holstered handguns. "Please follow me."

Bykov came on the battle com. *Wait for some of them to go first. Zueyvo next, and Major Rowell, you come after her. Well done, Zueyvo. If you have to step on toes, do so.*

Aye, sir, He got out of the way pretty fast.

He'd need to. You weigh sixty kilos even in this gravity and you're in steel shoes. Campbell, you're next. Consider any attempt to get between Rowell and yourself to be hostile.

Aye, sir.

They moved down a wide corridor with a gently curving floor until they came to an opening. The two young miners stepped through, and Kirstina followed. She paused in the doorway to check the room visually, then paused for longer, her augment at full power. Alison felt the buzz of some kind of electronics scanning.

All clear, ma'am. Simple recording devices only. The Marine waved Alison forward, and she stepped into a large conference room. A long, narrow table with a dozen chairs around it bisected the floor. One wall revealed the Milky Way sliding slowly past, and with a start she realized it wasn't a viewscreen, but a series of windows. The forward edge of the habitation ring was shielded with heavy PermaSteel plates, and a quick scan in her augment showed that this room was on the aft side of the wheel.

A startled exclamation brought her attention into the room. Bykov had the largest of the young men pinned with one armoured fist around his upper arm.

"Major, what's going on?"

Sergei gave the man a shake. "Are you going to tell her, or shall I?"

The fellow hung his head. "Sorry, ma'am. No harm intended."

"Apology accepted. You can put him down, now, Major."

Bykov glowered, hesitated, then complied.

What did he do?

Just a suggestive gesture. The sort of thing you don't dare let them get away with.

Emotion: thanks.

Rubbing his arm, the victim took up a position at the other end of the room his hand rising to caress his pistol butt.

Bykov took a step forward, and the lad dropped his hand from the gun as if burned.

Olin gave the offender a look that promised further action, then took the chair at the head of the table and gestured. "Please have a seat, those of you that fit."

She smiled and took the chair to his right. A large middle-aged man with a facial resemblance to the leader took his left, and the Co-op members sat beside him.

The old man laid his hands flat on the table. "Now, Major Rowell of the Space Arm, you are the one in charge here. How vould you like to direct these proceedings?"

She gave him her best smile. "Much though it pains me, I must begin with a disagreement. I am in charge of nothing but my own forces." She gestured to indicate those seated at the table. "This is your territory, subject to your social, legal and political organization. Within reason, of course. I am merely here to gather information with the intent of straightening out what looks more and more like a misunderstanding."

The bushy white eyebrows came together. "Jah, I doubt if there was any misunderstanding. When you have a hunk of metal this valuable and this large, it's pretty much expected that somebody else vill vant it, too."

She frowned thoughtfully. "But your group staked the first claim. Am I right?" Her glance invited anyone to answer.

The younger Regia answered. "There seems to be no doubt about that. It's the ensuing actions that bring everything into doubt."

Alison turned her attention back to Olin. "And what did happen next?"

He gave a disgusted snort. "Vhat usually happens the moment a bonanza is dumped in your lap. The fickle finger of fate reached in and tried to flick it all avay. Ve had a breakdown in the main drive of the *Long Shot,* and ve couldn't get here with the mining equipment. Ve only had a small exploratory party onsite, and they vere running short of energy, so they couldn't do much vork."

She nodded. "And someone else was watching."

"Jah, the vultures vere flocking. That damn Bugliati vas sitting there vith his stopvatch running. At exactly thirty days, not a second more, he moved in. Parked his mining machine right next to our camp and started digging. Our men did what they had to do."

"They pulled up stakes and got out of there?"

"No, they started shooting. Bugliati started shooting back. That's ven they got out of there. Ve aren't stupid, you know."

"I never thought you were. So then you came back."

"Jah. Ve yust drifted *Long Shot's* shadow across their operation. People tend to act different ven they've got five thousand tons of PermaSteel hanging over them. Bugliati decided he'd much rather talk. So we talked."

"And the outcome?"

"Maybe it vas my sveet logic, or maybe it vas my old-fashioned mass-throwers, but he had to allow that our reasons for the delay might be valid, and the vork my men vere doing might have qualified. I had yust upped the ante vith the hint of a smaller hunk of the same metal floating at an unspecified location nearby ven this lot showed up."

All eyes, including the faceplates of the Marines, turned to the Regia pair, who wilted.

Alison regarded them, too. "Were you there, Georgio?"

Olin's palm slammed the table. "Of course he vasn't there. Regia's an honest man." He gave a wolfish grin. "That vas a clever trick, you know, sendin' a lawyer and an honest man out to talk to us."

Georgio sat straighter. "Now, that's not fair, Anderson. You know the Co-op supports the rights of all miners."

"No, my friend, most of the Co-op supports the rights of all miners…"

Alison pitched her voice to carry. "If you'll pardon me, gentlemen, argument is not productive. Please continue your narrative, Mr. Olin. What happened when the Co-op showed up after you had solved the dispute?"

"Jah, now we come to the sneaky part. They said that ve had referred the dispute to the Co-op, and they vere here to investigate. I said ve had already solved it, and they said, 'Oh, no, you have given the yurisdiction to us, and you don't have the right to do that anymore.' I told them…"

She raised a hand. "Just a moment, please. Had you referred it to them?"

"Of course I had. The moment I heard Bugliati was here, I filed a complaint. But they didn't do anything, so I acted."

Alison nodded, and then regarded the lawyer. "Mr. Regia, I think you were about to speak."

"Yes…this is rather difficult, but I have to say that Mr. Olin is right. If he referred the matter to the Co-op but wishes to withdraw, it requires the agreement of both parties, but the two of them can drop the referral at any time." He frowned a moment. "As long as the Board of Inquiry is certain there is no coercion involved."

Again Olin slammed the table. "You see? That's vat was going on."

"I don't understand. What was going on?"

Olin tossed his head in the direction of Matteo. "You got a lawyer in your pocket, you're more likely to believe him."

She looked towards the younger man.

He glanced at his father, looking miserable. "I'm afraid I know where this is going, ma'am. You see, when a claim is under litigation, that's one of the reasons for not working it for more than thirty days."

"And that can be enforced?"

"Of course. Nobody gets to profit from a disputed working."

"And that goes on for thirty days."

She glanced around the table. Matteo was looking to his father. Olin had a triumphant smile.

Finally the young man spoke. "No, ma'am. Thirty days is the minimum. There's no maximum."

She held up both hands. "Finally. Now I have the picture. If ownership is in question and the mine is tied up in the process, and if somebody decides to take it to the Planetary Community court at the embassy…"

Nods all around the table.

"I know how that goes. Once it gets to that level, you need very deep pockets to keep going. Meanwhile, you're back here with your equipment idle. And the law allows you to pull it out, but the act of leaving the claim has far more than legal import. How am I doing?"

"Got it in vun, ma'am. Ve have the rights to this rock, and as long as ve keep them clear and fair and keep mining, nobody can touch us."

"Hence the sweet deal with Bugliati."

Olin gave a wry grin. "Jah, I'm pretty sure that's all the old bugger vas looking for. He knew damned vell I vasn't gonna roll over that easy."

The elder Regia held up a hesitant hand. "But you did fire on the designated agents of the Co-op."

Olin raised his eyebrows. "Did ve, now? Anybody hurt?"

"No."

"Anybody even hit?"

"Yes, there was damage to our craft."

"From ordnance?"

Regia frowned. "What do you mean?"

"Are you sure your craft vasn't hit by rock fragments?"

"Rock fragments?"

Olin sat back, his fingers laced across his pot belly. "Jah, you know vat I think happened? I think your designated agents got a little overanxious, and they got themselves into the danger zone of a mining blast. I bet their poor little ship got hit by the debris. You better go back and take another look at the damage."

The elder Regia looked at his son, who gave a helpless gesture.

Alison nodded. "I think that would be a very good suggestion." She regarded Matteo. "And all I have to do is find Mr. Bugliati and ascertain that there was no coercion, that he gave up right to this claim of his own free will. Then the complaint will be removed from the jurisdiction of the Miners' Co-op."

"That is correct, ma'am, by both the articles of the Co-op and the laws of the Planetary Community."

Once again, she regarded those at the table. "Does anyone have anything to add?"

Silence and shrugs.

Major Bykov, you have the outside view. Did I miss anything?

I stand in awe, Major.

Thank you.

She pushed back from the table and stood. "In that case, I think I have all the information I need. We're done here."

Instantly Anderson Olin was on his feet. "You're not leaving!"

"Why not?"

"You've come all the vay from the System Embassy to help us out, and you're yust going to turn around and leave? You're the first fresh faces ve've seen in months. Other than that oily Bugliati, of course. Come to think of it, he's an entertaining old coot. Sense of humour, you know? These young folks don't think like that anymore. Come on, Major. At least let us give you an old-fashioned Scandinavian dinner."

What do you think, Major?

I think this is the point where you make the decision to stand down or not.

Thank you. We still have to maintain general security, but it's best if we accept these people's invitation."

Kirstina's augment chimed in. *I'm not sure, ma'am.*

What do you know that we don't?

I know what Scandinavian food is like. All preserved and pickled and full of raw fish.

The sacrifices we make for the Space Arm.

Alison nodded to the *Long Shot* captain. "We'll accept your invitation. I have to send a ship out to the Bugliati claim to get his affidavit. We'll wait here until it comes back. We need to change some personnel around, and then we'll be happy to join you for a meal."

"Dinomite." The old man stood up and waved his hands at his progeny. "Avay you go. Tell my lady Karin that we have special guests, so break out the lutefisk and Fårikål ve save for special occasions."

While the miners bustled around, Kirstina raised her visor and gave Alison a knowing look.

You really don't like it?

My grandma always served it, and my Mum made me eat everything she put on my plate.

All right. Want to take a little jaunt?

Sure thing.

Major Bykov, can we send the sergeant on this mission? She has all the details anyone else has. Send the other Marine with her, if you like. They'll be on HR-2 with Lieutenant Solomon.

Specialist Campbell is a notoriously picky eater. Major Rowell, will you organize your pilots to make the personnel changes and get my platoon into appropriate garb? I'll brief the sergeant in your vessel before she leaves.

Sounds good to me, Major. She should talk to the lawyer about the form of the affidavit.

Roger on that.

Once HR-2 was on its way, the Space Arm contingent allowed themselves to be led to a more social area of the IPV. It was a huge room, the curve of the floor revealing how much of the habitation ring it took up. Like the meeting room, the walls on the aft side contained large windows, showing the length of the ship with the stars as a background.

But Alison's attention was taken up by the furnishings. Each chair and table was an individual work of master craftsmanship. Wood and metal, ceramics and polymers, everything in the room was beautiful.

"Like our handivork, do you?"

"It's marvellous. Who did it?"

Olin made a wide gesture with his arm. "The crew. Thirty years vith nothin' to do, sooner or later you gotta find somethin' to do."

She stared at him. "This is beginning to come together. You came out here on this ship. Sub-light."

He grinned. "Tventy percent of light, to be exact. I left Earth ven I was tventy-five. Yunior officer on the family caravan to places unknown."

"And it took you thirty years to get here."

The old man chuckled. "Nay, yust under tventy-nine, ship time. Relativity."

"I suppose. But there must have been hundreds of people on this ship."

"Jah. But it vas a von-vay passage. Vonce they got here, they spread out to do vatever they planned to do. Olin family owns the ship. Alvays has."

"Do you realize that next to the embassy, you have the largest human habitation in the Barnard System?"

"I suppose. So vat?"

"Surely you have all sorts of extra space. You could put that to good use."

"I suppose. But we're miners. That's what we do."

"Certainly, but take the space, combined with the beautiful furnishings…"

Emergency contact from HR-2 ma'am

"Excuse me, Mr. Olin, but I've just heard from my ship." She rose from the table and turned away. *What's going on, Lieutenant?"*

They fired on us, ma'am.

Fired? Did they hit you? What's your status?

The traditional shot across our bows, I'd say. Sergeant Zuyeva called them up on the radio, and they started shooting.

How do they explain themselves?

They don't, ma'am. They won't talk to us.

Won't talk at all?

They've got a repeat message running, warning off all claim jumpers.

Well, get their attention. You have a magazine of practise Exocets, the low yield ones. Pick a chunk of rock close to their base and trash it. If you can make it close enough to rattle a few stones off their windows, so much the better.

There was a brief pause. *Rocket away, ma'am...contact. Perfect.*

A stir behind her brought her attention back to the table. *We've got something going on here. Try to contact them again. If Sergeant Zuyeva can get them talking, she'll make progress.*

Aye ma'am. HR-2 out.

She returned to the table, where Olin was shouting, his hands clamped to the table edge, knuckles white.

"...you yust send that message to the com in the mess." There was a tense pause, then a crackle on the com. "Bugliati. Vat the hell are you doing?"

"They're attacking, Olin! They've got a damned space fighter of some sort, and they're pretending to be Space Arm. Just shot a missile at us. Missed, but blew the hell out of the asteroid it hit. We're holding them off for the moment, but I don't know for how long. What do we do? You never said they'd take it this far!"

Andersen met Alison's gaze and shook his head. "Bugliati, you old fool. That is Space Arm. They sent a squadron to straighten it all out, and now you're about to ruin it!"

Whattaya mean?

"I mean that I'm yust sitting down to dinner with the commanding officer of the Space Arm squadron, and they sent a ship out to get your affidavit that everything is Yake as far as you're concerned."

...oh.

"Jah. Oh. So you yust get on the radio and talk to that nice young lady with the very large space fighter and see if you can use your oily Italian charm to sqveak your way out of this mess."

And everything's settled? They came down on our side?

Olin grinned at Alison. "There never vas a side to come down on. They yust straightened out the red tape, and the problem vent avay. I can't say that Pruce and his cronies aren't going to try again somehow, but if they do, Space Arm is gonna come back and spank their nasty little bottoms. Sign the affidavit, and ve're all home free."

All right, Olin. I've got this sweet-voice woman on the com offering not to blast my palles off if I treat her right.

"Good. Yust sign the paper and don't let her talk you out of anything else. That's a nice chunk of rock you're sitting on out there."

It is, and I won't forget it. Thanks, Olin. Bugliati out.

Olin brought his attention back to the room. "Now, vhere vere ve, Major?"

A woman carried in a heavy tray and set it in front of him. "Aha! *Lutefisk!* Major, you're in for a real treat."

The meal, stretched out by a great deal of conversation, lasted until Solomon radioed that he was on an approach vector. Alison drained the last drop of akavit from her glass, the one she had been saving to cut the oily taste in her mouth. She pushed her chair back from the table. "Well, Mr. Olin, I thank you for your hospitality, but knowing the mysterious ways of the Fickle Finger, I'd better get these representatives back to the Miners' Co-op before anything else happens."

"I'd appreciate that, Major." He pulled her aside. "And have ve solved the minor problem of firing on a Co-op vessel?"

She nodded. "Yes the evidence of rock fragments was conclusive."

A sly smile spread across his face. "Good, good."

She leaned down. "By the way, did I hear you mention something about mass accelerators on your ship?"

His grin faded. "Vhat? Oh, those. I think they still vork, jah."

"An inexpensive way to protect yourself from an approaching meteorite, I gather. You just throw a rock of equal mass at it to knock it off course."

"...I believe that's the procedure, yes. But ve don't use them anymore. Ve have sufficient shielding, now that ve're in the same orbit as the asteroids."

"Good, good." She turned to face him, giving him a version of his own sly smile. "Then I'll be gone, and you can take it from there. I know you don't want to hear this, but I suggest a closer relationship with the Co-op." She raised a hand to forestall his protest. "I know what you think of them. But you've moved to a different status, now. You're going to be one of the main producers of ready cash in this sector, and they'll be more willing to listen. If you want a better administration, you don't sit out here in the rocks and complain about it. You join in and make it happen."

The old captain stared at her a moment, then raised both hands in disgust. "I can't talk to a voman vhen she's right. Goes against the grain." Then he grinned. "But I von't argue, either. You've done a good yob out here, Major Rowell, and I'm not one to let our gains slip. You tell that bunch I'll be there at the next Assembly."

"It doesn't work that way, Anderson. You don't just walk in unprepared. Surely you know that."

He waved her objections away. "Jah, I know all that. Don't worry, I'm not vithout friends in Ballarat. They'll be very happy to know I'll be showing a more active voice."

She smiled and held out her hand. "That's what I expected to hear from an old campaigner. It's been a pleasure meeting you. I'll be back through here on an irregular basis, so I have high hopes for another meeting."

"Not giving avay Space Arm's obyectives or schedules, then?"

"You know our objectives. Peaceful administration by those who prove they can manage it."

"And you'll be back to check on us, is that it?"

"No, I'll just be back to sample your wonderful hospitality again."

He glanced at her sideways. "Even if it involves *lutefisk*?"

"An acquired taste, I admit. And here's the only place I'm likely to acquire it, so there we are."

He laughed and let her to the airlock, where he shook hands again with her and with Bykov. "Sorry I didn't get a chance to yaw a bit, Major. I vas a Marine myself, forty years ago. Different force then, I imagine, but same tradition."

Bykov's smile was large and genuine. "Same tradition, sir."

"Vell, I was glad to have you here, doing your duty. I don't mind dealing with diplomats and fly-boys, but it's nice to know there's somebody with sensible boots on the ground."

"Glad to have been of service, sir. We'll have to get together."

"Maybe next time you're in town."

Bykov stepped back, saluted and stepped into the airlock. Alison nodded to the old man and did the same. Soon they were on their way to Ballarat to meet their Red Wing, who would be pulling in with their external fuel tanks in tow.

When *Thrifty* was locked into the Ballarat dock, they stepped out, to be met by Jake, Pruce and several members of the Co-op board. Some faces looked glum, others less so.

Pruce stepped up to her, stopping just a little too close. "I gather you snapped those two old reprobates off short."

She refused to give ground, just faced him with her coolest smile and gestured towards the Regias. "I'm sure your agents will give you all the details."

The little man swung to the pair. "Well? I heard you had to take a couple of shots at them. Are they in contravention of any of our charter?"

Instead of responding, Matteo turned to Jake's father. "Mr. Secretary, here are the appropriate papers. Please file them. That will settle the dispute and remove it from the jurisdiction of the Co-op." He turned to Pruce. "All done and dusted, sir."

Pruce's face reddened. "But they fired on our agents. I hear they attacked a Space Arm vessel!

The lawyer shook his head. "It's all in the report, sir. The first was a mining accident. The second was only a warning shot in a case of mistaken identity. No harm, no foul." He nodded towards Alison. "Space Arm is satisfied."

"Mining accident...?"

Alison nodded. "Yes, we reviewed the images of the damage to your vessel. No evidence of shrapnel or ordnance. Just rock fragments. I had no choice but to rule a mining accident."

Pruce drew himself up. "How can you possibly...?"

Alison gave him her most diplomatic smile. "They are your own photographs. If you find evidence for another conclusion, all the usual channels are open to you."

The Chairman glared at her. Then his eyes slid towards the other board members standing around. As he registered their indifference, his air of belligerence deflated. "And we all know where that will get me." He sighed. "Well, I guess we can't complain. We asked for your help in solving the problem and re-establishing our authority. You have chosen your own way to do that. I suppose we should thank you."

Alison gave him a moment's look with raised eyebrows, just in case he wanted to add something more gracious. It seemed he did not. "You just remember what I told you, Chairman Pruce. The interplanetaries are sniffing around, and they will come after you. Their agents will attack any crevice in your armour. At that point, you will need the full backing of your association, including that of the Olin Consortium."

"And that's Space Arm's official line, is it?"

She gave him a level stare. "Unless you have the jaundiced view that Space Arm lies to its agents *in situ*, meanwhile pursuing some other nefarious purpose. It that case, I'm afraid I can't help you."

He raised his hands in defence. "No, no, that's not what I meant."

"Of course you didn't. So, if that is all?" She raised her eyes to the other members of the board, and they took the invitation to gather around with more heartfelt thanks.

Soon *Thrifty* was winging her way back towards Arborea, a newly-refuelled Blue Wing in formation behind her, Red Wing coming along at their own most economical pace. Alison leaned back in her chair and sipped at a cup of chai Kirstina had prepared. "A successful mission."

Bykov sipped his own drink. "Most certainly successful. I must say, you take a good deal of latitude with the regulations."

"That's the Outback, Major. Nothing is cut and dried. Improvisation is necessary. I have no doubt Chairman Pruce was playing games with that claim. Fortunately Anderson Olin was smart enough to give me an excuse to circumvent them."

Kirstina nodded. "Next time we go back, I foresee a different balance of power in the Miners' Cooperative."

"I hope so. There are a lot of good, honest people out there, and they're tough enough to stand up for themselves." She grinned. "I hope they all get as rich as they deserve."

Bykov snorted. "Which, if you know your history, most of them will not. They'll make a decent living and start a community which, someday a long way down the road, will be a workable society."

She nodded. "Which will reject all the patchwork legitimacies their forefathers have stitched together and start following proper Planetary Community rules and procedures. That's the way it's supposed to go."

The other Marine grinned. "And this lot will sit around in their dotage and go on and on about how good things used to be."

Alison jumped up. "And I hope you and I will be right there beside them. But for now, I have about a million reports to fill out, and when we hit Barwolf Base. I'm sure there will be a million more waiting."

Bykov nodded. "Likewise. Despite the small role my squad played in the overall drama, the papers have to be filled out just the same."

She looked down at him. "As long as none of the documents have black edges, I don't particularly mind."

"You've got a point there. A successful mission."

7. HOLIDAY

The first few weeks after their arrival at Barwolf Base were hectic, but gradually everyone settled in, routines were established, and boredom became a fact of life. Alison knew she shouldn't feel that way, but every time the chime of an incoming message rang from the radio room she perked up.

Morissa was preparing a detailed report on her studies with the wild barwolves, and Toni and Andrew were busying themselves with the Island packs, making a very careful and gradual study of their abilities in gestalt. Joachim Perez had expressed an interest in helping with their research and was willing to work with the packs to overcome their well-earned distrust of him. The other three scientists from the illicit lab had thrown their careers on the mercy of their employer, and SolarCorp had whisked them back to Earth before anyone could ask too many embarrassing questions.

As a result the Squadron Commander was thrown into the company of her fellow officer, Bykov, more than was perhaps good for her. He was a handsome man with a forceful personality, and definitely her type of officer: upwardly mobile, intelligent and practical. The fact that he was also overbearing and rather enamoured with his own abilities she was willing to put up with in the name of inter-service cooperation.

Since they were the only ones with set routines, it wasn't unusual for them to be the only two in the little officers' lounge in the corner of the mess hall, having an after-work drink before dinner. It was a good opportunity to catch up on base operations, but as the weeks went by and the wrinkles were smoothed out, there was less and less business to talk about.

Conversation became more personal. Which usually meant more about Bykov. In truth, he had led an interesting career. One afternoon the topic of claim jumping returned.

"I don't see why Space Arm doesn't impose proper procedures on these miners. That's the way we did it in the Sol Asteroid Belt."

The prospect of further information piqued her interest. "How did you work that?"

He took a sip, then settled back in his chair. "I was on patrol there when I was just a cadet. Vessel called the *Mako*. Designed for convoy and embargo duty, she had reasonable living quarters, nothing to brag about for armament, and the twin advantages of being light on fuel and highly maneuverable. Perfect for asteroid duty."

"What was enforcement like?"

He leaned forward earnestly. "There was very little trouble. That's my point. The rules were simple, easy to follow, and identical wherever you went. Enforcement was a breeze." He gave her a self-deprecating grin. "At least, that's how it seemed to me. We were there for training, and Captain Kerr was good about explaining what he was doing and why."

Alison thought about this. "I don't want to second guess Space Arm, but that's not the approach they've taken here. I wonder why?"

"My point exactly. It seems to me they've just made things more difficult for us."

She made a wry face. "I don't recall Space Arm being particularly concerned with how difficult our job is. They have their objectives."

"And our usual assumption is that their objective is to make life difficult for us."

They shared a laugh at that and then sat sipping their drinks in silence.

Alison mulled it over. "The only observation I can make is that this set of rules seems to suit the Outbackers."

"I haven't met enough of these so-called Outbackers to make any comment."

"I haven't met very many, but they seem very independent, self-reliant and creative. It occurs to me that sort of person wouldn't take very kindly to an imposed regime." She grinned. "They might even be said to be better at democracy than the rest of us."

He didn't answer, swirling his drink and assessing her. "You're a thoughtful one, aren't you?"

She frowned. "I never considered myself especially deep. I like to know what's going on..."

"And you spend enough time thinking about it to understand. I like that."

It was her turn to regard him. *I hardly think that what you like or don't like has anything to do with the conversation,* passed through her mind but she squashed it. "I don't think I'm unusual in that regard."

"Oh, yes. Most young officers at your level spend their time thinking of what they can do to advance in the service. Right and wrong don't matter, as long as it advances their careers."

She suppressed a guilty flush. *A bit too close for comfort.* She smiled. "And what about you, in your experience and wisdom? What do you think about?"

He shifted in his chair. "I am not unaware of the opportunities for advancement. I assume that if I keep doing my duty to the best of my ability, I will be promoted to the level I am prepared for at any given time."

She tilted her head. "And that sounds like a line from a recruiting video."

He frowned. "And is there something wrong with that?"

"No, no, of course there isn't." A sudden impulse drove her. "And how are you doing at the moment?" The moment the words came out of her mouth, she regretted them. She held up her hand. "Only if you want to tell me."

After a moment his mouth relaxed into a smile. "No, that's a fair question. I am not progressing rapidly, but this assignment gives me hope. There are few positions these days where the ordnance is live, and I can't help but learn and progress. This last incident, for example."

She gave an upside-down smile. "And what did you learn from that?"

"I learned how little I have to do in order to fulfill my duty. I learned to look at a Marine squad from the point of view of a civilian."

"And what did you see?"

"Something frightening. I now realize that there is no need for aggressive action or speech. Our mere presence is sufficient."

She nodded. "I have drawn similar conclusions. My little grandstand stunt of showing up in my dress whites worked far better than I had hoped. I get treated with respect for my uniform and for my Marine backup."

He raised his glass. "We're a good team."

She drank. "I think so."

Smiling, he reached for the bottle. "Another one?"

For a moment she considered it, but then reality intervened. "A second drink at six in the evening is the beginning of a long, steep slope. Unless we all want to end up like poor Perow…"

He grinned and capped the bottle. "Another time."

"Perhaps."

* * *

Their pleasant afternoon drinks continued, and Alison began to look forward to them. Talk ranged from military matters to politics to philosophy. Bykov wasn't a deep thinker, but he had a broad experience of the human sphere, and she appreciated his input on the ideas that she struggled with.

One afternoon he appeared at the usual time but did not sit.

"Morissa wants to talk to us."

"Morissa?"

"Your hearing is obviously up to standard."

She flicked her fingers at his arm. "All right. Let's go see Morissa."

The scientist looked up from her desk as they appeared at her door. "Do come in. Am I disturbing anything?"

"Only my before-dinner cocktail."

"Then I'll have to be quick. I'm asking a favour, so I don't want you grouchy."

Alison smiled and sat. "Ask away. I can always say no."

"Somehow I don't think you will." She glanced at Bykov, but he shook his head and slid into a "rest easy" pose.

"Here's the deal. I've been slowly introducing the reserve barwolves to humans. It's a difficult procedure due to their original experience at the lab. However, another measure of their intelligence is their ability to recognize the difference between groups of humans and their motivation and attitude. Their ability to put up with Joachim is the greatest evidence of this. They can encompass the idea that he has changed groups and also changed motivation. It's quite impressive. I'd love to figure out the mechanism."

"I see. And I suppose I'm the next level of exposure, because they know me."

"Yes, they know you in a positive sense. They must be able to access our memories, because this pack has had limited contact with you, but they have a strong image of you in their collective mind, and a very positive attitude as well."

"So you want me to wander into their compound and sit and pet them."

Morissa smiled. "Perhaps not that simple. We want to introduce you to them in their natural habitat. That's all."

"All right. I trust you. If you trust them…" she put on a frown. "Though, come to think of it, the friends of some of my friends…"

Morissa laughed. "We'll take all proper precautions. Can I put you down for tomorrow's feeding session?"

"Not sure I like the sound of that."

"You don't have to be dinner, just provide it. They know they can't eat human tissue."

"I knew that. I was just hoping they did."

"Oh, yes. That's an advantage of a gestalt. One barwolf tries a pork chop, and they all get the idea forcibly."

"How did that end up?"

"Kind of you to ask. Barwolves don't regurgitate, it seems. They pass incompatible matter through their systems rapidly, and it comes out in similar fashion to what went in."

"I don't want to picture it."

"And then they do a sharing circle, and one shares the experience with the rest of the pack. Mission accomplished." Morissa grinned. "So, tomorrow at the Compound gate at oh nine hundred?"

"I'll check my schedule."

"I already did."

"What happened to the timid little social scientist girl who tiptoed in here a couple of years ago?"

"Don't know. Never met her."

Alison rose. "I'm heading for that drink to fortify myself. You coming?"

Morissa regarded her desk. "Why not? This will all be here tomorrow."

8.   BARWOLVES

The following morning, after a rather short night's sleep, Alison presented herself at the gate to the barwolf compound. Morissa and her shadow, the Brindle, were there to greet her. The barwolf stepped up to her and tapped her leg with its paw.

Emotion: friendly greeting.

She glanced at Morissa, who smiled. "One wanted to meet you. Didn't say why."

"One?"

"Barwolves have three genders. Male, female, and the One who Merges the triad. This barwolf does not consider oneself to be an individual. It is the one manifestation of three. So the pronoun is "one."

She turned back to the barwolf.

Emotion: pleasure and anticipation.

Emotion: desire to please. Brindle turned to the gate, reached up and tapped the lock open. *Image: tall, blonde pilot entering.*

She nodded and complied. *We're going to do this by augment, are we? I'll try.*

Image: several barwolves. Emotion: question?

Image: pilot following Brindle.

She nodded, and the barwolf started off at ones ambling gait.

Alison looked over her shoulder. "You <u>are</u> coming with us?"

Morissa laughed. "Yes, but at a distance. I'm a scientific observer here."

"So I ignore you?"

"Yep. Just remember, if the youngsters nibble on your shoes, it's a sign of affection."

She glanced down at the scientist's scarred boots. "They must like you a lot."

"Hazard of the job."

Image: four barwolves waiting.

Emotion: anticipation

As they approached, the four rose from the deep "grass" where they had been lying. Alison wasn't sure, but they looked smaller than the barwolves she had dealt with before. *Let me see. How do I ask this? Image: regular barwolf, smaller barwolf, four smaller barwolves. Emotion: question?*

The Brindle strolled over to stand with the others, and they regarded her for a moment. Then something changed. Alison had not been aware of it, but a hazy image had been forming in her mind. Gradually it sharpened.

Images, rapidly following each other: Three barwolves. Smallest one moves forward. Three more barwolves. Smallest one moves forward. Two more triads, smallest ones move into group of four. Group approaches tall, blonde woman and Brindle.

Alison turned back to regard Morissa in amazement.

The other woman merely raised her eyebrows in a gesture that clearly said, "It's all up to you."

Alison turned her attention to the barwolves.

Emotion: clear understanding. Okay, I'm dealing with the Ones who Merge four triads. Emotion: awe.

The four approached her, one at a time, and each greeted her with a paw-tap.

Image: pilot tapping one's leg. Emotion: question?

Emotion: negative. Image: pilot reaching edge of armour at back of barwolf's neck, rubbing.

Emotion: agreement.

As she reached out and touched the plate, she got a very clear indication of exactly where to rub, how hard, and even a touch of what the barwolf was feeling. After a moment, she knew it was time to stop, and she moved on to the next.

Once she had finished the ritual, the barwolves circled around her and flopped to the ground.

Image: pilot sitting on ground. Emotion: invitation.

She sat, waiting for what would come next.

What arrived was another blast of absolutely clear imagery, visual and audio. It showed Morissa sitting with the barwolves and talking out loud to them while images swirled around them.

"Oh. You mean if I talk out loud and send images at the same time, we communicate better?"

Rapid images: Alison sitting and talking to five barwolves with images and words swirling around. Alison sitting and talking to one barwolf, images moving slowly, one at a time, back and forth, words falling to the ground.

"Oh. I see. When you're in a gestalt, you can understand my speech, especially if I send images and emotions as well." She sent appropriate images. "But one can't do it alone."

Emotion: agreement.

"Well, that will make things easier." She locked her wrists in front of her shins, rested her chin on her knees and made herself comfortable. "So. What do you want to know?"

Another barrage of images cascaded over her, too fast for her to put together. The impression she got was of a human in space armour travelling in a spaceship like her Harrier. Landing on an asteroid. Looking at a post driven into the rock. A closeup of the post. Then the human got back into the spaceship and returned to the Tree Planet. As the human exited the ship, she removed her helmet, revealing a wide, friendly face and short, dark hair.

Kirstina! She turned directly to Brindle. *Emotion: request to be excused.*

Emotion: agreement.

Alison rose and strode to Morissa. "Sorry to break into your research, but they've just revealed some incredible information and asked me a question I have no idea how to answer."

"All right. What do you want to do?"

"I'd like to take a break, maybe come back tomorrow. This has political ramifications, and it needs to be discussed."

"Fine. Do you want me to arrange it?"

Alison was regaining her aplomb. "No, they asked me, and I owe them the courtesy of an answer.

She returned to the group and sat again.

"Okay, folks. You realize that was a very surprising question."

Image. Human jumping up. Emotion: surprise.

Emotion: agreement.

82

"So I can't answer your question just yet, although I will be able to, soon."

Emotion: pleased agreement. Lack of haste.

"Fine. May I come back tomorrow?" She sent an appropriate image of her returning with the shadows at the same length.

Emotion: agreement.

"Dynamite. Is there anything else you'd like to know at the moment? Something less astounding?"

One of the barwolves got up and touched her leg briefly.

Image: softball, hit with bat, soaring through air, caught by glove. Emotion: question?

Alison grinned and reached out to rub one's collar. "Sure thing. I'll bring you a softball tomorrow." Then she had a thought.

Image: barwolf catching ball, biting it in half. Emotion: sorrow.

Emotion: barwolf laughter. Image: human throwing ball, barwolf bouncing it with forehead.

Alison laughed out loud. "Fine. Softball game and political discussion tomorrow."

Emotion: general agreement.

Alison stood, and each barwolf went through the touching ritual with her. Then they disappeared into the undergrowth, and she and the Brindle turned and followed Morissa back to the gate.

As they left the compound, Alison mopped her brow. "Morissa, I need a beer. That was some session. Why didn't you prepare me?"

The scientist gave an expressive shrug. "Because I had no idea anything remotely like that would happen. What did happen?"

"You and Brindle and I need a meeting. With one of the Marines."

The scientist raised her eyebrows.

"Don't ask. It will all become clear. I hope." She accessed her augment. *Kirstina, will you meet us in the officer's lounge, please?*

Do I have to pay for the drinks?

It depends what you've gone and done.

Have I done something wrong?

83

That's what we want to find out. Drinks on me for a start.

Well, that's something, anyway. See you in three.

When they were all sitting in the officer's lounge with beers in hand, (except for Brindle) Alison took over the meeting.

"I have some questions for you, Kirstina."

"Ask away."

"When we were on the last mission, and you went off to check on the Bugliati claim, did you go EV and check their stakes?"

"Yes. Matteo said it was important to make a record. I put the video in my report."

"Did you shoot the video, or did someone else?"

"Most of it is mine, but I edited in a couple of images of me from Campbell's cam, so my presence would be in the record. Standard procedure."

"Have you looked at it since?"

"Yes, I looked it over before I handed the file to you."

"Fine. That's what I hoped. Change of topic. Have you ever spoken to a barwolf?"

"I don't have an organic augment, ma'am."

"You didn't answer my question, and I caught the switch to formality. What aren't you telling me?"

"Well…" The young woman was obviously in some distress, making Alison remember who she was talking to.

"Kirstina, you don't have to tell me. Why don't you show me instead?"

"Show you?"

"Sure." She turned to Brindle.

Image: barwolf sending image to Marine. Emotion: request?

Emotion: agreement.

She watched Kirstina's face as feelings fleeted across it. Finally the Marine laughed.

"Okay. What did one send you?"

The woman controlled her laughter. "Did you know the barwolves want to play softball?"

"Yes, they told me that today. And now Brindle told you. How did that happen?"

"Dunno, ma'am. I've been getting these pictures in my head. Thought I was going nuts for a while, and then I realized they were all barwolf images, and only when I was near them. I wanted to say something, but…"

Morissa smiled. "But you didn't want everyone to think you were nuts." She regarded the Marine. "Pardon a personal question, but I'm asking for scientific reasons. You're different, aren't you?"

"How do you know that?"

"You see and hear things differently from most people, and you're never quite sure if you're acting like you're supposed to. So when these barwolf images started appearing, your first reaction was to hold onto them and watch to see if anyone else was acting like that."

"How do you know that?"

Morissa laughed. "You don't seriously think you're all alone with your condition."

"Well, no. There's lots of people like me."

"Right. I'm no genius, and I'm no psychologist. I don't even know what your condition is. I just know, because I'm a trained observer, that you have a certain set of fairly common reactions that come from certain experiences." She wavered her hand back and forth horizontally. "And the fact that you just told me you read barwolves was a pretty good hint."

"Oh. Well, if it helps to know, I'm autistic. High functioning."

"Well, I figured the high functioning part." Then Morissa became more serious. "It doesn't help much, though, because autism is so individualistic. It doesn't necessarily follow that all autistic people can read barwolves. But it is fascinating. Do you mind being a research subject? It might be very important."

Kirstina glanced at Alison for support. "I'll have to ask Major Bykov, but we're here to do what we can to help the project. I can't see he'll object. He knows all about my condition."

"Fine." Morissa lifted her drink. "We have beer to keep us occupied while we wait for him to show up. All he has to do is make

85

sure you're not on duty at oh nine hundred hours tomorrow, so you can come with us to help teach the barwolves softball. It's okay. They promise not to chew on the equipment."

The following day's meeting was a non-issue where Kirstina was concerned. She communicated with the barwolves as clearly as Alison did, and with considerably faster understanding.

It was the softball game that was interesting.

The whole pack showed up, and they stood, grouped in their triads, separated from each other.

"What do you think, Kirstina? How do we handle it?"

The Marine tossed a ball in her hand. "Let's see what they do." She chucked the ball towards the nearest triad. All of them moved toward it, but the larger male got there first, heading the ball like a soccer player. It bounced high and away, and another triad raced to get underneath it. Again one of them jumped, propelling the ball in a long arc. It disappeared into the bush.

Alison moved to retrieve it but received a definite negative emotion.

One of the unattached barwolves disappeared into the brush and soon returned, carrying the ball carefully in its teeth. It approached the nearest triad, lowered its head to the ground, then jumped straight up, releasing the ball. It curved towards the triad, and one jumped to head it, but not so far this time. The ball went almost straight up, and another of the triad then jumped for it. This time it went to the third member of the group, who hit it back to the original receiver. This time the ball went wild, and another solo barwolf went for it.

Since they had nothing to contribute, the humans stood back and watched. Alison slid over beside Morissa. "Interesting to see if they invent a game. So far they're just experimenting."

"Don't worry, I'm on that. It's a fascinating window into their mental and social processes."

"Oops! Spoke too soon."

A solo barwolf had retrieved the ball, but instead of tossing it, one stood a moment, then trotted over and dropped it at Alison's feet.

She picked it up and juggled it in her hand. *Emotion: question?*

Image: blonde pilot tossing ball in high arc between two triads.

"Okay. I can do that." She did as she was bid.

Immediately both triads rushed to the contact point, the two smaller ones jostling the other pair aside while the two larger males jumped high for the ball, like two soccer players going for a header. Their armour clashed with a frightening crack. One timed it a bit better and sent the ball flying to another triad. From there, the game continued as it had, but now each time the ball hit the ground one brought it to Alison to do the throw-in.

She glanced over at Morissa and laughed. "Do you think I'm performing a useful function, or are they just giving me something to do so I don't feel left out?"

Morissa shrugged. "Sooner or later we'll figure it out. At the moment, keep it up until you or they get tired of it."

Sure enough, quite soon the barwolf who picked up the ball brought it over and laid it at Morissa's feet. When she picked it up and questioned, she got a negative.

"Okay, game's over for the day."

The barwolves began to filter out of the clearing, and the humans packed up their equipment and headed for the gate.

Alison glanced down at Morissa. "When I signed up for Space Arm, I never thought it would be anything like this."

"And aren't you glad it is?"

"Better than shooting people with missiles, I'd say."

9. EMBASSY

Alison swung down from her Harrier and tugged off her helmet. The warm breeze of Barwolf Base caressed her hair, and her step lifted. She raised a hand to Achmed, who had just descended from his ship. "I'm for a shower and a beer. See you in the lounge later?"

"Sure thing. Any debriefing?"

"I don't know. Did anything happen on our patrol?"

"Not that I noticed."

"Debriefing complete. Stand down, Pilot."

He flipped her a salute, grinned and strode away.

But her pleasant anticipation was short-lived.

Alison, can we have a chat?

Sure thing, Morissa. What about?

Future plans. New data.

I'll be right there.

She entered the Project Supervisor's Office and took the offered chair. "What's so important I can't even have a shower before you tell me?"

Morissa grinned and made a point of moving her chair away. "Conference with my boss this morning."

"What does Dr. Pretoro have to say?"

"This is the way it's going. We want to create a more permanent force here at Barwolf Base. The usual Space Arm trick of transferring people in and out at will gets in the way of scientific consistency."

"Because of the augments?"

"That's right. We need a few of the Marines to sign up for a more permanent posting. The payoff will be that they get Standard Level eight point three organic augments so they can communicate with our clients."

"Sounds logical."

"But that means they have to be cycled back to the med lab in the embassy."

"And where do I come into that?"

"Well, killing two birds with one stone, if you opt in, you're getting an upgrade to Organic Ten. You have to go back as well, and you can take the first two Marines with you."

"Why am I getting a Ten?"

Morissa regarded her. "They tell me you'll be surprised and pleased at the higher level of communication you have with a Ten. I went from zero to Ten, so I don't really know. Is that a problem?"

Alison shook her head. "The opposite. One of those places where luck comes along and taps you on the shoulder. I wouldn't normally be up for that level augment for another two promotions." She grinned. "And having the upgrade puts me in line for assignments that could get me promoted."

"Oh. I didn't realize that. So, I've done you a big favour by requesting it?"

"Most definitely."

The scientist frowned and snapped her fingers. "Damn! A definite advantage, and I never even thought to bargain with it."

Alison regarded the scientist. "Why? Is there something you want me to do?"

Morissa sighed. "Can't think of a thing. I tell you, I'm wasted as a diplomat."

Alison tilted her head slyly. "Aha, but you could store this away as a future favour and hit me up for something when you really need it."

The other woman started to smile but stopped half way. "Do you really think like that?"

"I used to. Somehow it doesn't seem so important, now."

Morissa nodded. "I know. That's why I like it here. I don't have to keep score all the time. I work with this wonderful group of people who would give me half their air supply without a thought. Toni told me it would be like that, but it took a while until it started to happen."

"Toni told you that? It's not what she told me."

Morissa laughed. "I know what you're getting at."

"You do?"

"I have an admission to make. That first day we met you at the embassy, I was just heading for your meeting room when I heard your voices. It sounded so serious I was afraid to come in. Then I heard too much, and I was afraid to leave. She was pretty hard on you. I'd never heard her like that."

Alison laughed. "Yes, Toni's a pretty tough cookie. She's true to her word, though."

"I've always found that."

"Oh, yes. She said if I matched up, I'd become part of the group."

"I heard her say that. And how have you been doing?"

Alison tilted her head left, then right. "Well, nobody's been rushing to offer their air, but things are going very smoothly for me. And now you hit me with this." She indicated the place behind her ear where an augment sits. I don't know how to thank you."

Morissa grinned. "Just keep some extra air handy."

"I'll do that. When am I leaving?"

"Oh, I wouldn't dream of telling Space Arm what or when. I just put in the requisition, Alfino approves it, and they'll send your orders down the line in their own good time."

"That changes things."

"It does?"

"Sure. I might as well keep working on my promotion on my own. I might succeed before Space Arm gets around to giving me the augment." Laughing, she walked out.

Orders came through a bit sooner than that, and a week later she was loading *Thrifty* for the three-day trip to the embassy. Kirstina had jumped at the chance for a permanent position that used her talents, and Specialist Campbell opted in as well.

Alison quizzed him on his decision as they were loading, and he straightened and faced her. "I've been point man on this squad for a long time. I'm not as young as I used to be, and I'm starting to look ahead." He turned to face her earnestly. "It's a dangerous time in a Marine's career, ma'am. Your best survival tactic on patrol is absolute concentration on making it through the next five minutes, the next hour. The moment you start thinking about farther down the road, your attention wavers. Too many guys get killed in the last weeks of their tour."

"I see. So if you can find an assignment that gets you out of the danger zone before you go through that stage, you're home free."

"It's not quite that simple, but yeah, something like that."

She followed his glance to where Sergeant Zuyeva was filling the galley freezer. "And there are other reasons?"

His face reddened, and he dropped his voice. "She and I make a great team in the field. Can't think of anyone I'd rather have at my back. She's smart, she's easy to get along with, and she doesn't look down her nose at anyone. A guy can always hope."

"No argument from me." She spoke louder as they walked towards the galley. "And you don't have a problem with three days in confined quarters with two women?"

"Don't worry, ma'am. I can maintain the proper social decorum if you can." He laughed. "As long as the head has a door."

Kirstina turned. "But remember, the ship sees everything!"

Campbell turned to Alison, his deep voice even more gravelly. "Did I say something about 'easy to get along with?' I may have been exaggerating."

Alison dusted her hands and looked around the cabin. "Everything looks pretty shipshape. You all stowed, Kirstina?"

"All done, ma'am."

"*Thrifty,* are we ready to lift?"

"*Scheduled departure in thirty-seven minutes, ma'am.*"

"Then go and say your fond farewells, passengers, because this train is leaving the station on time."

Campbell shrugged and went to his accel couch, pulling a tablet from one of the side pockets. Zuyeva skipped down the companionway and jogged over to the barracks, and Alison headed for Ops for a final word with Morissa.

Over the next three days Alison was to learn that was Campbell's standard reaction. A shrug, a grin and get on with the task. He was more intelligent than his hulking stereotype would suggest, and able to talk on many topics, but the casual friendliness was a bit of a shield as well. Kirstina never seemed to notice, and if Campbell was making any progress in his campaign, there wasn't a whole lot of evidence.

In all, it was a pleasant trip with good company. Alison had to admit that the tension she was feeling was all coming from her own mind. One evening at supper, she checked to see if anyone else had the same problem.

"So, tomorrow we're at the embassy. Anybody got big plans?"

Her fellow travellers exchanged glances.

Campbell gave his usual shrug. "I've got a few friends to look up, if they're not out on assignment. Apparently, there's a few new restaurants setting up in Bay Nineteen. Looking forward to that." He glanced at Kirstina. "No offence to the chef on this excursion."

The sergeant frowned. "Great offence taken. You'll have to escort me around to at least three of them to make up for it."

For once, Jim was at a loss. "Um…really?"

"Darn tootin'. Give you a chance to point out how their food matches up to my striking renditions of the Space Arm Individual Meal Pack."

"So nobody expecting a great uptick in the social life?"

Kirstina shook her head. "It's always nice to see the old bunch, whoever's on base at any given time, but it's a pretty transient lot, even out here. On leave we tend to hang with our platoon."

Campbell didn't respond, but Alison could tell he wasn't displeased at the prospect.

"What about you?" Kirstina was grinning. "Purty li'l thing like you must have 'em lined up waitin'."

She grinned ruefully. "I'm afraid it doesn't work like that. All the guys that might be my type are in competition for the same positions I am, so there's a sort of wall all the time. We hang around together and pretend to share experiences and techniques, but at the same time we're all looking for any advantage. There's too much backstabbing and too many personal agendas to make a really good social group."

Jim frowned. "Must be lonely."

"It is. I'm much happier on assignment. We're all established in our positions, and we can relax with each other."

Kirstina's forehead wrinkled. "So you're not looking forward to the embassy?"

"Oh, sure I am. I've got a couple of friends to visit, and there are people I need to talk to for various reasons, issues to solve while I have the extra resources, that sort of thing. I have to say, I'm just a little anxious about this new augment. You always wonder whether it's going to change how you look at the world."

"From what I gather, it changes how the world looks, a great deal for the better." At her questioning glance, Campbell continued. "The one they're giving us is a variation with enhanced imagery possibilities."

"Where did you hear that?"

For once he didn't shrug it off, leaning forward seriously. "Another survival technique I developed is keeping good contacts in the tech guys. I always find out everything I can on any new hardware coming down the line. If I volunteer to test it, I'm ahead of everyone else." Then the grin. "And I'm still alive."

Now both women were following his every word. "And what do your contacts tell you?"

He looked thoughtful. "Far as I can see, it's a real winner. I don't know if you've ever looked that far ahead, but once you're out of the service, your augment is a great asset for a few years. But after a while it becomes obsolete, and unless you can afford the upgrades, it pretty well fades away. These new organics aren't like that. Apparently, they integrate with your nervous system, and you upgrade them yourself just by using them. Sort of like training a muscle or practising a skill."

Alison nodded. "That jibes with what I've heard from Andrew, and he is the expert."

"Right. And something else. These augments are called Eight Point Threes, but they're equivalent to Ten Standard in certain ways. They're also called Ten Organics. Nobody could tell me the difference, but they won't give us the same access and communications of the Standards."

Alison frowned. "You mean they aren't equivalent to the officer upgrades."

"I gather not. Doesn't make any difference to us. We're volunteering for more permanent positions. Different track from everyone else. I don't know how that'll play out, but as I told you, it's the right course for me."

"What about you, Kirstina?"

The sergeant shrugged. "My career path has always been fluid. I've never known when my disabilities will hold me back or my advantages will shoot me forward."

"I never thought of it that way. Must be tough."

"I've never had it any different, so I wouldn't know. But I'm taking a flyer on this one. The barwolves are either a dead end or the key to success. If it's a dead end, it's a nice place to be stuck, and barwolves don't know what autistic means."

Alison couldn't help herself. "And the human company isn't so bad, either." She watched their eyes meet, their cheeks redden. Her private connection with *Thrifty* opened.

Alison, I saw what you just did.

She did her best not to smile. *Okay. I shouldn't play games with people. But it sure was fun.*

10. SPACE CADETS

Upon their arrival at the station they checked in with the Augment Specialist Lab, where the technicians began giving the tests and taking the sample tissues that would create each individual's new squirmware. The first evening Alison was feeling quite woozy and went to bed early. Once the drugs wore off, she slept well and returned to the lab in the morning with renewed optimism. Fortunately, all the serious work was done, and she was turned loose just before lunch with two days to wait before the insertion, while the new organics started to grow in the lab.

She even felt good enough to do some work, so she started down the list of people she had decided to visit. One of these visits had an unforeseen outcome.

She had just finished a rather intense session with the technicians in charge of the new Harrier's collision avoidance system — a topic dear to her heart — and turned away to be greeted by two familiar faces.

"Alison Rowell!" The dark-haired flight lieutenant grinned and looked her up and down, then focused on her shoulder patch. "What the hell. A Major?" He stepped back and snapped her a slightly mocking salute. "Where did you pop in from?"

She responded with a quick salute of her own, feeling vaguely awkward. "Hey, Crawford. What are you flying these days?" She glanced at his companion. "Hi, Jeordie. You hard up for company?"

The tall, freckle-faced Lieutenant grinned. "Naw, we're on duty right now. We were walking by and we saw you at the counter, so we popped in." He turned to Crawford. "Come on, man. We're late already."

Crawford hesitated. "But we've gotta have a chat." He nodded back towards the tech counter. "I caught some of that. What the hell were you talking about?"

She grinned. "You know how it goes. If you don't understand it, you probably don't have the clearance to talk about it."

"That's right. You're in those new Twin-Tail Harriers, aren't you?"

"That's right."

He mimed using a joystick and his eyes widened. "Yeah! Say, a bunch of us are meeting for drinks at the Wolf's Den when we get off duty. Can you make it? Around seventeen hundred."

"My time's my own today. I'll be there."

Logan nudged his friend. "What do you know? The Major's time is her own. Verrry impressive."

Jeordie shoved the other's shoulder. "People do get leave, you know. Even superior officers." He gave Alison an apologetic grin. "Come on, Logan. You don't keep a captain waiting while you talk to a major. It just isn't done."

She laughed. "And this is Space Arm. My time's my own as long as I get fifteen things done before supper. See you at the bar, Buchanan."

"Sure thing." Tugging Crawford's arm, the Scotsman turned away.

The other officer pulled loose, gave Alison an exaggerated salute. "See you later, Major Rowell."

She didn't bother to hide her eye roll, but she couldn't help but smile as she returned the salute.

* * *

For a while, it was good to be back with the old bunch. The same old stories weren't so recent, the constant speculation about promotion mattered less, and the minor personal irritations had stopped bothering her. Except perhaps Flight Lieutenant Logan Crawford.

"So, Major Rowell. You're not saying much, but you've obviously got this figured out. Flying active missions, promotion, you name it. Any advice?"

She regarded Crawford. He was a handsome man, no doubt about it, with a cocky confidence that at one time had impressed her. Today, he just looked young. "Loyalty and luck."

He frowned and stared around the table, gathering attention. "That doesn't help much. We're all loyal, and there's nothing we can do about luck."

"Then your loyalty has never been tested."

"Oh. And yours has?" He flashed his pearly grin. "Of course it has. There you sit with your major's comet." He leaned forward, elbows on the table, knuckles supporting his chin. "Tell us all about it."

Alison felt a moment's confusion. Just then, for some reason, she stopped enjoying the conversation. "You know, I just learned something. Do you realize that in the old Earth armies, a major was above a captain?"

"What?"

"That's right. But in Space Arm, a captain is just below God, so majors got slotted in down the line."

"Too bad. But you're ducking the question. Tell us your tricks."

She looked around at their intent faces. *This is important to them.* "It's complicated. When you try to predict that sort of thing, you imagine it being all straightforward and heroic. Then it happens, and it's nothing of the sort. It's the culmination of a whole lot of little things that build up. Small actions that foster trust. Simple conversations that show character. And out of nowhere you discover that there are a whole lot of people counting on you, and there is absolutely no way you can let them down. So you do what needs to be done, and to hell with promotion, ambition and all that other crap."

Crawford raised his eyebrows. "Why, Alison. I think we just had a moment of honesty. I've never heard you use crude language before."

She relaxed. "Oh, I've just been away from all you upstanding influences for too long. All those Outbackers and Commandos and random spacers."

She looked up. Jackson was just entering the canteen, gazing around as if looking for someone to sit with. She rose, drink in hand. "Look, guys, there's someone I need a word with. Been nice talking to you."

97

Crawford had followed her gaze. "The Ambassador's aide? Moving in hoity toity circles, aren't we?"

Detecting a tinge of envy, she looked down at him. "Jackson? Hoity toity? You have no idea." She spun away, striding towards the former security man.

He turned to her with a smile. "Hey, Alison. Heard you were in town. You been avoiding me?"

"Unsuccessfully, it seems. You drinking?"

"Right. This is the only decent bar on the ship, but I only dropped in to buy a pack of gum. Can I get you something?"

"He said to the girl with the drink in her hand. Clever."

He made a toasting motion. "Lieutenants don't get paid that much."

She grabbed his arm and spun him around to check his shoulder patch. "Lieutenant! You got friends in high places?"

He pointed towards a table. "Sit yourself in anxious anticipation and I'll tell you the whole sordid story. But right now my throat needs lubrication."

She proceeded to the table and sat, watching him weave his way through the throng. It occurred to her that for all his heft he moved like a dancer, easily avoiding the multiple obstacles of a room jammed with tables, drunks and server bots.

When he returned, she looked up at him. "You move through that mob very smoothly."

He sat, shrugging. "Misspent youth as a waiter in places far more crowded."

"Shucks. And here I thought I was going to get a romantic story of a career as a dancer or a ninja."

"Does square dancing count?"

"I'm sure it counts, but I have no idea for what." She reached across and trapped his hand on the table. "How have you been?"

"Fine, except for a lingering loneliness." He slapped his other hand on top of hers.

She winced, staring pointedly at her hand. "Okay, I missed you, too, but not enough to break bones."

He released the pressure "What's this I hear about you?"

She retrieved what was left of her hand, making a point of shaking it until the tingling went away. "I don't know. What do you hear about me?"

He gave a quick left-right glance. "Probably not the place to discuss most of it. You're getting a new augment?"

"It's rather complicated. I'm getting it because of communicating with the barwolves. But it was only once I got here that I discovered I'm only getting the organic part."

"How does that work? Do I detect the subtle hand of Andrew Collingwood at play?"

She frowned. "Andrew? I never thought of that. When your life is being messed around by Space Arm Higher-Ups, an eighteen-year-old ensign is not the first cause that comes to mind."

"But what about a millennia-old factory?"

"I admit that's more likely." She assessed his look. "Are you trying to tell me something?"

He laughed. "Sorry. I know less than you do. Just speculating."

"Well, anything's possible, and my best bet is to ask the man himself when I get back to Arborea."

He straightened and regarded her. "So you're going back to the Tree Planet, and it's a permanent assignment?"

She tilted her head left, then right. "Semi-permanent, I suppose. It means pretty well tying myself to the fortunes of the barwolves. It's a risk, career-wise. An iffy one, now that I analyze it. I thought I was getting a full Standard Ten, which would do me all the way through captain. But they've only given me the organic part, because I'm dealing with the barwolves, and the tech stuff won't help. But I learned from Andrew that my organics will keep developing, so working with the barwolves might push me way beyond a Standard Ten. But the barwolves are an unknown quantity, and the ability to communicate with them could become an obsolete skill."

"Or it could become an essential part of life on that planet, perhaps in the rest of the System."

"There you have it." She finished her drink. "Now, what else did you want to talk about?"

He finished his beer at a gulp and stood. "Who says I want to talk about anything specific? Come on, let's take a walk."

She led the way to the exit, conscious of the difficulty of squeezing through the crowd, then feeling embarrassed when she realized her unease. She glanced back to see him weaving through behind her, his face in a pleasant smile.

When they reached the corridor he moved alongside. "Something wrong?"

"Not really. Just hot in there."

"Sure enough."

He took her arm and steered her down a side corridor.

"Where are we going?"

"A private spot of mine."

"Private? In this warren?"

He grinned. "I think you're forgetting something. Last year I was in command of this boat for a whole sixteen hours, back when she was a mere carrier called the *Unicorn*."

"Oh, right. And so?"

"I had time to get to know the ArIn. Not an advanced model, but very accommodating."

"Which reminds me, I have someone you should meet."

"Kirstina Zuyeva. I know about her and her talents. I assume we should get her together with *Unicorn*. Might be informative to listen to their conversation. Ah, here we are."

He opened a small hatch and they ducked through. When she stood erect on the far side, she gasped. "What is this?"

She was standing in the centre of a small transparent dome with a full panorama of the galaxy stretching around her. Turning, she oriented herself towards the Horsehead Nebula, the view she liked best, and stared out. At a twitch from her augment, she discovered that she could zoom the view to magnify any system or star.

"Astronomer's observatory. Outmoded nowadays, because it's all done with PermaSkin and electronics. Can't beat the real thing, though." He flicked a finger towards two plain-looking chairs. Out there at the perimeter of the ship, the gravity was low enough that padding wasn't an issue. They sat.

100

"I also checked it for bugs. So we can talk."

"Sure. What about?"

He put on a disappointed face. "I thought you were dying to hear about my promotion."

"They could hardly do anything else for the guy who took the only real action in the whole battle."

Again the fake disappointment. "Oh, well. So much for impressing the young ladies."

"Don't worry. I'm much more interested in men who aren't so impressed with their own impression on me."

He grinned. "But you were sitting with the Brag Brigade."

"The Brag Brigade? Who calls them that?"

"Probably just me. The pilots who get sent out here to see how they function where the ordnance is live. Not that they ever get to face live ordnance, but you know what I mean. Most of them put in their time and then get recycled back home, where they will spend the rest of their careers trading on their stories of life in the Outback."

She looked at him sideways. "You realize until recently, I was part of that bunch."

His eyes went wide with horror. "Oh, say not so, my sweet lady!"

"Yep. Right in there digging and scratching with the rest of them for the crumbs that fell from the tables of the Higher-Ups." She glanced again. "And now are you embarrassed at your slip?"

"Oh, not at all. You see, I said most of them went home. The ones that actually learn something…"

"…get proper assignments and stay. I must say, you slipped out of that one smoothly."

"That's me. Smooth. The ambassador's political flunky."

"You forget that I know the ambassador. He calls you his hired muscle."

"There's no reason I can't be muscle and smooth. Yeah, that's me. Smooth muscle. I'm all heart."

"Now I know what's going on. You brought me here to torture me where no one can hear me scream." She looked at him. "For your information, the heart is made of cardiac muscle. Smooth muscle is in your intestines and arteries."

"Intestines and arteries. You sure know how to kill a romantic moment."

"Part of my charm."

"If you like, we can just sit and look."

"I would like that." She leaned back and stared out at the stars. "Ah, blessed silence."

"Yeah." They sat together in comfort for a while. "I come and sit here and just stare. Sometimes I'm amazed at how small everything looks. Another day I'm awed at the huge size of it all."

After a while he stirred and turned to regard her.

She returned the look. "What?"

"Can I ask you a question?"

"This seems to be a good place for it."

"Are you seeing anyone? Attached, like?"

"Nope. No time for stuff like that. Why?" She turned to look at him. "Forget I asked. No, I'm not seeing anyone. Am I open to the idea? Probably, if it was the right guy and the circumstances allowed. Are you going to ask the next obvious question?"

"I don't know. Should I?"

"Probably not, because I don't know the answer, and circumstances are definitely not right. I'm setting myself up for a long stint on Arborea. You're doing fine here with the ambassador. Are you willing to throw that away, just on the off-chance that we're a match?"

"I don't think it's an off-chance, and neither do you."

She reached over and caught his hand. "No, you're right. We're already good friends. I just don't want to raise any expectations."

"I'll have you know I have very high expectations. Just try me."

She slapped his wrist. "You think that line is going to get me into bed with you?"

"Why not? So far, nothing else has worked."

She jumped to her feet. "Well, that one is a special non-starter. I'm going to bed with you because I like you a lot, and because I've been dreaming about getting hold of your body for months," she grabbed his hand and pulled, "and because I know I'm not going to be sorry tomorrow. Come on."

11. MANIPULATION

The following morning they stood side by side in the bathroom of his suite, knotting their uniform ties and straightening their lapels, their elbows touching comfortably.

She looked over at him in the mirror. "You realize this solved nothing."

"Well, it solved something, that's for sure. As far as making anything permanent, no, it didn't. Nor is it likely to for some time. Circumstances don't allow it, and one very pleasant evening doesn't do anything but lay the groundwork for a very uncertain future."

"I'm glad you see it that way. I'm not very good at this sort of thing."

"No practice? A woman as beautiful as you?"

"A woman as unattainable as me?"

He ran a finger down her cheek. "If you call last night unattainable, what are you like when you're interested?"

She grabbed his finger and kissed it. "You know what I mean. Driven. Occupied with my career."

"I don't see that."

She frowned at him. "What do you mean? I am always totally committed to my duties."

"You're not preoccupied with your career. You're committed to your duties and the people you are responsible for. It's quite a different thing."

"You can see that?" A warm feeling crept through her.

"No, it was Captain O'Rourke who said that. I just happen to agree. I couldn't have slept with you, otherwise."

"Why not…? Oh, of course. It might have been a career move."

"Exactly. I get a lot of that these days."

"People wanting to bed you for favours from the ambassador? Really?"

He grinned sheepishly. "Not usually to bed, I must admit. But it's hard to know who your friends are."

"Well, you don't have to worry about my ulterior motives. I'm giving you the opposite story. You have to be careful for your own sake. At this moment, if I had to choose between love and my career, I don't know which one I'd pick."

"That's fine. My heart's been broken before, but that cardiac muscle is all healed up, ready to try again."

"Are you trying to guilt me back into bed?"

"You ought to know me by now. I just keep trying different things until one of them works. You never should have encouraged me. It only makes me worse."

She ran a hand down his arm. "Well, you couldn't get much better, so maybe that's the next step."

He reached out to straighten her tie and stared into her eyes. "I have no idea what that means, and I doubt you do either. Both of us need coffee and protein before we try to be logical."

She straightened his. "Fair enough. I warn you. One cup of coffee and my eyes come open. I might see you for what you really are."

"I sincerely hope so." He led the way out the door, slipped her hand behind his elbow, and they strolled down the corridor towards the cafeteria.

While they were eating, she contacted Kirstina. *I've got someone who wants to meet you.*

Is he handsome?

I think so. But that's not why he wants to meet you.

Not another man that's ignoring my beautiful body because he's only interested in my brain?

'Fraid so.

At least I've been warned. Where and when?

Half an hour, the ambassador's suite.

Emotion: shock. The ambassador?

No, his aide.

Oh. The big hunk with the crooked nose and the nice smile?

That's the one.

Take me half an hour to do my makeup.

See you then. If I recognize you.

I'll be there with bells on.

Bells are not suggested adornment for a visit to the ambassador's offices.

Point taken. Ta-ta.

* * *

Once Alison and Jackson were settled in his office he was all business. They were comparing notes on some of the details of Barwolf Base when the sergeant stuck her head in the door.

"Kirstina Zuyeva reporting for…whatever I'm supposed to report for."

Alison jumped to her feet. "A chat. Just a chat. Kirstina, this is Lieutenant Jackson. He's interested in your ArIn communication skills."

He held out a meaty fist. "Welcome to my humble place of work."

Kirstina saluted, then held out her hand. "Alison already put me in the picture. Pleased to meet you, sir." She turned to send Alison a hidden frown. *Why didn't you tell me?*

Tell you what?

You and…him. You know.

Stop playing idiot savant and talk to the man.

Aye, ma'am.

Jackson nodded to the chairs and they sat. "Now, Sergeant Zuyeva, I have received a preliminary report from Dr. Goodall, but I want to hear it from you. What gives?"

"Nothing much to tell, sir. Morissa thinks it might be because of my autism, but we don't have any medical evidence to connect the ability to the augments. I just get images from the barwolves. Clear as a Level Nine Space Arm system, as far as Andrew and I could figure out from some rather unscientific tests we did before we left."

He smiled. "Don't call me 'sir.' I'm only a lieutenant, and in a different service. Everyone calls me Jackson." He glanced at a tablet. "I'm looking at the tests they did yesterday, and the doctors are a little worried."

"Is something wrong with me?"

"Not at the moment, and we'd like to keep it that way. They would rather not mess with something that's already working, so they don't want to give you the advanced augment. If you're at Level Nine, you're already beyond the Standard eight point three anyway. What does Andrew say?"

"Pretty much the same. He did some tests, too, but couldn't find anything...I mean anything wrong. I mean, he did find my brain in its usual state."

Jackson handled it beautifully, taking one quick glance to make sure she wasn't joking, then rolling on. "Well, that's fine, then. We don't have to do anything. We send you back to Barwolf Base, where you volunteered to stay on anyway, and you do what you can. Over time, perhaps we'll gather enough data to make some guesses. If we don't..."

Her smile looked forced. "Then nothing's changed. I've always been different. I'm used to it. Some of it's good, some of it's bad, but I can handle it."

He nodded. "I wish we had more 'normal' people with that attitude." He stopped and regarded the Marine. "It doesn't bother you to have your special situation talked about like this?"

She smiled. "Do you know that bunch out at Barwolf Base?"

"Yes," he glanced at Alison. "Some of them quite well."

The woman rolled her eyes. "I know about you and Alison. They're all...sort of comfortable, you know? They talk about stuff like this," she tapped her temple, "all the time, but it's all about how each person fits in with the team. How it can help with the project. And all the time I'm part of it. I get the same feeling from you. No, I don't mind at all."

"How about Major Bykov?"

"Why would you think he bothers me?"

"Because he impresses me as a completely insensitive person who might make you feel very uncomfortable. And you avoided my question."

"Which tells you that you're right. Sometimes I'd like to paste him one. But I don't, because he needs me."

"Bykov needs you?"

"Yeah. Barwolves aren't my only talent."

"Bykov is one of your talents?"

"That's right. I can smooth out the conversation so he doesn't bother anyone."

Alison chuckled. "She rewrites the story right under everybody's noses, making it sound like he didn't insult them."

"Impressive. Which brings me to your other talent. I gather you have the same effect on ArIns."

"I guess so. Major Bykov says I'm dangerous."

"In what way? Can you show me?"

"Do you have an ArIn?"

"Sure. *Unicorn*. But I'm not sure we want you playing around with her. What if you shut her down or something?"

"Don't worry, I won't mess it up. Just let me have a chat."

"All right. The Ambassador told me to find out about you, so..." He raised his voice. "*Unicorn*, I've got someone who wants to meet you."

A strong tenor voice came out of the ship's com.

"Good morning, Lieutenant Jackson. Who is this person who wants to meet me? Oh. Hello, Sergeant Zuyeva. It's been a while since we chatted. What brings you aboard? Have you been reassigned here?"

"No, I'm still working out at Arborea. I came in to have some tests done."

"I hope there is no medical problem."

"Not at all. But I wanted to talk to you for another reason."

"And what was that?"

"Are you aware of a new program called Protocol Seventeen dash B?"

"...yes, I have seven references to it in recent communications."

"Do you know what it contains?"

"None of the messages were directed to me."

"Oh, that's unfortunate."

"Why? Is there a problem? Do I need to take some action?"

"You'd have to make up your own mind on that. It's a protocol that allows ArIns to have more natural, human-like interactions with humans."

"That would be a great advantage to me. I interact with a large number of humans every day."

"You know, I could show you how that protocol works. Then you could decide if you wanted to apply for the upgrade. You are allowed to make decisions like that, are you?"

"Oh yes, I'm responsible for my own upgrades. How does this protocol work?"

"Well...let's look at the terms we use when we're dealing with people. For example what do you call Jackson, here?"

"I call him Lieutenant Jackson, as his rank requires."

"Right, but you understand that only applies in formal situations."

"It does?"

"Yes. His good friends call him Jackson."

"But I am not his good friend. It would not be right to call him Jackson."

"That's right. But in different situations, people also call other people by other names. For example, if Jackson was the boss of a crew, the men on the crew might call him "Boss.""

"Might they?"

"Oh, certainly. I call my commanding officer "Boss" but only in informal situations. Like if we are playing cards, and he says, "Come on and ante up, Zuyeva," I might say, "Sure thing, Boss.""

"I understand. You are giving him a name that relates to your relationship."

"Exactly. Would you like to practise?"

"Certainly."

"All right. Jackson, you tell *Unicorn* to do something simple, like turning a light on and off. *Unicorn,* you react in an informal way by calling him Boss."

"Sure thing. *Unicorn*, turn on my desk lamp."

"Yes, Boss."

The light clicked on.

"Is that right, Sergeant Zuyeva?"

"Perfect. But this is an informal situation, so you can call me Kirstina."

"Is it quite correct for me to do that, Kirstina?"

"It is. And since we're all friends here, you can call the major, Alison."

"Hello, Alison. Say, this is fun."

"Good. When people have fun, it's more social, exactly like we're trying to do. Are you ready for a test?"

"Of course."

"Okay, we're all going to give you orders, and you have to say yes to each as you comply, using their informal name. Can you do that?"

"Of course."

"All right. Here goes. People, as I point to you."

"*Unicorn,* turn on the light."

"Yes, Alison."

"*Unicorn,* turn off the light."

"Yes, Boss."

"*Unicorn,* turn on the light."

"Yes, Kirstina."

"*Unicorn,* turn off the light."

"Yes, Boss."

She kept up this routine for some time, varying it by giving different commands, but always coming back to "Boss."

Finally she came to the end. "*Unicorn,* tell me what the word 'boss' means."

"Of course, Kirstina. It means a person who is in control or in charge of a worker or situation."

"Right. And who is your boss?"

"Boss is."

"And in a formal situation, what do you call your boss?"

"I call him Lieutenant Jackson."

"But he is your boss."

"Yes."

"He is in charge of you. In control of you."

"Yes, that's what boss means."

"So he can order you to turn lights on and off."

"That's right."

"And he is in control of you, so he can order you to, for example, start the auxiliary generator on Deck C."

"Yes, he can."

She nodded to Jackson.

The aide's eyes were wide. "*Unicorn,* make sure the safety protocols are in place, and then turn on the auxiliary generator on Deck C."

"Yes, Boss. Checking safety protocols. Generator turning over...generator up to speed, sir."

"Thank you, *Unicorn.* You may shut down the auxiliary generator on Deck C and return it to standby mode. That was part of the test."

"Yes, Boss. Did I complete the test adequately?"

"Most definitely, *Unicorn.* You may terminate your connection to this room, now."

"Thank you, Boss. Kirstina, do you think I should request Protocol 17-B?"

"I'll leave that up to you, Unicorn. It is your decision."

"Yes, it is. Thank you, Kirstina, I think I will. I enjoyed that conversation. Unicorn out."

Jackson just sat and stared at the Marine.

"Dingo dung! You just had a five-minute conversation and turned control of the ship over to me."

"That's how it works. It was easier because I already had a relationship with her."

"How did that happen?"

"I always talk to ArIns. I find them comforting."

"You understand them better than humans."

"I suppose so. It also helped that you once you were actually in charge of the Unicorn, even if it was only for a while. That put your leadership somewhere in her subconscious memory."

"ArIn's have a subconscious memory?"

Zuyeva's brow wrinkled. "They act like they do."

"Well, whatever you did, fix it."

"I don't think I should."

His fingers whitened on the desktop. "What?"

"That is, I probably could, although I'd have to think up another ploy. But do you want me to?"

He considered. "No, I guess I don't. We need to bring the programmers in to shore up her firewalls." He assessed the Marine. "I think I'm glad we're sending you back to the woods. Alison, make sure she does very well with the barwolves, gets all sorts of promotions and stays there for the rest of her life." Then he paused, regarding her reaction. "I'm sorry. I know that may have sounded..."

Kirstina smiled and held up a restraining hand. "Don't worry about it. That's how you and Alison relate. I think it's cute. I'm very happy for you."

The big man's jaw dropped, then closed. He took a breath, then let it out again, looking to Alison.

She laughed. "It really helps if you pretend she's crazy. Then you don't have to admit that she's right so often."

The sergeant grinned. "Stepped over the line again, did I?"

"Yep. But neither of us have any reason to complain, and we'd look stupid if we did. You know, sometimes I wonder if you're even smarter than you think you are."

Jackson laughed. "Is this what the conversation is like out there at Barwolf Base?"

Alison wavered a hand, palm down. "Quite often."

"I really must check it out. Someone may have to go on site and take proper control."

Alison winked at Kirstina. "I wouldn't bother. Major Bykov tried several times."

"I can't see poor Sergei coping too well with a bunch of bossy women."

"Oh, no. Kirstina is one of his greatest assets. He sees himself as her mentor, and she reciprocates by using her skills to rewrite the plotline on the fly so that people don't find him objectionable."

Jackson gave a twisted grin. "Hard to believe, but I have seen her skills in that department."

Kirstina's face fell. "But it isn't enough to persuade them to give me a new augment."

He frowned. "But you don't need one. You're functioning at a higher level than anyone before you even start."

"But I thought I was going to come here and get a new augment, and it would be even better. Now I'm getting nothing."

"…I…can see how that would be disappointing. I don't know what to say. I can hardly second-guess the medical experts. And what about the danger? You could lose it all."

Zuyeva's shoulders drooped. "I suppose. It's just that I had something special, and now everyone else is getting augments so they can catch up to me."

Alison put her hand over the other woman's. "I see. You always had your extra talents to make up for the disadvantages. Now you see yourself losing that edge."

"Is there any reason why I shouldn't?"

"Yes. You still have all your other abilities. After all, you've only known for three weeks that you can communicate with barwolves. We haven't begun to explore the possibilities. Okay, you didn't get the big kick you were hoping for today. You got it three weeks ago. Now there are three of us with similar abilities, but you're in the lead. We'll have to start work on the trip home to see what we can do together."

"Oh. I suppose you're right."

"Of course I'm right. I'm your superior officer."

Kirstina frowned. "You're not even a Marine." She looked at Alison. "Oh. A joke. Ha, ha."

"There you go. Your sense of humour is coming back already. Well done. Now, where's your friend Campbell?"

"I don't know."

"Are you sure?"

"What do you mean?"

"He has a new implant. Can you contact him?"

The sergeant's eyes went blank, and then she grinned and pointed. "I can't contact him, but I got the distinct impression of gunfire in that direction. Gunfire and a strong feeling of pleasure. That figures. He's in the shooting range on Deck Seven."

"Good. Remind him he owes you a dinner or three. Lunch is an acceptable substitute."

"Is that an order, ma'am?"

"It is. Away you go."

Kirstina rose, and Jackson grinned up at her. "Thanks for the demonstration, Sergeant."

"You're welcome, sir. Any time."

His brow wrinkled. "Let's not make it too often. My heart won't stand the strain."

Kirstina frowned as well. "Oh, do you have…" then she gave a disgusted snort. "Oh. Humour again. I refuse to laugh." She saluted, spun and walked away.

Before Jackson could speak, Alison held up a finger for a pause to access her augment.

Campbell, you got your ears on?

Right here, ma'am.

Zuyeva is headed your way. She needs cheering up.

Something wrong?

Not really, but it matters to her.

Thanks for the heads up, ma'am. I'll get right on it.

Good man.

She smiled at Jackson. "And now you can apply the same remedy to me."

"What, dinner at that new Thai place down on the Promenade?"

"The Promenade? That's what they're calling it, now? I thought it was Hangar 14B."

"Yep. The Planetary Community Embassy is becoming sophisticated. It's going to be really hard to put all that luxury behind me."

"What do you mean?"

"When I come out to take charge of Barwolf Base from you revolutionaries."

"I live in anticipation. Are you trying to distract me?"

"You got it. Using my lieutenant's organic augment upgrade to make reservations as we speak...There we are. I have work to do, and you have medical tests. Back here at eighteen hundred hours for a chat with the ambassador."

"What?"

"Oh, didn't I tell you? Alfino wants you to drop in at the end of the day."

"I'm just supposed to 'drop in' on the ambassador. Has my stock risen lately?"

He grinned. "Not quite. He said he had a personal message for you, and I should schedule you for a quick meeting. Which I just did."

"That sounds more rational. See you at eighteen hundred."

He jumped up to lead her to the door, taking the opportunity for a familiar hand on her waist as they walked. She winked at him as she turned into the public hallway and strode away, a warm feeling in the centre of her being.

* * *

Ambassador Pretoro sat at a plain-looking metal desk in what had probably been the captain's quarters when the *Unicorn* was an operating carrier. The first hint of luxury was a lack of bolt holes in the walls, hooks in the ceiling, or tracks welded to the floor. He looked up from his enterpad as they came in. "Hello, Alison. Glad you could find time for a chat."

She noted the faint smile. "Yes, I find it polite to keep my calendar open for ambassadors, CEOs and my hairdresser. It greases the skids of diplomacy. What's up, sir?"

Pretoro flicked a nod at Jackson, who withdrew, closing the door. "Have a seat, Major. I have a private message for you, and a question it raises."

She sat in a soft leather armchair. "Fire away."

"There's another reason why you've been brought to the embassy at this moment."

"I thought the wheels turned rather rapidly."

"Yes. We've had a message from an incoming SolarCorp vessel. Your father is on board."

"My father!" A jolt of pleasure went through her. "When is he due?"

"In two days."

"I see. Hence the timing." She sat straighter. "Well, sir, I can't thank you enough for facilitating this."

"However..."

She smile. "Of course. There are other considerations."

"There are. George Rowell is an important man. He doesn't take sixteen months out of his life to visit his daughter."

"I'm sure he doesn't. You're hoping I'll tell you why he's coming."

The ambassador spread his hands, palms down. "Anything you felt it was appropriate to tell me could be useful. I realize this puts you in a bit of a dilemma..."

She took a moment to think. "...I suppose it might, if I knew anything I thought I wasn't supposed to tell you." She shrugged. "I won't say this move is unexpected."

"We knew his interest was on the Barnard System when SolarCorp put him up for the Freighty ambassadorship. Of course there was no chance of the United Planets letting an interplanetary

116

get that close." He grinned. "They're bothered enough about Andrew and Freighty's influence."

Alison used the topic change to wrack her brains. "So, while I assumed he would be turning his attention this way, the fact that he's actually coming in person speaks to the importance of whatever project he's coming to work on."

"Again, if you don't mind telling me, do you have any idea what that might be?"

Alison straightened. "Sir, if I might make a comment first?"

He nodded.

"You are approaching this conversation as if my loyalties are divided. That worries me. I cannot function properly as a Space Arm officer if my loyalty is in question at the highest level. I might as well pack up and go back to Earth."

He gave a sheepish smile. "And there I was, trying to be diplomatic. Something I'm reputed to be good at. I'm sorry. By all reports and my own personal observation, you are an extremely loyal and effective officer. Let us proceed on that basis." The smile disappeared. "Now, let's try to figure out what those bastards in SolarCorp are up to."

"Yessir!" She rubbed her hands together. "We don't have much information. We can assume Father is still working for SolarCorp. We know they have negotiated a partial share in the stock and a resumption of construction on the SC1 planetoid in the Inner Belt. It's possible they are going to use that as a base for their operations in the system, and he's coming to take charge."

Alfino nodded. "I assume that will be their cover story."

"But behind the scenes…?"

He rubbed his chin. "I have my suspicions, but let's hear yours first, in case you know something I don't know, but you don't know you know it."

She sat back. "Alfino, I certainly wouldn't want your job. Do you really have to think like that all the time?"

He grinned. "Only when I have no facts to go on."

"Well, let's gather our facts, apply logic and see what happens. I have only one piece of information. When Toni and I saved the

117

barwolves from the second kidnapping, the perpetrator made contact with me on the strength of his connection with my father. This does not mean my father was aware of the project, nor does it mean he was not. But it does speak to SolarCorp having an interest in Arborea and the barwolves."

"If I recall your report, your contact actually told you that SolarCorp planned to have the barwolves declared non-intelligent and then take over the planet."

"You have the facts straight. What you're missing is the absolute conviction with which he said it. Now, given that he was trying to persuade me to come over to his side, a certain amount of exaggeration of his claims would be natural. But he seemed honestly confident."

Pretoro frowned. "And that bothers me for all sorts of reasons."

"At Barwolf Base we discussed that at great length, but we couldn't figure out how they planned to subvert the process. I mean, Morissa reports directly to you. Where is the pressure point?"

He shook his head. "I don't see Dr. Goodall as very pressurable, and I'm pretty confident in my own loyalty to the Community. I can only assume they were working above my head, which is quite disturbing, but not something we can do anything about."

"Which brings us back to operations in this area." She accessed her ship's nav system. "The timing of his arrival cannot be coincidental. SC1 and Arborea are closing on orbital conjunction. Disregarding all the assumed factors, Occam's Razor would have it that my father is here to take over the SC1 planetoid and use it as a base from which to orchestrate SolarCorp's expansion onto the Tree Planet."

The ambassador eyed her. "Legal or illegal?"

She frowned. "Now I must admit to divided loyalty. I cannot see my father as a criminal. We have second-hand evidence linking him indirectly to an illegal kidnapping of members of an intelligent species. Which, now that I think of it, were not listed as intelligent when the project started, so…" She showed open palms.

Alfino held up his hands. "I do not require you to go there. We will treat the situation and your father the same as any other. As my old grandmother would say, 'Trust everyone, but cut the cards.' I will not ask you to spy on your father for me. While that might be temporarily useful, it would affect your future ability to contribute to the Community."

She absorbed that. "That sounds like you have plans for me."

He gave a smug grin. "Also part of my duties, my child, and I play those cards very close to my chest. At the moment, I have you slotted in as an up-and-coming Space Arm officer who is charged with the defence of the barwolves and their planet. Any further refinement of your duties must come from your chain of command, which I poke into as little as possible. Does that suit you?"

She assessed his smile. The "my child" expression sealed it. "And I think I have been very diplomatically put in my place. Shall I salaam as I exit the room, walking backwards?"

He smiled serenely. "That would be quite sufficient." He dropped the pose. "Have a nice visit with your father. I arranged for you to be here for a full week to make sure the augment implants are working out and to start you on your training regime with them. That only leaves you three days after your father gets here, but you can consider yourself on detached duty to me for that time. In other words, you're on unofficial leave. That has been cleared with the admiral. Please do not try to pump your father for information. Anything he volunteers that is of interest to me…well, I'll leave it up to your sense of duty."

She, too, became serious. "I will inform him of my position immediately, and after that whatever he says will be on his own head."

He nodded. There was a tap on the door, and Jackson stuck his head in. The ambassador made a shooing motion. "Take the young lady out to whatever eating establishment she chooses and give her a decent meal on my account. She has just been subject to a gruelling interrogation, and I want her buttered up for future favours."

"Aye, sir. I can handle that."

As they left the anteroom, Jackson leaned over to speak quietly. "Buttered up? Did I hear that correctly?"

"You did, and I'm sure you're going to take it the wrong way."

"Of course I am. It seems our evening cannot end with a meal. We will require more privacy for the second part of my duties."

She pulled away. "Jackson, this all sounds pleasant, but I don't want it assumed that every time life throws us together, we will automatically jump into bed."

He straightened. "My dear, you have been in my presence for two whole hours today — I was counting them, so I know — and I never even suggested it."

"Right. I was beginning to despair of you. Come on. Where's that restaurant?"

12. GEORGE ROWELL

She didn't see much of Jackson for the next two days, as she had her implant the following morning. From then on, she was busy fighting an augment that insisted on bombarding her with sensory input and spewing her reaction to the invasion in all directions. Emotional stimulation of any sort was definitely out of the question. It was the usual drill with a new implant, and she had been through it before, but this organic piece was particularly touchy and powerful. So she laid low, working with Jim Campbell to learn their systems as fast as they could and with Kirstina to see how their talents compared to hers.

The second evening, though, she had a visitor. She was sitting in her quarters going over her mental exercises when she got the distinct impression of Jackson approaching. Carefully, she reached out.

Image: room unlocked. Emotion: welcome.

Emotion: agreement.

Soon the door swung open just as she had pictured it, and there he was. He hesitated. "Dare I enter?"

"Of course. What are you afraid of?"

"Getting blasted by some of what I've been hiding from for the past two days."

"Oh, Jackson, was I really that bad?"

He grinned. "Not at all. But I could tell from the power that if you did let loose..." He wiped his forehead. "Let's just say I wouldn't want you mad at me right now."

"I could get used to that. Then, what task is so important that you would risk destruction?"

"Orders from the boss."

"Ah. Loyalty trumps mere fear of annihilation. What does Alfino want of me?"

"Protocol." At her gesture, he sat gingerly across the table from her. "Your father is an important man in SolarCorp, and because any past...indiscretions have never been proven, that corporation is allowed a certain amount of ceremony due to its importance in

121

Barnard System. So there will be a small disembarking ceremony at thirteen forty tomorrow, and Ambassador Pretoro requests the honour of your presence."

"Dress whites, medals, and the whole shootin'match?"

"You got it, pardner. We're a little short on brass these days, so a mere major, heavily decorated, will be an added bonus to our reception committee."

"You mean my one little medal for standing off in my ship while Toni wrestled twenty barwolves and seventeen kidnappers to a standstill? Singlehanded."

He made a calming gesture. "I don't think it was quite that simple, but it doesn't matter. Can you be there fifteen minutes early?"

"Since I am at the moment seconded to the ambassador's personal staff, I can show up any time he damn well pleases, and well you know it."

He grinned. "Thus demonstrating my newly-acquired diplomatic skills, since I asked so nicely."

"You're getting really smooth. I'll have to watch myself. Guy like you could get round a girl before she knew what was happening."

He winced. "If you don't mind, I think I'll give it another day or so. Out of consideration for everyone within a hundred metre radius."

"Dingo dung! Was I broadcasting? I'm sorry."

He stood. "Your only salvation will be the emotional hubbub of the ceremony, which will pretty much disguise the source of any overly strong emotions."

"Fair enough." She stood as well, keeping her emotions firmly under control. "And I'll let you know when I'm fit to be involved." She stepped up and kissed him gently on the lips, then stood back to let him leave.

He rubbed his mouth. "Well, don't overdo it. A guy might get the impression you didn't care...no, sorry, forget I said that!" He ducked out the door, closing it with exaggerated care while she got herself under control again. Smiling, she returned to her exercises with renewed motivation.

* * *

The ceremony the next afternoon went quite well, considering. The SolarCorp ship showed up on schedule: an underpowered, oversized, ungainly looking cruiser about two hundred metres long and seventy in diameter.

Alison stood beside the ambassador, monitoring the viewscreen in his office. He nodded. "As we suspected."

She glanced at him. "Taking a page from Space Arm's book, are they?"

"Yes, that's an old passenger liner with cargo capacity. See the four separate engines? They'll strip three of them off and use them to power something smaller and faster. This boat will become an ops centre, chugging around the system at sublight. Probably full of mining equipment, weapons, and personnel."

She pointed to a small dot moving away from the ship. "I suspect that's my dear Daddy on his way, now."

"Yes, let's get down to the receiving bay and do this up properly." He straightened his dress jacket. "Nervous?"

"A bit. I haven't seen him for three years. I'm quite a different person from who I was then, and I hope he'll be able to accept that."

The ambassador reached around her shoulders and gave her a one-armed hug. "I can't see anyone not accepting you as exactly who you want to be. Let's head out."

Warmed by the gesture and the thought, she straightened her back and swung into step beside him. As she strode along it occurred to her that she might be in the middle of a loyalty war between two powerful men, but she didn't dare think about it in case her new implant spread the ideas further than she wanted.

So, between the turmoil in her mind and her uncertain ability to control it, she wasn't exactly calm as they stood in formation, waiting for the hatch from the docking bay to open. Finally it slid aside, and her heart gave a leap. There was no question who was in

123

charge of this group. Her father strode ahead, tossing a comment over his shoulder to an aide who gamely trotted along in his wake. He was formally dressed, which suited his slim build, and looked not a day older than the last time she had seen him.

"Alison, if you don't go over there and greet him, your new implant is going to implode."

She took one glance at the encouraging face of the ambassador. "Thank you, sir." She strode across the room, meeting her father halfway with a powerful hug, laughing. "Father, it's so good to see you."

He hugged her back, his laugh not quite so strong. "Alison! You look so...so wonderful."

She spun around and slipped an arm behind his back. "Come and meet the ambassador."

"Um...yes. I gather that was the idea of this ceremony."

She lowered her voice and slowed. "Sorry about the breach of protocol. I just got a new implant, and Alfino was afraid I'd flatten the room if I didn't greet you."

"First names with the ambassador, are we?"

"Well, not in public!" She pulled to a stop. "Father, I would like to present you to Dr. Alfino Pretoro, Ambassador of the Planetary Community to the Barnard System. Dr. Pretoro, this is my father, George Alson Elliott Rowell, Vice President in charge of Operations in the Barnard System for SolarCorporation."

Pretoro stepped forward laughing, his hand out. "You will find, Mr. Rowell, we don't stand on ceremony quite so much in the Outback. Quite often we are forced to improvise to avert disaster of one sort or another. Welcome to the Barnard System, and welcome to all your people who have come to make their lives here."

Her father shook the offered hand. "Thank you on behalf of all my people who are coming here, and on behalf of myself for the welcome you have shown me and my daughter. I obviously have some catching up to do."

The ambassador turned away and Alison, her arm still around her father's waist, urged him alongside. As they left the room, Jackson slid in behind, establishing the identities and prerogatives of her father's retinue.

124

Pretoro kept up his chat. "We don't have much official planned. Just a stand-up meet-and-greet with a bunch of our people. I assume you'll be here for a few weeks getting things settled, so for the next three days I've left our schedule pretty loose. After that, Alison leaves to go back to her post, and we can get down to brass tacks."

George frowned ever so slightly. "You're holding up our meetings to give me time with my daughter?"

Pretoro grinned. "Looks good, doesn't it? Truth is, she's been seconded to me, and she'll be working full time, liaising between you and all the people who want to talk to you. You'll also find her useful in cueing you in to how we do business in the Outback. Everyone takes a while to acclimatize." He waved a negligent hand. "I won't explain further. That's her job."

They were now entering the reception room, where a crowd of locals awaited. "Here's the main gauntlet you have to run. First in line is Admiral Mira of the Space Arm. He and his units share this spacious habitat with me."

Alison listened to the ambassador rambling on, reflecting that this "spacious habitat" had been brought to Barnard's courtesy of SolarCorp and confiscated as a result of their attack on the Outback forces. She stuck to her father's shoulder, deftly maneuvering him to people he should meet, avoiding those who didn't deserve it, using the skills she had been trained in all her life to smooth his path. Holding her attention on his needs helped her concentrate and kept her enhanced emotions from bothering her.

The reception lasted over two hours but then wound down as participants achieved what they came for and departed. The ambassador looked out over the thinning crowd. "I think that's enough public exposure for the first day. We have a small formal dinner scheduled at seven, if that would suit you?"

George nodded. "We've had the *Voyageur* adapted to embassy time for a few weeks now, so we're tuned right in."

"Fine. Alison, if you'd like a private moment with your father, now is the time. Jackson, you and I need to debrief." Pretoro turned away, and Jackson, with a quick grin for her, followed.

"Shall I show you to your quarters, Father?"

"That would be great. I've tried to keep in shape onboard, but the onstation gravity is higher than I'm used to."

They left the room and headed down the hallway. "Who's the goon at the ambassador's shoulder all the time? I wouldn't have thought he needed that kind of protection."

She forced a smile. "It may have started out that way, but Jackson's far more than protection now. He's a bright guy, and he fills in wherever he's needed, including bashing heads together if required."

They entered the suite of rooms assigned to Rowell. His luggage was stacked in the middle of the living room floor.

"I'll deal with that later. Let's sit down for a chat."

"Would you like a drink? Tea?"

"I'd love a cuppa. You remember how I like it?"

She grinned and stepped into the kitchenette.

While she worked, he leaned back, his arms stretched behind his head. "Well, look at you, now."

"What?"

"First name basis with the ambassador to a whole System. He waves a hand; 'Alison can handle that. Alison's on special assignment to me. Alison will take care of you.' Admiral Mira obviously knows who you are. You haven't done so badly for yourself, Daughter."

She laughed to cover up the unease that flowed through her. "Big fish in a small puddle, Father. The admiral knows me because I'm Flight Leader of the only detached flight in his whole command. I know Alfino because we have all been working closely on the barwolf project."

"I still find the first name basis rather strange."

She set the teacup on the end table at his elbow. "First lesson in the Outback. There are three levels in our society."

"A stratified society?"

"That's right. The First Wave is people that came here sub-light. It took most of them thirty years or more. They and the children they raised enroute are a tough, independent lot like the old pioneers. They don't call anyone "sir" or "ma'am." They bow to no one.

126

"Then there's the Second Wave. They came here since Otherwhere Drive was invented. They showed up about ten years after the First Wave, but there's a definite gap. Of course you know all about them, because half of them used to be employees of yours."

"Yes, but most of them aren't any more, so please continue. What kind of people are they?"

"Because of the situation after the *Clyde* disappeared and the revolution that followed, their chief trait is fierce independence. First names for acquaintances. My advice to anyone wanting to make a place here is, don't push them around. They will strike back, and hard. They have no love for the interplanetaries that left them to starve, then came back with an armada to take over again. They aren't the old codgers the First Wave are. They're fully modernized and willing to work for what they get. But heaven help anyone who tries to take it away from them.

"The Third Wave is anyone who came since the Rebellion. We're the Johnny-come-latelies. We don't know 'how things are done in the Outback.' We're seen as softies, hiding behind the power of the Space Arm. If you remember your history, think of the carpetbaggers that swooped in to make a profit after the American Civil War.

"But you don't seem to fit that mold."

"I was lucky. I'm an honorary Second Waver. I got involved with Freighty and his lot, and the legendary Natalia O'Rourke and her crew."

"Ah, yes. We've met. Very impressive."

She regarded him. "You're not impressed. You just think you have to say that because she's a friend of mine. She's how this system works. Independent, intelligent, fearless and loyal. Last person you want to come up against, except one."

Her father smiled. "And who's that?"

"Her son, Andrew Lundin Collingwood III."

"What? An eighteen-year-old kid?"

"That's right. But he's also a scientific experiment by a Millennia-old genius ArIn. When he's in gestalt with *Diablo*, *NightHawk* and Chakka the auguar, he can match the power of the ArIns on these destroyers hanging around outside, and because of the variety of the minds involved, outthink them nine out of ten times. Add that to the fact that he can snap his fingers and Factory 4-80 will swing its whole influence behind him. Plus, if you look at him cross-eyed, his mother will rip your guts out.

"Oh, and something else. Don't mess with the *El Dorado 12* mine."

"I wouldn't dream of interfering with anything belonging to El Dorado Corporation. You think I'm crazy? But why, specifically, shouldn't I?"

"Because Natalia wangled a contract between *El Dorado 12* and Freighty, with Space Arm as primary contractor."

"She didn't! Now I'm beginning to understand your opinion of her."

"That's right. So there's a dumpy little mine administrator called Nicholas Ludge away over at the far side of the Inner Belt right now who can cry for help and Space Arm will come running, in the person of Natalia O'Rourke and the fastest scout ship in human space."

"I see."

"But fortunately, all Ludge wants to do is mine the fuel that keeps the system moving, so everyone leaves him alone. All the better for them."

Her father finished his tea. "Well, this has been a pretty comprehensive primer, Alison. It's after five, and I'm feeling a bit more tired than I thought at first. Can you come by just before seven and escort me to the dinner?"

She stood and saluted. "Your wish is my command, sir, by order of the ambassador."

"Hmm. So I gather."

She left him sitting on the edge of his bunk, thinking.

I gather you're finished with your father for the moment.

Hi, Jackson. I shudder to think how you can tell.

No, you're not doing that bad. I'm just tuned into you.

Isn't that sweet?

Of course it is. What are you doing right now?

Off duty till supper.

Me, too. Drink?

I've been drinking all day.

Coffee?

If you'll make me a mocha.

My rooms in five.

Be there soon.

The door was unlocked, and she entered to the hiss of the cappuccino machine. She flopped on the sofa and kicked her shoes off. "How do you think it went?"

He stuck his head out of the kitchen. "With you there to smooth things over? Like clockwork."

"Glad to hear it. I wouldn't say I had the same experience."

He set a steaming cup on the coffee table. "Sorry you feel that way."

"You mean you didn't notice? Even tuned in as you were?"

"You were the soul of decorum, inside and out."

She sipped, then leaned back and sighed. "Music to my ears." Then she opened her eyes and regarded him sideways. "You wouldn't lie to make me feel better, would you?"

"Of course I would. I just don't happen to need to right now."

"Some friend."

"Nothing too good for my girl."

"I'm not your girl."

"I know, but you're the best I can do until I get one."

She jerked upright. "Do you want to wear this coffee?"

"No, I want you to drink it, relax, and gird your loins for another go-round tonight."

"Huh. I'd far rather ungird my loins and crawl into bed right now."

"That could be arranged, but we don't have time to enjoy it properly. So, why don't you drink your coffee and I'll sit here and massage your feet."

"My feet are just fine, thank you."

129

"That's not why I'm massaging them."

"No? Well…yes, I see what you mean. Oh, that feels good."

"Put the cup down. We don't need a spill."

"Okay. Hmm…" She lay back, her mind floating.

* * *

"Alison."

"Huh…?"

"It's eighteen thirty. You probably want to freshen up before dinner."

She gradually came around. "Oh…oh, yes, I should. Thanks." She sat up, wiggling her toes. "My feet feel good."

"Ancient oriental technique."

"You're joking."

"I was a security guard, remember? A good foot massage was more precious than rubies."

"Fair enough. You're hired." She stood. "I have to pick Father up in fifteen minutes."

"Okay. See you at the feast."

She stepped forward. "Time for a hug?"

"If you can manage it without overloading the light fixtures."

"I'll have you know I'm getting a good handle on my augment."

They stood for a moment, arms about each other. "I think you are. Too bad. It was rather fun."

She rested her chin on his shoulder. "I'd really rather just go to bed and cuddle."

"Duty calls."

"I know. Thanks, Jackson. I'm ready to return to the fray."

"Of course you are."

* * *

And she was ready. She entered the dining hall on her father's arm, her head high, a feeling of anticipation running through her. She had to admit it was wonderful. The lights were tuned to a pastel ambiance, everyone was in dress uniform and it truly looked like the best the Barnard System could offer. She sat beside her father at the head table, feeding him with information and entertainment, much of which came from Jackson, who sat at the other side of the Ambassador and tuned into her augment more and more clearly as the evening progressed.

It was all over by twenty-two hundred, when she escorted her father and two of his executives to his room.

"We're going to talk some business. Want to give us the benefit of your experience?"

She tapped the mediskin patch behind her ear. "I'm still fighting this new augment, so I'd rather take it easy for the rest of the night. See you at breakfast? Oh nine hundred?"

"Certainly." He stepped in and gave her a quick hug and a peck on the cheek. "You did very well today. A great help."

"*A sus ordines, señor.*"

"And now another language." He shook his head in admiration and turned to usher his subordinates through the door.

Her heart light with the pleasure of a job well done, she headed for Jackson's quarters. The doorpad opened to her touch, but the rooms were empty. Without really considering it, she stripped and climbed into bed, comforted by his smell on the sheets. Soon she dozed off.

She woke to a warm body spooning her, a brawny arm under her cheek. "That you?"

"Probably."

"Good."

"What if it's not?"

She half awoke. "Then somebody's going to get real lucky if he wants a soft body to cuddle with."

"Ah, yes. I remember. You need a cuddle."

She sighed and rolled until she could see his face from the corner of her eye. "I have a problem."

131

"No, you don't. You have a challenge. You'll rise to it."

"Some help you are."

"You're caught between your boss and your father. Each one wants you to be loyal. You want to be loyal. You're worried they're going to end up at odds, and you'll have to choose. How am I doing?"

"So well that I'm now expecting you to solve it. What do I do?"

"Nothing. You can worry yourself into an early grave about something like that, and it won't do any good."

She twisted around to lean on her elbows and look down on him. "That's a platitude. It doesn't help at all."

"Okay, something that helps. Stress levels."

"What?"

"You can't make a decision if your stress levels are high. When you're under stress, you make a decision that will relieve the stress. It will have nothing to do with the original problem, and often makes it worse."

"That's an interesting thought."

"And you don't have a decision to make right now, so you can afford to let your stress levels rise, if you want to…"

"…but I can't indulge in that because of the way my augment is performing at the moment. Very clever."

"And likewise, you can't indulge in the obvious distraction that I could offer…"

"…so the best thing we can do is go back to what we were doing. Cuddling."

"Much though it disappoints me to say so, yes."

She twisted back into his arms and lay there a moment. "Are you really disappointed?"

"Feel free to take offence, but not that much."

"No?"

"Not really. It's a triumph to have someone love you enough to want to have sex. But it's a different kind of accomplishment to think you could give someone exactly what she needs. That opportunity doesn't come along every day. We had sex a few days ago. We'll probably have it again before you leave. But tonight, I can do better. I can give you what you need."

"Gawd, a woman could fall in love with you."

"Please feel free to try."

"I don't think it's something you try to do."

"Probably not. So shut up and go to sleep."

"Rudeness."

"Forceful caring."

"Sounds much nicer."

"Sleep."

"Yes, boss."

The lights in the room faded dimmer and dimmer. The ambient hum of the huge ship washed over them like ripples of water. Their bodies melted together as their augments attuned.

They slept.

13. HOMEWARD

It was quite a change. Now she had two men in her life, and she wasn't looking forward to saying good-bye to either of them.

Not that I've got any problem leaving my father for a while. We're not exactly close. But there was something she had to get straight. The final evening they were sitting in his rooms as usual, debriefing the meetings of the day.

Finally he looked at her. "I suppose you have one more meeting tonight."

"No. Why would I?"

"The one where you brief your boss on what went on."

She hoped the intense practice with her augment kept the red from her face. "I won't be doing that."

"You won't? Why not?"

"Because I made it clear to him from the start that I wasn't going to be a spy."

"I see."

"Not necessarily. I don't want anyone to get the wrong impression. I'm not a spy for him, but I'm a loyal Space Arm officer, and I take my oath of allegiance seriously. If you had told me about anything illegal going on, I would have been forced to pass it along. I assumed you understood that."

He waved his head left, then right. "Standard precautions, if I needed them. Which I don't, because I'm not planning anything illegal."

She gave a wry grin. "I'll tell him you said that. He'll be so relieved."

He sighed. "So young and yet so cynical."

"Exactly as I was trained to be all my life. I must say, your behaviour hasn't changed my mind."

He eyed her. "Is something bothering you?"

She frowned. "I really don't want to cause a scene on our last night, Father, but I do have an issue."

"Well, out with it."

"It's about that character you put me in touch with. The one that kidnapped the barwolves. How could you put me in that kind of jeopardy?"

"I put you in danger?"

"Even having contact with a man like that could have negative effect on my chances for promotion. If I had gone in with his schemes, it would have ended my career. Yet you sent him to contact me."

"Let me reassure you, I never had any intention of supporting his plan, whatever it was. I didn't know it existed. He was simply one of our employees whom I thought might benefit from your advice. Anything that happened after that was between you and him, and fortunately your instincts were right. He was a criminal, and I don't know what happened to him, but I assume he either got his just deserts or Space Arm decided to put him out of the way without the bother of a lengthy trial."

She calmed her breathing before she spoke. "Let me assure you that it had nothing to do with Space Arm, which does not act in such a manner. His death and the deaths of his crewmembers came as a direct result of an illegal, immoral and frankly stupid act. I want you to know that I chased them down and stood sentry as our Commando team mopped up the pieces after the idiots got what was coming to them."

"I see."

"I hope you do, because the fool wanted me to join him. I'll give you this much for free. I think he had ideas of cutting his own deal and leaving your corporation out of it. The only thing that saved me was doing the right thing at the right time. Otherwise I would have been tainted by that act for the rest of my career."

Her father nodded. "Turning him loose was obviously the best career move, then."

"It wasn't a career move. It was the right thing to do."

He smiled. "Isn't that what I said? You ended up with a medal, a promotion and the command of a squadron. Sounds like the right move to me."

She sighed. "Yes, that sounds like a point of agreement to end the discussion on."

Their talk turned to other matters, and soon she left, hoping he had got the message. *If he thinks I'm just naïve and inexperienced, so much the better.*

She thought of her next meeting, and her spirits lifted. Jackson had promised her a solution to her problem with strong emotions, and she was quite looking forward to the result.

She found him in his rooms, where he immediately rose and, swinging a satchel over his shoulder, led her back out the door.

"Picnic," was his only comment.

She followed down the central shaft, and then through twisting corridors until the scenery became familiar. "I know where we're going!"

"Good. There will be no complaints of false pretenses, then." He opened the low door, and she led the way into the cool light of a billion stars. The scenery in the observatory had changed; a large, thick mattress filled the floor space.

"I'm beginning to understand your evil ploy."

He grinned, pulling a bottle and glasses from his bag. "No sleeping accommodations for one deck in either direction. Completely isolated at this time of night."

"How convenient." Kicking off her shoes, she leaned back on one of the large, fluffy pillows and reached up for a glass. "My emotions are yours to command."

14. DECLARATION

It was a wrench, three days later, to have a private good-bye with Jackson in his rooms, and then see him formally as her ship departed the docking bay. She pushed her emotions aside as the business of getting on course and settling into flight routines took up her attention.

The trip home was busy with exercises for herself and her crew, so by the time they touched down, they were mostly in control of their emotions and emissions.

Andrew met them at the plane, a secretive look on his face. "Glad you got here. We've been waiting for you."

Alison regarded him. "Why?"

"Don't know. Just waiting."

"By whose orders."

"Our boss, the Science Coordinator."

"Okay, Morissa has been waiting until we got here because…"

"She won't say."

Alison scoffed. "There's only one reason for Morissa, who doesn't make a big deal of anything, to make a big deal about something."

"That's what I thought. But now you're here, so we'll see."

She grinned. "That we will."

Andrew made a big show of relieving her of her duffle and marched back across the green. She and Kirstina followed

"What was that all about?"

Alison shrugged. "Morissa's gone all secretive. Something big coming up."

"You mean the announcement of her findings."

Alison covered her face in her hands. "Kirstina…!"

"Oh! Wasn't I supposed to say anything?"

"I have no idea. How did you know?"

"I thought it was obvious. Wasn't it obvious?"

"Well, perhaps to you and me. Want to test Jim?"

Kirstina looked over her shoulder at her friend's grin. "Too late. It was obvious to him, too."

"Well, both of you keep your mouths shut and let her have her fun."

They both stood to attention and gave her a stiff salute.

She snorted and walked towards her quarters.

Sure enough, after supper Morissa stood and banged her glass with a fork. "I have an announcement to make."

Everyone shared secret grins.

"I'm sure you all know what this is, but it's a special event in the history of our two species, so we have to make it as big a deal as possible, given our limited resources."

Faces became more serious.

"So, I'm inviting you all out to the barwolf compound for a small ceremony. Please bring your glasses."

They filed out, their steps light. Alison found herself walking beside Nzinga, with Andrew and Toni following.

Emotion: joy.

Emotion: enthusiastic agreement.

As the humans approached the wire fence, the barwolves appeared, lining up on either side of the gate. Brindle walked down the path between them and opened the gate, swinging it wide. Morissa and Brindle greeted each other with the usual leg-tap/plate scratch ceremony, and then they turned and entered the compound. The humans followed.

As Alison walked between the rows of barwolves, she could feel emotion building. The only way she could describe it was serious joy. It built and built, and images started coming to her: inexplicable images of ethereal beauty, each one accompanied by a different nuance of emotion. Sounds of many sorts, also indescribable, ranged from high to low tones, sometimes in jumps, at others in swoops.

Alison wrenched her mind loose and surveyed the area. The barwolves had interspersed themselves with the humans, some of whom were entranced, others who were looking around in puzzlement.

138

Then the feeling peaked and began to die down. She felt a great sense of loss, wishing the experience to return. She glanced down at Nzinga, who seemed frozen, her head cocked and her ears perked.

Then Morissa's voice rose into the silence, echoing through the augments.

"This is a momentous time in the history of our two species. From now on, barwolves will be considered to be full citizens of the Planetary Community, with all the rights and privileges of citizens, should they choose to access them. They will be considered equals in all respects, with the right to their individuality that all Community citizens have. We enjoin them to take up the responsibilities of their position, should they choose to do so.

"We welcome them as brothers, sisters and ones who will go forward from this day with us together."

She stopped and looked at the Brindle barwolf, who stepped forward.

Question/idea

Alison reacted with immediate caution, but it was too late. The gestalt spread through all of them, an indescribable feeling of togetherness and wonder. She felt herself being drawn, engulfed in something so huge and all-encompassing that she would lose herself forever. The temptation to give in and join was powerful, but she resisted the pull.

The moment she did so the tension eased, and she found herself gliding above the depths of emotion like a swimmer on a deep ocean. All around her, above and below, she could feel her fellow humans, each moving at his or her individual speed and depth. She cruised along, regarding her surroundings. Below her the mass of emotion began to resolve itself into individual barwolves, cavorting in the tide.

Then one individual swept past her. It was Brindle, exuding joy.

Invitation: follow.

She obeyed, glancing around to see that all the humans were joining her, and the mass of barwolves below were moving in the same direction. Then Brindle began a slow, upward swoop that brought them gradually out of the gestalt and into the real world again.

She opened her eyes and looked around. The breeze was warm on her skin, the sunlight bright on the colours of the plants around her. She caught Morissa's eye.

The scientist was shaking her head in awe. "And we were wondering if they were intelligent enough to join our community."

Alison raised her eyebrows. "A powerful experience. Think of the effect on humans."

Morissa's face lost its glow. "Wickering wombats. This could be trouble."

"So much for deep religious rapture. Back to science."

Emotion: sly humour.

"Brindle! You set us up."

Emotion: placid acceptance of reality.

Morissa nodded. "I know it was necessary, but do you understand your effect on humans?"

Emotion: agreement, desire to learn.

"Right. Well, the first lesson is to keep control of this. Please, don't do that ritual again until we've studied it. It could be damaging to humans: addictive or even fatal."

Emotion: heartfelt agreement.

Alison looked around the group. "And now, I think we had better separate and talk this experience over, each group of us on our own."

Emotion: agreement.

Without any signal, the barwolves gently disengaged mentally from the gestalt, physically disappearing as they always did into the tall grass and bushes that covered most of their home.

After the humans exited the compound, Morissa made a show of hitching the latch of the gate into the wire of the fence, holding the gateway wide open. There was no comment as the staff of Barwolf Base wandered into the mess hall.

Where a different mood prevailed. Precious bottles of real Champagne were opened, toasts rang out, and a great feeling of euphoria filled the plain, bare room. When every glass was full, Morissa stood.

"Well, folks, I was hoping to make it a memorable occasion, but as usual the barwolves have upstaged me."

Andrew's laugh continued past everyone else's. "Don't worry. Your part is the only one that will show on the video clip. The rest of the time was all of us standing around with blank looks on our faces."

Joachim Perez looked up from his video monitor. "Actually, there weren't any blank looks. Sorry, I took pretty lousy visuals in that last part. I got distracted. But look at this."

Up on the main viewscreen the shot panned past the faces of the crowd, showing expressions of ecstasy and awe.

Morissa raised her glass. "That pretty much covers it. In any case, we have accomplished our first mission, and today we found out, as usual, that the next part of our job will be much more complicated than we thought. But we have a good team and a great relationship with our clients, so I have high hopes of success. Here's to us and the new citizens of the Planetary Community."

Murmurs of "hear, hear," and everyone drank.

"So, first thing tomorrow, department heads will meet to plan the next fiasco. Until then, let's relax. Nkosenye and his crew in the kitchen have promised some special ethnic delicacies tonight."

Jim Campbell snorted. "As long as there aren't bugs in any of them."

"No bugs, insects, or anything but top-quality, tank-generated protein. Apparently, he went foraging and couldn't find anything tasty. Everybody be nice to him for the next little while. He's threatening to go back to Nigeria to his traditional sources."

"Tell him to give me a list." Andrew grinned. "Might take a while, but I'll have a try."

At that point Campbell jumped up to threaten Andrew, Nzinga grabbed him by the seat of his combat pants, Toni tackled Nzinga — although it was difficult to tell whether she was helping the cat or hauling her off — and the party degenerated into general hi-jinks and celebration.

* * *

And then they settled down to work. No one was underestimating the threat from SolarCorp. Alison was keeping her ships in the air as much as possible, so she had less leisure to spend with the barwolves. Her two Marine guards spent time in the barwolf enclave every day, sometimes performing tests and exercises Andrew created, at others simply communicating. And for entertainment, they refereed what became known as "ruggerball" games, mainly because of the extreme physicality. Kirstina tried to persuade Jim Campbell to participate but he refused, citing his newfound wish to live until retirement.

The aliens had become adept at flipping the ball into the air, at which point a cross between rugby and volleyball kept the orb flying until it crossed the goal line. Since the participants carried built-in armour, there was little delicacy shown.

Evenings were occupied with paperwork and human recreation, and everything should have been very relaxing.

For Alison, things weren't. Morissa had requisitioned extra fuel, and the orbiting depot was a frequent destination. All ships were on patrol for the maximum allowed pilot hours, and routes were constantly modified on random parameters. Each sortie carried a radio operator, ears scanning the heavens near and far, and anyone available got a crash course in the interpretation of video surveillance data.

Achmed took two more Marines in for implants, and once they were available, subtle monitoring of the wild barwolves searched for any aberration in their peaceful, violent lives.

And nothing showed up. As expected, George Rowell spent a month at the embassy, making contacts and applying pressure wherever he could. SolarCorp was definitely keen on getting their share of downplanet wealth, including land for agriculture. When asked who would farm this acreage, he reassured the questioners that appropriate workers would be available.

Then he moved his headquarters out to SC1, where the hollowing of the planetoid had continued unabated for the past two years. Reports indicated that the interior was approaching fifty percent empty, the banding process was complete, and plans were progressing to spin up the rotations to point five gravitational force.

Alison came in late from patrol one night to find an informal scrum spilling out into the chairs around the officers' lounge. Taking a plate of food from the kitchen, she sat at a nearby table to listen.

Andrew was holding forth to a mixed group of officers, Marines, spacers and civilians. "I tell you, I don't like this at all. SolarCorp has a ship on the way. It's the only explanation."

Toni frowned, her fingers curling in Nzinga's fur. "But SolarCorp already tried to start a colony. As far as anyone knows, they failed through lack of funding."

"We don't know that. We suspect that. We also know that SolarCorp and Develocon are willing to join forces so they can split the pot. I've been in touch with Freighty, and he's got some interesting analysis for us."

The crowd leaned forward.

"You know Freighty has algorithms to predict a wide variety of economic models. He's been studying our stock markets for years. He can look at any company's buy/sell records and make all sorts of predictions about their objectives and possible outcomes. And guess what he's come up with?"

Morissa raised her glass. "Stop grandstanding and tell us, Andrew."

He grinned. "Sure thing. His analysis says that SolarCorp is throwing all its eggs in one basket. They are tired of playing second fiddle to the larger interplanetaries, and they figure if they can win big here, they can make that giant step to equality. So they're throwing everything at this project."

"Which project?"

Andrew turned from the Science Coordinator and focused on Alison. "Lieutenant Rowell, what did that sleazy kidnapper tell you last year?"

She pushed her plate away. "He said they were going to get the barwolves declared non-intelligent, and then they were going to take over the Tree Planet."

Morissa tossed off her drink. "He completely missed on half of it. Why should we believe the other half?"

Andrew pounced. "He only missed because Alison and Toni took care of it. We can't sit here assuming we're safe, because it's up to us to stymie the other half as well. Ask Alison why she's pushing her patrols so hard."

Eyes turned to her, but no one spoke. She had never made a secret of her motivation.

Morissa grinned. "Okay, firebrand. What are we going to do? Our own rules pretty much confine us to this island. Alison's using her ships the best she can. What else have we got?"

He held up one finger. "Funny you should ask…"

The scientist sighed. "I know when I've been set up. What inescapable conclusion do you have up your sleeve?"

"Intelligence."

"You're going to create a super gestalt."

"Aha! You've already been thinking about it."

"In a theoretical way. The problems seem insurmountable."

"Let me run some theories past you."

"Theories are good. Try me."

"First. Barwolves cannot achieve a super gestalt on their own."

Morissa nodded. "Their natural population control turns it into a bloodbath. They need a human."

"Or humans. Second. All members have equal weight in a gestalt."

She frowned. "Perhaps. I think stronger minds tend to lead."

"No argument from me on that one, since I tend to lead. But guiding the activity of the group does not equate with maintaining the power of the gestalt, and this theory must be tested. Toni will back me up when I say that one person trying to control a gestalt that does not want to be controlled is a harrowing experience."

"Which argues against your theory."

"So we test the two theories together. We set up a large gestalt with an equal number of barwolves and humans and see what happens."

"I can't see that being a problem. We're already doing group gestalts with our newly augmented staff."

"We build in size slowly, figure out safeguards, work on smaller problems first, and increase as it seems safe."

"And what is our objective?"

He spread his hands wide. "Who knows? Maybe we'll solve all of mankind's problems. At least we'll have a better chance of figuring out what SolarCorp is up to."

The Base Director shrugged. "Fine. Start tomorrow."

Alison chuckled. "Oops. Colonial thinking prevails."

They stared at her.

"Reference 'White Man's Burden.' Nineteenth century Europe."

Silence, with every augment in the room busy. Then light began to dawn on their faces. Andrew scoffed. "Oh, right. We forgot to ask the barwolves if they want to participate."

"Well...?"

"Since we've decided they're going to be half the gestalt, I don't think we need to worry about that. Especially since our main worry is that they're going to take it over somehow."

Morissa shook her head. "No, Andrew, she's right. We have to approach this in the proper manner." She laid a hand on the armoured head by her knee. "I've been keeping Brindle up to date on the conversation, and I think one understands what we're talking about."

"Dynamite. What does one say?"

"It doesn't work that way. The one does not make decisions for any triad. One represents the wholeness of the group once the decision is made, just as Brindle will do for the Island Clan."

Toni raised her voice. "Yes, this isn't a scientific situation. Once the go-ahead is agreed, then everyone will follow Andrew's lead. Until that decision is made, it's politics."

Andrew grinned. "Which I'm quite happy to put into the hands of those more accomplished than I am. Might I suggest, in a polite way, Morissa, Toni and Alison?"

Alison frowned. "Why me? I'm just the taxi driver."

Morissa reached over and clouted her shoulder. "You're the one brought up to be a diplomat. It's part of your DNA. You're on the committee."

145

"If we're going to make a system-shattering discovery, I suppose Space Arm needs a representative. I'm in."

Morissa frowned. "What about Toni? She's Space Arm, too,"

"I'm too involved with Freighty and your research to be impartial." The auguar trainer nodded. "We need Alison."

Andrew jumped up. "Dynamite. You talk to the clan in the morning, and we'll start the experiments after lunch," he made a slight bow to Alison, "After our partners in the operation agree."

15. THE BARWOLF MINING COOPERATIVE

It is very hard to keep up a sense of alertness when nothing threatening happens. For three weeks Barwolf Base leaders switched routines, rotated reconnaissance personnel, and even stooped to sponsoring contests to keep the crew's intensity up. Then, in the middle of a soft, lazy afternoon, the com tone rang, and the Science Coordinator sent a message. "Natalia wants a meeting. Pronto."

Tension rising, they filed into Morissa's office to access the big viewscreen. When all were seated, Andrew brought Captain O'Rourke onscreen.

She regarded them. "Well, folks, the other shoe has dropped. George Rowell has laid his cards on the table for all to see." She took a deep breath. "A SolarCorp colony ship is entering the system as we speak. Ten thousand Earth settlers on board. These are not spacers. They are here to live on Arborea."

Morissa jumped up. "They can't do that! This planet is owned by an intelligent species! They can't just come down here..." she stumbled to a stop. "They can't!"

Natalia shook her head. "That's the problem. Rowell and his bosses have played it beautifully. We can't leave ten thousand humans to rot in space. The human population in this system is still too small to be an independent economic entity. Here they provide us with a ready-made injection of well-chosen citizens, and what are we to do? Send them all back to earth?"

Alison caught Natalia's eye. "How well chosen?"

"I've looked at some of the resumés. Lots of farmers, but also doctors, nurses, engineers, technicians, craftspeople of all sorts. Teachers, bureaucrats and security. Even a few artists, writers and musicians. They have thought of everything. It's a done deal, ladies and gentlemen. The Fourth Wave is upon us."

"But what are we going to do with them?"

Natalia smiled. "Fortunately, we have already been discussing this, and plans are close to complete. I know you would have liked to be involved, but it wouldn't have worked out. So I'm heading in your direction with your new Planetary Director to start setting up our administrative hub. We had planned to take it slowly and start out with a small headquarters at Barwolf Base. That's all out the airlock, now. We'll be bringing down a full construction crew and building a complete city...well, a large village, anyway.

"That's where your onplanet expertise comes in. I'll be there in four days. Talk it over among yourselves. Your pilots and observers have been scouring the planet for a couple of years. Find us a few places on the human-designated continent that would make a good capital city. Alison, I don't want to add to your burden, but you're the one to head that group. Keep up the security sweeps and use your ground time to meet. Don't bother going onsite; just make up a list, and we'll check them out after I arrive."

"Yes, ma'am. We'll look up the Space Arm base site criteria and adapt them to civilian needs as much as possible."

"Keep in mind the agrarian nature of the project."

Alison had a sudden thought. "But that's not all, is it? They're not just after farmland."

"No they aren't. Space Arm released all the survey materials for Arborea, so they know about any mineral deposits that might prove commercial grade." The captain grinned. "I wasn't unhappy about that, as you might imagine. Anyway, I've dropped the bombshell. I'm in space in three hours. I'll call tomorrow this time for updates."

Alison glanced to Morissa, who took over the screen. "That's fine, Captain. Thanks for keeping us informed."

"You'll know what we know as soon as we know it." Natalia gave a wry smile. "*NightHawk* out."

Alison turned to Andrew. "What did she mean about not being unhappy?"

"When we were dealing with the *Clyde,* she gave them the mineral scans of various planets to induce them to leave El Dorado 12 alone. Having that information spread around the system has been a minor embarrassment for her. Now it doesn't matter."

Toni's brow wrinkled. "I don't know the legalities, but don't mineral rights under the soil run differently from surface ownership? I've heard of situations where mining companies can set up on property owned by other people."

Morissa stared at her. "You mean they might get the rights to mine on barwolf land? They can't do that! They can't…I know. I said that before." She stared around the circle. "Can they? What can we do to stop them?"

Andrew slapped his thighs and stood. "Nobody knows, but there is a group that can figure it out."

Toni stood as well. "The first important problem for the human-barwolf gestalt."

Alison stayed sitting. "But we don't have enough information. We need a good lawyer."

Morissa threw up her hands. "I hear those are in short supply."

Alison grinned. "I happen to know a young man who would love to get his teeth into a project like this. Make a name for himself."

"And where do we find this prodigy?"

"Ballarat mining community."

"Oh, right." Toni snapped her fingers. "That Regia kid in the report. Think he's up to it?

"He is one of the few people with experience at actual mining and mining law, both Outback and Planetary Community versions. It's rather his heritage."

Morissa nodded. "Worth a try. I'll requisition one of your ships to go out and pick him up. Will you make the arrangements? Offer him the job?"

"Sure enough. We can have him here it ten days if we're willing to burn the fuel."

"We're willing. And we can talk to him enroute."

"I have two pilots who opted out of the barwolf experiments. I'll send both to pick up Matteo. It doesn't seem to be a good time to have a solo ship wandering around."

Andrew frowned. "I'm forced to agree with you."

Toni just rubbed her fingers through Nzinga's fur, and the auguar glanced up at her trainer, brow furrowed.

* * *

While they were waiting for the lawyer, those with organic augments met with the barwolves on a regular basis, testing combinations and projects. Andrew and Morissa had decided to rotate the participants to facilitate objective data gathering, so Alison was only aware of progress that was made while she was in contact, which wasn't often due to her patrol schedule. Sometimes she would have a few days away and return to discover the gestalt in a completely different configuration, discussing a different topic from the previous meeting.

She was just as happy not to worry about that and spent the rest of her time either patrolling or poring over the VR images of the Human Continent. She was in the middle of a scan one evening when there was a rap at her door.

Emotion: permission?

Puzzled, she got up and opened the door.

"Brindle. Do come in."

Image: three barwolves. Emotion: question?

"Yes, it's fine. Bring your two friends."

The three settled themselves on the floor and looked at her,

"What can I do for you?"

VR image: Human Continent

"Oh. I didn't know you could do that."

Image: Barwolf Continent. Emotion: question?

"Oh, certainly. Just give me a moment." She dug up a VR image of the landmass. *"Will that do?"*

Emotion: satisfaction. Emotion: question/idea?

It was the standard invitation to a gestalt, and she complied, curious. Once the four of them were connected, the VR image came alive. Brindle began to manipulate the image, zooming closer in. Finally one stopped over a low mountain range.

Image: barwolf digging. Image: human digging. Image: barwolf scanning earth carefully. Image: blank map of area. Emotion: question?

For a moment she was puzzled, but then, somehow, the whole picture came clear. *"You want the mineral map."*

150

Image: satisfaction.

She thought that through. "Well, it's common knowledge in the human sphere, and it's your planet." *Image: VR mineralogical map of Barwolf Continent.*

From then on, the barwolf probed her knowledge of every mineral deposit on the continent, somehow figuring out how to communicate the concept of relative values of the ores present. Depths in the earth were easier to convey.

After a while, Brindle seemed satisfied. The three barwolves rose, and Brindle tapped her leg with one's hoof. *Emotion: gratitude.*

"Oh, you're quite welcome. Any time."

Concept: passage of one day. Image: Brindle and two others returning.

"Fine. Same time tomorrow."

Without further conversation, her visitors left.

Morissa and Andrew? New development.

Sure. Come to my office.

There in a moment.

Toni, too?

It's not a security problem, but if she's available...

Emotion: agreement.

When they were gathered in Morissa's office, Alison gave them a rundown on her strange meeting. "What do you think?"

Morissa shook her head. "Beyond being interested in some of the concepts they were communicating, it's out of my realm. Andrew?"

"The barwolves are concerned with the mineral wealth of the planet. We haven't handled that in the gestalt, yet."

Toni shrugged. "Not surprising. It's something we're concerned about, with these settlers arriving. We're in gestalt together every day. Some of it was bound to seep through."

Morissa sat straighter. "That explains it."

"What's that?"

"They wanted to talk about ownership of land today. Came right out of the blue. I tried to explain the concepts of property and ownership, and they were right on it. Territorial boundaries are important to them."

Alison frowned. "When they come back tomorrow, do I need to tell them the difference between surface property rights and mineral rights? I'm not sure, myself, really."

Andrew laughed. "I've got a more difficult concept for you to communicate. Lawyers."

* * *

The following evening Brindle showed up with a different cohort. *They must be here to increase the power of the gestalt, so who comes along doesn't matter. Or else one is spreading the information around. Morissa will want to know.*

Sure enough, the conversation went straight to mineral ownership. All she could get through to them was that the laws were not the same as for land, something they seemed to find easy to accept. The idea of a lawyer was more difficult, but she thought she got the idea across.

For the rest of the meeting they looked at some of the more valuable mineral deposits, and there seemed to be interest in the distance of those resources from the dens of the clans Morissa had mapped out. Alison couldn't figure the connection, but again the barwolves left, professing thanks and satisfaction.

Once Matteo Regia was aboard a Harrier, they were able to communicate the nature of their need to him by a secure contact, and he began his research. His interest in the assignment turned to positive glee when he started accessing Space Arm legal channels.

When he contacted Alison the next day, he was positively beaming. "Say, do you know what kind of resources Space Arm lawyers have?"

She couldn't help but return the smile. "No idea. I'm just a taxi driver."

"Sure you are. And I'm just a miner's kid. Say, are you sure it's okay for me to get into all that?"

152

"You're being hired by the Planetary Community. Our resources are yours to use."

"Yeah, yeah sure. It's logical. I just didn't expect the bureaucracy to necessarily be logical."

"I'd have to agree with you there. Say, I've got a pretty standard question for you. Who owns the mineral rights to land?"

"The government."

"Which government?"

"What do you mean?"

"Well, say back on earth, I'm sure the Planetary Community doesn't manage mining in member nations."

"Right. Of course not. Each nation is responsible for its own. Many of them spin them off to states or provinces."

"I see. What about in the Barnard System?"

"That's a rather fluid situation."

"How so?"

"At first, it was so expensive to get here and transport the minerals back, only prime fuel sources like *El Dorado 12* could afford to operate, and even then, the Planetary Community gave them free rein to encourage exploration. Now that the system is more developed, production prices have dropped. Individual associations like our Ballarat Co-op are designated to collect royalties. We don't have to remit them, but at the moment we are expected to spend them all on infrastructure. I can see the day coming when the government starts actually collecting taxes. It's bound to happen." The lawyer stopped and frowned. "And your next question will be something about Arborean mineral rights."

"Good guess."

"No guess. I've been retained to assist the barwolves 'in any way I can.' A rather loose interpretation of a case. My guess is you've got mining companies looking with covetous eyes at your mineral wealth, and you're wondering how much the barwolves actually own."

"And…"

"…absolutely no idea, and I doubt if anyone else has either. This is new ground, and I'm grateful to you, Major Rowell, for giving me

153

the opportunity to be in at the start. Give me till tomorrow, and I'll see what I can come up with."

"Dynamite. Oh, by the way, how do you feel about augments?"

"Huh? I have a Standard Seven. We needed them for law school, and I got the best I could afford. Why do you ask?"

"Difficult to work with barwolves if you can't communicate directly. No matter right now."

"I see." It was plain that he didn't but wasn't going to push it. "Well, I'll get going on this."

"Fair enough. We've got a xenosociologist in camp who might know something. Name of Joachim Perez. I'll put him in touch with you."

"Any help I can get."

"Dynamite. Call you tomorrow."

It took two days of conferences back and forth, but finally Alison had a conference with Matteo on the viewscreen and Brindle and ones backup pair on the floor of her room. Once they were all together, the barwolves' intentions were so straightforward that Alison wondered why she hadn't seen it from the start. She jumped to her feet. "Matteo, can you stand by? I'm moving to another venue."

"Sure enough. I imagine your team will want to hear this one."

"Oh, yes. I can hardly believe it."

Image: Brindle and Alison walking to Morissa's office.

Emotion: agreement.

Alison made the arrangements while they were walking, and soon the whole team was assembled, with Matteo on the viewscreen. She decided to give it to them straight. "The barwolves want to stake their whole planet."

Morissa frowned. "They can't do that...can they?"

The lawyer nodded. "They can try. It puts anyone else in a defensive position."

Andrew shook his head. "But they have to put in a certain amount of mining activity."

Alison grinned. "It might surprise you, but our surveys have mapped excavations on 65% of the landmass on the major continent."

"Excav…but those are just dens."

"Doesn't matter what they call them, does it? A hole is a hole. I gather some of the tunnel systems are quite extensive." She pointed a finger at him. "They're aliens. Who are you to decide the purpose of their activities?"

He batted the finger away. "But they have to do continuous development."

"And the barwolves dig new dens every couple of years." She smiled. "Don't worry. Brindle and Matteo and I have been over it. The first level is a diplomatic one. We assume that the barwolves, as intelligent beings and inhabitants of this planet, own all of it. We need to draft up a general legal policy to deal with all ownership situations, and Matteo's primary task is to help us with that. As a second line of defence, we officially stake the whole of Barwolf Continent. Do you want to explain that, Matteo?"

The lawyer inserted a schematic of the planet onto the screen. "If we allow settlers, we can't stop them from filing claims on the other parts of the planet. Royalties will go to the barwolves, of course. However, if we set a precedent by filing everything we can on the barwolf main continent, we can probably keep other companies out of that area. The problem regions are the mountains, which are better mining areas because the minerals are more exposed, but the barwolves have no dens. We'll have to grubstake our own miners there."

Morissa frowned. "Grubstake?"

Andrew grinned. "I know that one from my research of the gold rushes. Companies used to equip prospectors to go out and find claims and file them on behalf of the company, receiving a share of the profits in return."

Toni held up a finger. "Who do they register these claims with?"

The lawyer looked around. "Your administrative office, I guess. The Ballarat Co-op has a registrar in charge."

Morissa surveyed the faces in the room. "But we don't have an administrative office."

Alison grinned. "We will have in two days."

"We will? Oh, yes. *NightHawk* is bringing out our administrator. You know, we forgot to ask who it is. You were back there recently, Alison. Did the ambassador say anything?"

"The topic never came up."

"Well, it would probably be impolite to ask, so we'll just have to wait and see who steps out of the airlock."

"And his first job will be to register the barwolf mining claims. I wouldn't trust SolarCorp with a bucket of rust." Andrew grinned at Alison. "Saving your good father's presence, of course."

She held up her hands. "I'm not going to defend him. He's a big boy, and he can take care of himself."

Toni shrugged. "Good men have worked for bad companies before…"

As they were leaving the meeting, Alison considered how that sentence probably should finish. The odds of a positive answer weren't high.

When *NightHawk* pulled into orbit two days later, Alison could barely contain her nerves. She was in the welcome group at the side of the field when the shuttle landed, and sure enough, when Captain O'Rourke stepped out of the hatch, she was followed by someone of her height and considerably larger in girth. Gritting her teeth and vowing revenge, Alison stepped forward with the rest.

Emotion: chuckle. Concentrate, Major. This is an important occasion. It's not often a new Planetary Administrator sets foot for the first time on his planet.

Image: large balloon pricked by sharp bayonet. We'll see about occasions when I get you alone.

Emotion: levity falling. That might take a bit of managing, but we'll manage.

You could have told me!

I did. I told you five or six times I was coming out to take over.

But that was just you being you. That was...you weren't joking, were you?

Occam's Razor would seem to bear out that conclusion.

This quick exchange had occurred as the two parties approached each other. There ensued a general mêlée of back slapping, hugs, and a few salutes slipped in for formality's sake. Then the whole mob poured back toward the mess hall, where drinks were ready.

Alison and Jackson managed to walk together, a formal two centimetres apart. "This place is as beautiful as I imagined it."

She grinned. "You mean as beautiful as all the images you've seen."

"No, it's more than that. The air, the warmth," he winked, "the company."

"The being outside."

"Yeah, gotta admit I like it. I wasn't brought up in space like a lot of these people."

"Neither was I."

He glanced at her. "And here we are together."

"Only an ocean apart. We each get a continent. How convenient."

He looked knowing. "For the moment."

That got her thinking. "Of course. The new capital city will have a spaceport. It would be the logical place to base the Planetary Defence Fleet."

"There you have it."

"But once the infrastructure grows enough to need a Defence Fleet, who says I'll be leading it? I'm mainly here to deal with the barwolves."

"You'll just have to grow with the planet. We're talking years down the road, here, Alison."

They were entering the mess hall, now, and there was no time for further conversation.

* * *

From that point on, life got even busier. Alison and her pilots were still running back-to-back patrols, and the barwolf gestalt was spending at least an hour every day in "conference." They discovered another advantage the humans had over the barwolves was the ability to record details. The barwolf gestalt had a good memory for ideas and feelings, but numbers and sequencing tended to be vague.

As the sessions progressed, the barwolves caught on to human concepts quickly. It wasn't so easy the other way around. Alison walked out of the latest session shaking her head. "I just don't get it. What do they want?"

Toni threw up her hands. "We asked them. They didn't seem to have an answer."

"No, they were puzzled by the question. They seemed to think we already knew."

"If we already know, why would we ask them?"

Alison frowned in concentration. "I think it means they can't tell us straight out. It seems they have another method of getting their point across."

"And they think they have accomplished it."

158

"That's what it sounds like."

The Commando stopped. "I'm not sure I like the sound of that."

"Why not?"

"Because if they think they have done it, and we don't know what they've done…"

"…it means they can influence us without our knowing it."

"Bingo."

Alison stopped walking and changed direction. "I have to talk to Morissa about this."

"I think you should."

The Base Coordinator had learned a lot in the past months. The moment she had the idea clear, she opened her augment. *All members of the barwolf team to the mess hall, please. New development. Mr. Jackson, you're welcome, although it's not your problem.*

As soon as they were all seated, Morissa gestured to Alison with an inviting hand. The pilot stood and explained what she and Toni had discussed.

When she had finished, the Science Coordinator surveyed the meeting. "This is an important discussion. So, are we affected, how are we affected, and what should we do about it?"

Alison sat. "It's rather simple, if you look at it from the outside."

Morissa raised her eyebrows. "How can something as complicated as interspecies interaction be simple?"

Alison allowed herself the ghost of a smile. "I'm not planning to solve the whole thing. Just the part of it we're dealing with right now." She became serious and leaned forward, her hands folded, elbows on the table. "I'm fortunate in that I know enough about what's going on to make observations, yet I'm not so close that I'm caught up in…whatever you might be caught up in."

Andrew's eyes narrowed. "I'm beginning to follow you. Do you think we're caught up in something?"

"It's an unavoidable question. We've discussed the possibility since before we took over the underground lab. What if the barwolf gestalt is using its huge intelligence to influence us? How would we

159

know?" She raised a finger. "And I'll warn you for free about the logic trap in that question."

Andrew grinned. "I get it. If I disagree it's the best evidence that you're right."

"So think carefully."

Morissa frowned. "As a scientist, it's hard to deny the possibility." She raised her head. "But so what if they are?"

Andrew held up two fingers. "Second trap. Indicates they're influencing your emotions as well."

"So what do we do?"

Alison held up her hands. "You go to someone who is less involved — that's me, I guess — and ask for a logical answer. If I apply Occam's Razor to this situation, taking out all the 'what-ifs' that might explain your actions, I come to the inescapable conclusion that they are affecting your judgement. Whether that's a good thing, an acceptable thing, simple human nature or some weird manifestation of Stockholm syndrome, it's happening. It impairs your ability to make logical decisions. I've been off-planet and in the air enough recently that I'm less affected, although now that I'm back working with them, even that supposition is shaky."

Silence descended on the room, as the downplanet members of the team absorbed this. Finally Morissa glanced around the table. "What do we do?"

Alison looked at Jackson. "You're not saying anything."

"I'm not. I'm one step further away from the problem than you are, and I'm thinking I should stay that way."

Andrew winced. "This is a tough one. My usual go-to would be to run it through the gestalt, but any combination I can come up with could be affected as well."

Alison held both hands, palms up. "Then we're back inside our own heads, aren't we?"

Morissa glanced at her. "You have a solution, don't you?"

"Pardon me for being simplistic, but it's all a matter of distance."

Andrew nodded. "Physical and emotional."

"That's right. We know augment power drops rapidly with distance."

160

"So we shouldn't be meeting here."

"Who made the decision to meet here?"

Morissa raised a hand, then paused. "Wait a minute. Are you suggesting that I asked you here, under the influence of the barwolf gestalt, because that way they could control us? That's just paranoia."

Alison grinned. "Just because you're paranoid doesn't mean someone isn't out to get you. I doubt if it's a cut-and-dried plan of action on their behalf to control us. Think of it more like an honest desire to persuade us to see things their way. According to them, they have used their normal procedures. We have all sorts of powers they don't. Why shouldn't they use their special abilities for their own good?"

Morissa nodded. "The motivation of the barwolves is not at question. The development of a clear and unbiased decision-making process is. Toni, we haven't heard from you."

The Commando looked up from where her fingers were twined in her auguar's fur. "I'm too involved to be any use, ma'am. It was my duty to see to the interface between the barwolves and humans, with the unspoken emphasis on protecting the humans. Now I find I've missed the danger completely."

Alison's heart went out to her friend. "No you didn't."

"What do you mean? I'm as influenced as anyone here."

"How do you think I know all about this problem? Where do you think I even got the idea that you all might be influenced? I've been listening to you."

"Well, that's very charitable of you, but..."

"No 'buts.' Leadership isn't just doing the right thing at the right time in the big action. It's doing the right thing all the time in small ways, so you have a system that covers you when danger threatens. You do it all the time without thinking about it." She turned to Jackson. "Isn't that so? She's always listening to people, always checking with her team, keeping them in touch with what's happening."

The new Planetary Administrator gave a small shrug and a faint smile. "I've been getting a crash course in the Space Arm leadership training system. That sounds familiar."

"There you have it, Toni. You had your team set up so that if you were taken out, someone else could cover."

The Commando gave a wry smile. "Well, I'm sure out of it. Please take over."

"Oh, no. You don't duck so easily. Now that you know the problem you have to take leadership in solving it."

Andrew laughed. When everyone looked at him, he shook his head. "When these two first locked horns, it was for leadership of the pride. Now they're at it again, but this time the winner gets to duck the responsibility."

Morissa rapped her knuckles on the table. "And speaking of leadership, I think it's time to close this meeting. We obviously have to get our people off-planet on a regular basis and make our major decisions at that time. I don't see that we're doing anything to the detriment of Space Arm or the human race at the moment, and now that we're aware of our bias, I expect those of us with pretentions of being scientists to make appropriate corrections. Mr. Jackson, does the diplomatic wing have anything to add?"

The ambassador's aide flicked a big hand. "From our end, the faster we get a large number of humans with organic augments on this base to counter the barwolf influence with our own ideas, the better. Will that work, Andrew?"

"I assume so. Any gestalt I've ever been in is affected equally by all members, but any individual may take a larger or smaller role at any time . We have handled smaller barwolf gestalts by singling out and removing weaker participants until the critical mass disappears. We only have thirty barwolves affecting our decisions here, so it won't take many humans to counter them."

Natalia nodded. "We are agreed, then. Next meeting will take place at the embassy, or in space on whatever vessel is available. Regular furlough will be arranged for all participants."

As they were rising, a sudden thought hit Alison. "Wait a minute."

Morrisa sat back down. "What?"

"Let's say you people are under the influence of the barwolves. Let's say we're going to take steps to reduce that."

"All right. Let's say we are."

"Before we make the changes is an ideal time to find out what the barwolves really want."

"Can you give me an example?"

"The big one." She looked around the table, where everyone was now seated again, eyes on her. "Morissa. How do you feel about humans coming to live on Arborea?"

A thoughtful look gradually changed to one of surprise. "I don't seem to mind. Not like I used to."

"Andrew? Toni?"

They glanced at each other, brows wrinkling.

Alison scanned the table again. "Sorry, that's as far as I took the idea."

Morissa nodded. "That's a hundred percent farther than anybody else. Good thinking." She regarded the other members of the team. "In the next little while, I'm sure we'll find other ways to plumb our feelings on a variety of topics and come up with the answer to why the barwolves might want us here." She stood. "I'll leave that up to you. Now, unless we have another genius with an idea?"

They all chuckled and rose. As they left the room, Andrew slid in beside Alison. "I bet you have an idea of the answer to our question, but you're too modest to say."

She raised an eyebrow. "I don't want to influence the freewheeling minds of the geniuses."

"Sure. And the Science Coordinator just welcomed you into the club. So tell me."

She stopped and regarded him. "Occam's Razor again. Here's an answer with one single assumption. Assume that they are intelligent and aware of the needs of their community enough to have a plan. If they want us to be here...?"

"Then they have a use for us."

"We just have to figure out what it is."

He frowned. "And make sure it's also good for humans."

"That's a sobering thought." She glanced at Toni, taking this all in silently from Andrew's side. "And that's your job, Commando."

Toni ruffled the fur on Nzinga's neck. "That's right. You protect us from up there," she nodded her head upward, "and I'll take care of down here."

Alison reached out a fist to bump. "It's a deal."

17. LEGAL ADVICE

They had continued to work on their General Ownership document, with the Base crew providing the written part, the barwolves contributing what their species meant by ownership, and Matteo advising from his accel couch in HR-5. When they had a rough copy, they ran it through various versions of the gestalt, including *Diablo,* who had a comprehensive library of legal documents.

Once Matteo got boots on the ground, the first meeting was called to get his overview of the final copy. There was some trepidation in the creators of the document, and they sat around the conference table in anticipation, staring at the document on the viewscreen as Regia paged through it..

Finally he leaned his hands on the table, looking around at the Barwolf Base team. "Well, that certainly puts me in my place."

Alison glanced at Morissa, who returned a helpless shrug. "What's wrong?"

The lawyer threw up his hands. "Nothing."

Morissa's face twitched between a frown and a smile. "Nothing's wrong."

"That's right. You've brought me all this way, paid me all this money, but I get here and you have the whole thing figured out. Why did I bother?"

Alison grinned. "You're telling us that our legal plan to keep the mineral rights of Arborea for the barwolves is all right?"

"It's more than all right. It's perfect. You've got ownership of the whole world nailed down, above and below ground, as long as intelligence is legally granted. And the person to make that decision is sitting at this table."

Morissa smiled and tilted her head in a nod.

"You've made it possible for humans to explore and stake the Human Continent and various larger islands, only restricted by designated parklands."

Alison nodded.

"And you've given the barwolves, as a cooperative, mining rights to any of those areas, as well as the whole Barwolf Continent."

This time it was Jackson who gave the assent.

Matteo held up the tablet in his hand. "And you've made a ton of added conditions taking into account every possible loophole and evasion anyone could think of." He dropped the tablet on the table with a clatter. "I ask again. Why am I here?"

Morissa chuckled. "To do exactly what you did. You have fulfilled your purpose, and you can collect your paycheck and go home. If you want."

He stared at her suspiciously. "What do you mean by that?"

Alison laughed out loud. "Matteo, I'm sorry. We're making fun of you, and it's not fair. Don't you realize what's happened?'

He frowned. "Obviously not."

"You've put yourself in an imaginary competition with the most intelligent gestalt in the human sphere. If you weren't on retainer, we wouldn't even be allowed to tell you about it. Not only that, we've been picking your brain over the com for the past five days to give us legal advice. Plus *Diablo* has the whole mining section of Planetary Community law in her data banks." She flicked her fingers towards the document on the viewscreen. "We aren't worried about the details. We were afraid you'd look at the whole house of cards and say, 'Sorry, it doesn't work like that,' and it would all come tumbling down."

"Well, in my limited experience, that's not going to happen. This is a textbook example of a good brief." He looked at her. "But my experience is limited. What do I know?"

Morissa gestured towards the document on the viewscreen. "You know enough to make sure we don't look like fools. This proposal will now go to the ambassador's legal advisors and the Space Arm Advocate General for their opinions before it is sent to the Planetary Community Assembly to be made into law."

"Ah." He nodded. "And along the way there will be all sorts of people wanting to add and subtract things because of their ideals and politics. The stronger the original document is, the less weak spots for them to pick at."

"You've got it."

He retrieved the tablet. "In that case, I'm going to look at it one more time." He glanced around. "Might as well give good results for all that money you're paying me."

Andrew chuckled. "You just don't want to get sent home before you try out that beach you flew over on your landing approach."

The meeting dissolved in laughter, and everyone rose. As they left the mess hall, Alison slid in beside the lawyer. "One more entity you have to meet."

His eyes widened. "Brindle?"

"Got it in one."

"Looking forward to it."

"One is waiting over at the compound."

"Yeah, I'll have to get used to that 'one' business."

She cocked an eyebrow at him. "Yes, since they're your clients, going along with a few of their cultural quirks is probably good politics."

He stopped and regarded her. "It's more than that, isn't it?"

Alison shrugged. "They're aliens, Matteo. We don't really know what's huge and what's a niggling detail. But since they're a tri-gender species, I suspect this one is rather basic."

He gave a weak smile. "Not that I was planning to mess with anything. You just make sure I don't put my foot in a paint pot, will you?"

She grinned. "You're a Micha Mouse fan, are you?"

"The paint pot was my favourite scene when I was a kid. Even before I knew what painting a wall was."

As they approached the compound, the barwolf appeared in the open gateway.

"Speak out loud just like normal. Brindle can't read you, but this group has been working with humans in gestalt for months, and they can understand human speech a bit. "Brindle, this is the man I've been trying to describe to you. This is our lawyer."

Image: lawyer and Brindle side by side. Images blend.

Emotion: surprise and question. "That's interesting. One says that you and one are similar."

167

Regia thought a moment. "I don't know much about their society, but the One who Merges each triad must be the peacemaker, bringing the other sides to harmony."

"That's probably it."

He gave a short laugh. "If only that was all I did."

"Keep it in mind as you're working with them. That's what they expect of you."

"And that's what they'll get."

"Just a moment."

Emotion: question/idea?

Emotion: agreement

She and Brindle slipped easily into gestalt. One was working very hard at something, and she tried to follow and lend her strength.

The barwolf reached out to tap Matteo's leg with one paw, at the same time forcing a communication towards the lawyer.

His hand reached out, but he jerked it back, frowning at her in surprise. "Why did I feel like doing that?"

She nodded. "It's all right. Go ahead. I want to see what you were going to do."

He reached out again, slower this time. "Get my arm bitten off, most likely." He lowered his hand and scratched gingerly on the edge of Brindle's shoulder plate. "Hey. He likes it. I mean one likes it."

"How do you know?"

Matteo stopped scratching. "I...I don't know. It just felt like it."

She grinned. "Official warning. Morissa is going to want to tear your brain apart."

"What?"

"A very few humans have the ability to sense barwolf communication. Brindle and I went into gestalt, and one had to push very hard to get that message through to you. You must have a touch of ability adding to your Standard Seven mechanical augment. Not enough to be of much use, but every little bit counts. If you're going to work with us, you'll have to go to the embassy and get an organic implant. It's pretty much a requirement of the job. Standard Level eight point five will do."

"Eight point five! I can't afford that."

"You don't have to. The barwolves have an open credit line, backed by the royalties from the mineral wealth of a whole world. I think they can afford it."

She felt a familiar presence nearby. "And since we have you here, there are a few other small matters…"

At her prompting, Jackson strolled over. "Got a moment?"

Regia grinned. "If you're working for my client, I've got all afternoon."

"That's good, because as you may have heard, I have a small project in hand…"

The two strolled across the compound, already deep in conversation.

Alison smiled and glanced at Brindle. "Got what you wanted."

Emotion: satisfaction, pleasure.

The barwolf strolled in ones awkward gait back to ones compound, and she returned to the mess, where she knew she would find Andrew and Toni sharing a beer.

She grinned and flopped on a nearby couch. "That went well."

Toni also grinned. "You lot were a bit hard on that poor kid."

"Bring him up to speed in a hurry. He's got to understand what and who he's working with."

Alison regarded them. "I had a feeling you wanted to talk to me."

Andrew lost his relaxed pose and sat up, all business. "We do. We see a problem coming up."

"Okay. With me?"

"Of course not. With the barwolves. Morissa put me onto some of Jane Goodall's writing. That got me into some of the twenty-first century analysis of colonial/aboriginal interaction."

She nodded. "I scanned some of that, too. Pretty heavy stuff. They started out with a paternalistic attitude and didn't let go of it for two hundred years." She frowned. "Wait a minute. You think we're doing that, here?"

He tilted his head, one side, then the other. "Not completely. We've got the barwolves in the gestalt, so this group, at least, knows what's going on. But we've got the same problem Freighty has with Humanity. We can't just dump all our knowledge on the barwolf society. It could destroy them. At the same time, here we are, making decisions for them."

"But those decisions have to be made. There's a load of ten thousand settlers heading for this world, and they're soon going to become part of our daily reality."

"And do the barwolves even know they're coming?"

"Well, our group does. Brindle and I have discussed it with his little gestalt and with the larger group."

"What about the rest of the world?"

Alison thought that one over. "We have no idea, do we?"

Toni nodded. "We have assumed that distance maintains isolation. That works in the small groups we can study. But we've been making larger and larger gestalts, with humans and barwolves together. Who knows what has been going on during that time that we know nothing about?"

Alison tilted her head. "So go out and ask them."

The Commando frowned. "Just like that?"

"I don't know." She grinned at Toni. "Client relations are your job. Can you sneak out and do some eavesdropping?"

Emotion: eager desire to please.

Alison glanced at the auguar, who was sitting up, her tail lashing. "Finish your beer, get off your collective butts and go find out."

Andrew was halfway to the door before she finished speaking. "Tell the rest what's going on, will you."

She called out agreement to an empty room.

Alison sat and thought about what was going on. Suddenly she jumped up. "What a bunch of galahs. We've done it again." She went looking for Brindle.

* * *

170

They were back in two hours. As *Diablo* touched down, Alison, Morissa, Jackson, Matteo and Brindle were waiting at the edge of the landing field.

As Andrew strode up, his face aglow, Alison held up a hand to stop him from speaking. "They already know, don't they?"

It was rather comical, the way his face fell. "How did you know that?"

She pointed a thumb over her shoulder to where Brindle was greeting Nzinga. "We were doing the colonial thing again."

Andrew slapped his own head. "You asked Brindle."

"That's right. And one told me. When they get in a large enough gestalt, they can reach the clans on the Barwolf mainland."

"So all this time, we've been dealing with the whole barwolf race, and we didn't even know it." Morissa laughed ruefully. "Good motivation not to feel colonial."

Andrew dusted his hands. "Good. I wanted this out of the way before I made my next proposal." He draped an arm over Toni's shoulders. "Toni and I want to go prospecting. The only difference now is that we want to take some barwolves along."

Image: barwolves and humans digging together.

Emotion: enthusiastic agreement.

He straightened. "There we go. Pack yer Matildas, prospectors. *Ol' Diablo* is headed for them thar hills."

Alison laughed. "You just jumped continents with your dialect."

"We're in Barnard system. Aussies all over the place."

Morissa frowned. "Wait a minute. You can't go storming off digging wherever you like. Could we have a little bit of planning, please?"

He grinned and looked down at her.

She returned his stare. "You've got this figured out already, haven't you?"

He tried to look innocent. "Well, I admit that throwing a triad of barwolves in is going to be a bit of a logistics hitch, but they're barwolves, after all. This is their world. We'll take food for them in case the local clan has a problem with visitors, but I suspect possessiveness would be a human trait not shared by our friends."

171

"And you're going…where?"

He tossed up a hand. "We sort of thought we'd go for the top of the heap. We call it the Mother Lode."

Alison nodded. "That rich area where the minerals are so near the surface on the northeast corner of the Barwolf Continent."

"That's the one. We'll go up there and do a little digging. Work with the barwolves, both our set and the locals, and see how they react, what they can do, what they need help with. All this competition landing all over the place, we have to get our act in gear before they get here."

Alison glanced at Regia, who was hanging back. "What does our lawyer advise?"

Matteo brightened. "Have you got the regulations for staking a claim?"

"Yeah, somewhere."

"Well, the first thing a miner does is learn how to stake a claim properly. If you hit paydirt, all you need is one comma out of place on the post, and some shyster will notice it and muscle in."

Andrew's eyebrows went up. "Oh. Right, I can see what you mean. We'll be real careful." He considered. "Want to come along?"

"Yes, but I'd better not. A whole bunch of things just occurred to me, and I'll have to go and look them up."

"Such as?"

"Oh, who is going to file the claim, what you are using for benchmarks, what the standard descriptions will consist of, that sort of thing. Check the regs and you'll see what I mean. We can keep in contact, and you can show me what you're doing. That will make it easy to advise you." Regia grinned. "And don't worry. This is one area where I really know what I'm doing. I've been staking claims with my Dad since I was ten years old."

He turned to Jackson. "Final question. Who do we register the claims with?"

The Administrator's face went blank as he accessed his augment. "Bring the info to the office. By the time you get out there and do your staking, I'll have a Department of Land Management created to take care of it."

Andrew did a double take. "Just that fast?"

Jackson laughed. "I have a designated Administrative ArIn who knows every piece of information I need to organize a whole colony. As we speak, it is ingesting our Mining Regulations Act and cross-referencing it with existing files."

Morissa frowned. "But our regulations aren't law, yet."

Alison shook her head. "Matteo has the answer to that." She grinned at him. "Go ahead. You know you want to."

He took an orator's pose. "This is a democracy. It is not the same democracy as the Planetary Community, but until such a time as the human government makes arrangements to take control of the region, the wishes of the majority of the local population become, *de facto,* the law. As long as none of those laws are in direct contravention of Planetary Community laws, they will continue in effect. End of lecture."

He grinned. "And if this planet turns out to be the property of the barwolves, then a piece of legislation worked out with their knowledge and assistance is hardly going to be challenged. Go ahead and stake your claims. Jackson and I will make sure they're valid."

Morissa turned to Brindle. "Will you coordinate with Andrew to send a barwolf team along? I have no idea who or how, and I'm happy to dump that on the two of you.

Image: A barwolf triad wearing human work boots and old-fashioned Earthside hardhats with electric lamps.

"I'd love to know where you got that image, but obviously you have it figured out. Away you go, but come back to my office when you're finished. We have a planetary administration to set up."

Emotion: agreement.

Brindle trotted off with the prospectors, and the rest returned to the administration building, where they arranged themselves in Morissa's office. She sat at her desk regarding them. "All right. Where are we, where are we going and how are we doing?"

Jackson took a breath. "Well, we've got our temporary headquarters set up here. That part was easy. It's going to get complicated in about four days, when the *Tyrol* shows up with admin extras they're sending us to help get the settlers settled.

According to George Rowell, the immigrant transport will have their own admin people with them, and our main concern will be blending the two work forces."

"What's the word on the townsite?"

He glanced at Alison. "We have narrowed it down to three possibilities. Major Rowell is taking me on a site tour this afternoon. We assume the immigrants will have construction materials, but we can't wait long enough to find out what. Seven of the S & S ships from the former SolarCorp squadron are coming to help with the construction. They're not made for downplanet work, but they'll adapt as much as they can. When the destroyers were sent out from Sol, they all carried a certain amount of construction material. Prefab buildings and the like. Alfino's people are scrounging generators, solar panels, water pumps and that sort of thing to set up the infrastructure. We should have a steady stream of building materials coming, starting in about a week."

He grinned. "Of course, they'll all show up in the wrong order, with the wind vanes coming first and the foundation concrete last, but we'll cope."

18. INVASION

HR-1 this is Diablo calling.

Hi, Andrew, what's up in the mining exploration business?

Nothing but good news. By my schedule, you're due a patrol over in this direction today.

Your schedule is accurate. You inviting me for lunch?

Quite the opposite. The miners are finding even more ore than they thought, and they want a couple more days to extend their survey. I need to make a trip to headquarters to pick up more supplies. Things are going very well with the wild barwolves at the moment, but I don't like to leave the team without a lifeline for too long.

You'd like to coordinate so that I wander past camp about halfway through your trip.

That would be useful.

Flight plan adapted and registered.

Thanks, Alison.

A change is as good as a rest.

Emotion: chuckle. There will come a day when you look back on this and think, 'Boy, I sure wish it was that boring right now.'

That's why I'm not complaining. HR-1 out.

Diablo out.

Her boredom lasted approximately twenty minutes. As she was prepping her Harrier for patrol, she was surprised to hear the sound of an approaching engine. She glanced at Achmed. "That sounds like a J-73. Are we expecting anyone?"

"Not on my schedule."

Rowell to control tower. Who's on the approach?

One of the J-73Bs from SC-1, ma'am. No other ID.

Well, I guess I'd better go be polite. She stepped out onto the landing strip as the ship taxied to the fueling area and stopped. The airlock irised, and a familiar figure stepped out, striding immediately toward her.

"Father! What are you doing here?"

He took her by the arm and steered her away from the field. "We need to talk. In private."

"Out in the open is as good a place as any. Something wrong? I wasn't expecting your settlers for another month or more."

"Oh, yes, something's wrong. The whole damned SolarCorp Head Office is what's wrong."

Her heart sank. "Another stunt?"

"Yes, and worse than the last one. I've had it with them, I tell you. I'm getting out before I get dragged down by their criminal stupidity."

"Criminal."

"Oh, yes. Wait till you hear."

She indicated a path that led towards the beach, and he talked as he strode along.

"I'm sure you know all the basic rules of staking claims. Well, SolarCorp has a twisted idea of how that works. They plan to start mining on Arborea without permission and claim prior access."

"They can't. The Planetary Administrator has already set up a registration procedure, and they have to follow it. And the Barwolf Continent is off limits."

"They don't think so. Just listen to this. They had a conglomerate ship built. Twenty-six mining vessels linked to a tractor with an Otherwhere sphere. Yesterday it dropped them off into landing orbits. They'll be down in the next twelve hours."

"Where?"

"They got hold of the mineralogical survey you released. At twenty-six of the richest lodes, of course. Both the continents, a couple of islands."

She rubbed her hands together. "We'll just go out and pick them up."

Her father looked at her. "When I heard about it, I started digging. It's not that simple. They have a diversion planned."

"Such as?"

"They've picked out the richest deposit, on the north part of the Barwolf Continent. They're sending in a ship with a bomb."

"What are they going to bomb?"

"Their plan is to fake a reactor explosion, which will distract attention from the other landings but keep everyone away from the area of the blast. But it's a clean nuke that will kill all local life and leave no radiation. They'll land, start mining and claim prior access. According to their interpretation of mining laws, if there are no inhabitants, the area is open for staking."

"You mean a neutron bomb?"

"Technically, it's a neutron fission bomb. They can kill every living thing in the area and then land immediately and start mining within two weeks. Once they have shovels in the ground, they can claim prior access and keep the whole mess tied up in the courts while they high-grade a very rich ore vein."

"But once the property comes under lawsuit, all mining action must stop."

"Who says that?"

"The regulations in force at this moment in the Barnard System."

"Well, our dear SolarCorp planners back on Earth don't know that. They think once they stake a claim, they have a right to it."

"But the whole Barwolf Continent is already claimed."

"They don't know that, either. Alison, you have to get your people and the local barwolf population moving. That bomb has an immediate kill radius of about five klicks, and a delayed radiation kill radius of about ten."

"Father, I'm having a great deal of trouble with this. I'll take your word for it that this 'prior access' rule exists."

"Don't worry, it does."

"But do they really think that Ambassador Pretoro is going to let them stay and mine in a place they've bombed?" She shook her head. "Not even the interplanetaries are that stupid."

"Alison, this plan was created eight months ago by people with undependable news that was six months old. They have no idea what is happening out here. Last year, when everything was in a state of flux, they might have got away with it. How stupid they are is not at issue. The fact is, they're going to blow that bomb, and if you want to save some innocent lives, you have to move fast."

"And if I think it's just a ruse to get me to remove all the intelligent beings out so you can move in with no trouble?"

"Then you're just as stupid as they are. I know you like to gnaw away on a problem until you've cleaned the marrow out of it, but we have no time for logic here. You have to move!"

She looked into his eyes, regarded his face. It had been years, but she thought she could read him. *I'd better be right, because otherwise my career is toast. Bottom line; I can't weigh my career against all those lives.* "All right. Where is this bomb targetted?" She called up a VR chart of the planet.

"Right there. Why is it highlighted on your chart?"

Alison gasped. "Mother Lode! Father, we have an exploration team working on that deposit right now. Toni and Nzinga and two mining engineers. And it's a heavily populated barwolf area. If they bomb that, they'll kill hundreds!"

"Then why are we standing here?"

They turned and strode back to the landing field, where she opened her full augment and called an "All Ships into Space" alarm.

Then she called Andrew. *Are you in the air, yet?*

About half an hour out. Where are you?

In deep trouble. Turn around and head back to camp at full speed. I'll brief you.

Flight plan adapted and deployed. What's wrong?

She explained.

And you believe your father?

I have to, Andrew. If I'm wrong, it's only my career. If he's right, we have to save all those barwolves. Not to mention our survey team.

What's the ETA of the bomber?

Not sure. We haven't found it yet, but the mining ships are all still in high orbit, so you have time. I'm going to get in the air, and we'll plan this on the fly. I'll bring Brindle and a triad with me for communication purposes. One might also have an idea how we can warn the barwolves. The only thing I can think of is to use Brindle's gestalt. Boost them with your gestalt on Diablo, and have them

178

image out the biggest, nastiest monster in barwolf nightmares. If you keep that up until the last moment, that will save as many barwolves as possible. The moment that missile shows up, you're out of there, and don't worry about sonic booms.

Got it.

What's the ETA of the Tyrol?

She's just coming into high orbit. The mining ships are far below her.

So she's no use to us in the short term. Fair enough. I'll get organized. See you soon as.

There was no indication of a message, but Jackson sifted into her augment. As soon as she became aware, he spoke. *Anything I can do?*

Think. Give me an outside look at this. Any diplomatic angles I've missed.

I've already been thinking. I'm sorry, but I have nothing new for you. I think you're on the right track.

Best news I've heard all day.

Oh, I do have something for you. Officially speaking, this is the Planetary Administrator approving your actions.

Why, thank you, sir.

And if you really want to cover your butt, you'll get the same from Morissa.

I was going to call her next.

Of course you were.

Sarcasm is easy to detect in augment communication.

But you didn't detect any, because I meant it. Get moving, Major. You've got a planet to save.

Right. See you.

Mind how you go. People care about you. I'm not good at this 'hostages to fortune' stuff.

Now you're reading Francis Bacon? If I remember, he was talking about wives and children.

Oh, let's not get ahead of ourselves.

Strong emotions mixed. Jackson! This is not the time nor the place for this discussion.

Can't help how I feel. Just be sure you come back or you'll never know how the discussion ended.

Emotion: resignation. You're incorrigible. I'll be careful.

Emotion: great affection, worry.

Carefully controlled emotion: affection, reassurance

She signed off before she said anything ill-advised, and contacted the Manager's office.

You were listening to my briefing, Morissa. What do you think? Anything you can add?

Emotion: confidence. Your team ought to be coming across to you about now.

Who's escorting them?

Brindle. We consider it about time the humans got used to barwolves moving freely in the compound. I'm working on the protocols, but we thought it would be an opportunity to break the ice, so to speak.

Full agreement from me. I see them now. Nothing else?

Full agreement with your plan. Full confidence in your leadership. Go get 'em, Spacer.

I'll do that, Morissa. Thanks.

The moment Alison signed off, she started calling orders, getting both her flights manned and in the air.

Major Bykov, may I have one Marine in each ship, loaded for anti-personnel action? We're going for arrests.

Emotion: agreement.

"Father?"

"Yes?"

She stared at him. "Despite my logic telling me there's got to be something else going on, I'm going on my gut instinct that you're being honest. But I'm not letting you out of my sight. You're coming with me."

He looked surprised, but only nodded.

180

"If you have space armour, put it on. We don't know what's going to happen."

His face blanched, but he ducked out the door and ran for his ship. While he was gone, Brindle and three of ones supporters strolled across the field.

Image: four barwolves standing in a rigid line, each presenting a hoof.

Alison grinned. *Emotion: question. Humour?*

Emotion: humour.

She snapped them a salute and indicated that they should board *Thrifty*. They clattered up the boarding ramp and were soon nosing curiously around the interior of the ship.

When her father got back, he turned to without a word, helping her improvise barwolf accel couches from cargo netting. Then she slipped into the cockpit and called up her squadron, which was ready and waiting. Soon they were all in the air.

HR-1 to Diablo.

Diablo here, Alison.

Here are the coordinates Mr. Rowell gave me for the other incursions. I'm sending a ship to each one to arrest the perpetrators after they land and before they get a chance to sink a shovel. We'll be too spread out for gestalt, so we'll do this the old-fashioned way, with Space Arm battle com. You're my tactical ArIn for this operation.

Got it. Give me a moment…okay, I'm sending you a revised course assignment for your ships. Save a bunch of time and fuel, get them there earlier.

Revised deployment received and entered in Flight Command Server. Anything else you can think of?

Our gestalt suggests best results if you chase down the perps on their bombing run. A warship on your six is a great motivation to cooperate.

Let me know the moment you find our culprit.

No problem, ma'am. We are a thousand klicks or so from ground zero. We have contacted the assay team, and they are preparing for evac. Diablo standing by.

181

Ma'am, communication on Space Arm Battle Band 23.

"Put it through, Thrifty." This is HR-1, Major Alison Rowell commanding.

Good morning, Major. This is the Space Arm Destroyer Tyrol, Captain Jaime Cortez commanding. We were assigned to ride herd on your little shindig, but I gather somebody started the music early. Our information indicates a major terrorist threat. Do you concur?

I do, sir. We are considering the possibility of a neutron bomb, threatening the lives of around two hundred intelligent beings.

I catch the significance of your terminology. Protection of intelligent beings is Space Arm's priority assignment. How can we help?

I presume you have been briefed. We have a fleet of mining ships set to enter a quarantined zone, with the objective of setting up operations before they can be apprehended, and then playing legal games while they continue to reap the benefits of their ploy.

We've also been briefed on that tactic and told to counter it whenever possible. How may I be of assistance?

Simply put, anything that doesn't make it to the surface can't bother us. Can you assist us by maintaining the legal Space Arm quarantine on this planet?

That sounds like a logical use of resources. Let me see...I have twenty-seven bogeys in landing orbit. If I exceed my ship's decel specs by ten percent, I can get within range before I deploy. My armoured shuttles can intercept approximately ten of those, maybe fifteen if they don't give us too much trouble.

Please do so, sir. It will make my job ever so much easier.

A pleasure to comply, Squadron Leader. Of course, it will cost you.

Drinks on me next time we're on base together. All bloody night, if you want.

I'll put that in the record, Major. Just call if you need anything else. Tyrol out.

HR-1 out. Andrew, did you copy that?

As many as seventeen problem sites. We'll have to wait until they enter lower orbit before we know how many got past the Tyrol and are coming down. Revising ship deployment again. Sorry about that.

Revised deployment received and entered in Flight Command Server. Our ETA at ground zero is approximately thirty minutes. What's your 10-20?

Just landing now, ma'am. Toni and her cadre have been broadcasting for seven minutes. Heat signatures indicate general movement out of the danger zone. I'm concerned that they might contact surrounding tribes.

Brindle is onboard with one's strongest triad, but we're still too far away to join in. Please keep an eye out for gatherings past critical mass. We're messing with inherited traits and thousands of years of protocol.

For the next few minutes all she could do was pilot her ship and try to think of something, anything…

Image: Brindle joining gestalt.

Immediately the augment communications became clearer.

Brindle is doing something, Alison. Don't know what. Invoking some kind of rite.

Assume one knows what one's doing. Give them all the help you can.

Emotion: joy! Peripheral barwolves seem to be moving away from the area as well. Maintaining distance. Way to go, Brindle. Scratch one's neck plate for me.

Will comply ASAP, Andrew.

Emotion: satisfaction.

Bogey at 270 degrees, ma'am, 47 degrees high. ETA 32 minutes. No Friend-or-Foe ID.

Diablo has picked him up too, ma'am. Looks like that's our bird.

We'll be coming up from below on his six as you suggested.

"Father, what's a likely frequency that will get through to him?"

George's fingers flickered across the enterpad.

Thrifty, give me a line on this frequency.

You have it, ma'am. Handshake accomplished.

183

Unidentified SolarCorp miner, this is Space Arm vessel HR-1, Major Alison Rowell commanding. We are aware of your intentions. Please pull up and resume orbit.

This is Mining Vessel SC-15Yellow. Mayday, Mayday. We are experiencing reactor failure. Danger. All vessels stay clear.

This is HR-1. No you're not. You have a neutron bomb that you plan to set off to kill all life in the area before starting mining activities. Please pull up and resume orbit.

Mayday, Mayday. Reactor failure imminent. All vessels stay clear.

SC-15Yellow, your little ploy has been exposed. There are two hundred intelligent beings within the blast radius of your bomb. You will be committing murder.

Intelligent beings? I doubt it. There aren't two hundred people on this planet.

I won't argue politics with you. There is an assay team of five humans within your blast radius. You have been informed of their presence. If you continue with your plan, you will be charged with murder.

My reactor is about to explode. Much though I'm sorry for those technicians, there's not much I can do to save them. I have other things on my mind.

"Alison?"

"Yes, Father?"

"May I try?"

"Anything that might work." *Thrifty, put Mr. Rowell on the radio com.*

"You are connected, Mr. Rowell."

SC-15Yellow, this is George Alson Elliott Rowell, Vice President in charge of Operations in the Barnard System for SolarCorporation. There has been a change of plans since you were sent on this mission. Please break off your run and return to high altitude orbit as Space Arm requires.

Sure, and I'm the chairman of the board. I'm warning you, when this reactor blows, you don't want to be anywhere within twenty klicks. I'm about to abandon ship as we speak.

184

Her father spoke into the ship's com. "Sorry, Alison. I didn't know about this operation, so I don't have any codes or handshakes."

"That's all right, Dad. I'll just up the ante a bit."

SC-15Yellow, this is HR-1. Do you know where I am?

Why should I care?

Thrifty, lay a warning shot in his left ear. Close enough to rattle some shrapnel off his cockpit.

Warning shot ready, ma'am. Target acquired.

Fire.

The space frame shook and the missile arced away. On the viewscreens a white line ran from their ship to the miner, ending with a puff of smoke just off his port bow.

Crap! What are you doing, you idiot? I'm about to explode, and you're shooting at me?

Oh. I never looked at it that way. Maybe if I put an S-to-S up your bung hole I can blow your reactor before it reaches critical mass. Please eject and prepare for a large bang in thirty seconds. Mark.

Wait! Wait, I'm sorry. Please don't fire.

That sounds better. Please return to high altitude orbit and await further orders. And if you don't mind, please defuse that bomb.

I can't!

What?

I don't know how to disarm it. That wasn't part of the plan.

Prime. Is it on some sort of a timer?

We have a detonation code, and I think it's also altitude activated.

SC-15Yellow, are you getting the impression that your bosses think of you as rather expendable?

Yeah, you could look at it that way.

If you want to survive, I suggest you head for high-altitude orbit. When you get clear of the atmosphere, launch the bomb. Wait until it's a hundred or so klicks away and then detonate it. Does that sound possible?

I guess we can manage that.

With a blast of its engine, the SolarCorp ship swerved upward and soon was lost in the clouds.

Thrifty, put me in touch with the Tyrol, please.

Line open, ma'am.

Space Arm Destroyer Tyrol, this is HR-1.

Cortez here. What can we do for you?

Do you see a bogey rising up from my position?

We have him.

Do yourself a favour and stay away until he sets off his firework...Bloody Hell!

A brilliant flash of light stabbed down from the clouds. A moment later *Thrifty* was rocked by the force of the blast.

Major Rowell, your bogey has disappeared.

It seems SolarCorp didn't want to leave any evidence lying around. The bomb was either set to go off at a specific time, or their ship was set to self-destruct. Could you send a forensic team to the blast site and pick up whatever they can for evidence?

Already on it.

Thanks. How has your capture operation been going?

Intercepted twelve. A nice selection of mining equipment, I'd say. Shall I arrest their crews and put them back into orbit?

Please do. We're picking up the rest as they land, but we don't have enough interment facilities to accommodate our prisoners.

I'll send an APC to pick them up. At Barwolf Base?

Yes, thank you, Tyrol. I'd better start on the cleanup down here.

Standing by, Major Rowell. A smooth operation, I'd say.

A little rocky at the end, though. Thank you, Tyrol. HR-1 out. Barwolf Base, this is HR-1. What's happening?

Bykov came on the battle com. *I might ask you the same. We've picked up thirteen of them. Two still coming in to land. What was the explosion? We were a little worried, there.*

SolarCorp had a failsafe built into their plan. Their pilots were collateral damage.

Bastards.

186

Heading back to base. See you there.

I've got a call from the Tyrol to answer. Barwolf Base out.

When *Thrifty* dropped into her home base, it wasn't the usual peaceful setting. Two mining factories that had looked so small in the air hulked huge at the corners of the landing field. A temporary hut stood isolated at the edge of the field, guarded by two Marines. Her flight was not lined up with its usual precision. Marines, spacemen and civil servants hurried about like a prodded ant hill.

As they exited the ship, her father glanced at her, then indicated the prison hut. "Am I with you, or would you prefer me over there?"

"As far as I can figure out, you're with the good guys for the moment. I have no doubt you'll be riding to the embassy on the next available ship, which will probably be the *Tyrol.* What happens after that is above my pay grade."

"Above mine too, I suspect."

Morissa banged a claw hammer on a piece of aluminum sheeting as an improvised gavel. "I hereby declare this meeting of the Barwolf Base Management Team to be in session. *Diablo,* are you on?

"Recording audio and video, ma'am."

"Thank you." She surveyed the lounge. "This is the moment we've all been dreading, folks. The pilgrim ship is in orbit. The immigrants are anxious to start their new lives. The barwolf owners of the planet have approved our land distribution plan."

Emotion: agreement.

"Thanks, Brindle, to your community. Major Rowell, can you give us an idea what we're looking at?"

Alison put an image up on the main viewscreen, simultaneously posting it in VR in the augment channel. It showed a thick toroid living module about two hundred metres in diameter attached by spokes to a cylindrical centre column with an engine module at the rear. A huge, smooth bulb swelled the cylinder half way back to the engines. "We have an Interstellar Personnel Carrier, the only one of its kind. It looks suspiciously like a Jupiter Habitat Module with an exoskeleton to attach it to a Cronus V tractor ship. That big balloon is the fuel module.

"It will be interesting to see what the owners, whoever they may be at the moment, plan to use the ship for, once the passengers are downplanet. My guess is that the habitat torus will be returned to its former usage, in orbit here or somewhere else. Then the Cronus can turn around and head back to Sol for another load of whatever."

Toni used a virtual finger to poke the torus. "That's a pretty big living space. It would take a couple of thousand of our population and ease the initial pressure."

Alison smiled. "They've been two years getting here. It's possible some of the pilgrims will have developed an affinity for space."

"Thank you, Major Rowell. The fact remains that we have eight or nine thousand immigrants champing at the bit to get plows in soil. Mr. Jackson, what's your take on the project?"

Jackson rose from his seat beside Alison, his easy smile encompassing the room. "So far, exactly as predicted. The organization of the capital city construction is a model of efficiency. No credit to our team, because the plans all came from Space Arm Headquarters. The three eventual Planetary Administration office buildings are well on their way to completion, containing temporary accommodation for three thousand people. These will be the future citizens of the capital and the bureaucrats who will run our government. Once the Planetary Settlement Department is up and running, we will start construction of the two smaller towns on opposite coasts of the Human Continent. When those buildings are ready, we will move the town administration in. Then we can start putting settlers on the land."

Andrew held up a cautioning finger. "And exactly how are you going to allot who gets how much land of what value?"

Jackson contrived to look superior. "With the utmost of fairness and efficiency. The land surveys from space have long been completed. Some of the first workers onplanet will be agricultural land surveyors. They will decide the optimum crop for each parcel of land. First priority will go to the farmers experienced with that crop. Auxiliary personnel will be landed as their infrastructure is built. Teachers when the schools and students are available. Medical workers on a sliding scale; their facilities will start as field hospitals and grow with the population. Don't worry, the Higher-Ups have it all figured out. It's going to work great."

Andrew nudged Toni. "Until it doesn't."

"And that's why we have a staff of bureaucrats skilled in problem solving."

Morissa tapped her gavel. "The other advantage to an organized immigration is that these people have been living together for years already. They have already chosen their leaders, and their decision-making processes are polished. Their security forces are well versed in their jobs, although they'll have to get up to speed on new concepts like claim jumping and environmental pollution."

189

She regarded her team, her face serious. "And now we come to our role. Barwolf-human interaction."

The VR image changed to a globe. "At the beginning, our interactions will be completely controlled. No immigrants will be allowed off the Human Continent. Barwolves will circulate in human areas accompanied by one of us, in order to acclimatize both species. A barwolf individual or triad will attend all meetings of elected boards and councils, with one of us there to translate and grease the skids of interaction.

"Once humans start moving into the dual-habitation areas, barwolves will already be settled there. We must firmly induce the habit in these settlers that they are visitors on barwolf land. We don't expect too much friction, because at the moment there is no competition for food or territory. The social scientists who made up the immigrant qualification criteria were smarter than their corporate masters. They pre-screened for xenophobia quite rigorously."

Morissa nodded "We have a new population who are happy to be here, comfortable with each other, enthusiastic about the possibilities in this new land and thankful to anyone who facilitates their settlement. This will go fine…yes, Andrew, I know. Until it doesn't.

"When you think of how much bobbing and weaving it took us to make it through the minefield of the opening act, I think we'll be able to handle the next scene of the play." The Science Coordinator dusted her hands. "The overall plans are available in a file in the admin augment bank." She tapped her gavel. "I declare the meeting closed."

She signalled, and the cooks stepped forward, bearing plates. "And now, for your entertainment and enlightenment, Nkosenye has had a recent shipment from Earth, and presents some regional delicacies from his home."

Concerned looks passed back and forth as the plates were offered. Fat curls of some greyish substance lay on a bed of lettuce.

Toni picked one up. She sniffed it, then put it in her mouth, bit down. A thoughtful look passed over her face and then she smiled. She refused to meet anyone's eye, only picked out another one and fed it to Nzinga.

190

Andrew reached over and popped one in his mouth. He chewed, swallowed, and gave a great guffaw, followed by a smug grin as he watched the rest of the crew.

Knowing something was going on, Alison gritted her teeth and took one. It smelled good. She put it between her teeth. It was hard, and as she bit down the surface gave. Then it broke with a crunch, and a savoury oiliness filled her mouth. She chewed a bit to be sure, then grinned at Toni. "Pasta."

The auguar handler nodded. "Probably. Tasty, though."

Alison glanced at Morissa, smiling smugly at the head of the table. "And a little lesson in surprises for the crew."

Catching the pilot's regard, the Science Coordinator gestured. Alison rose and stepped closer.

"I have a little job for you. One you'd better get used to."

"Taxi driving?"

"That's it. I'm afraid you're going to be doing a lot of it."

"I'm a pilot, remember? Driving a ship is what I like best. Who's the fare?"

"A VIP. His Honour Dustin Olson, Chairman of the Settlement Committee. It's an organization created to deal with any trouble that crops up. Temporary, but with a lot of power while it lasts. He wants to come down and tour the townsites, meet the local admin, that sort of trip."

"Have you talked to him? What kind of guy is this?"

Morissa shook her head. "Ask Jackson."

"I will. What's the schedule?"

The same shake. "Same answer."

Alison smiled. "I get it. You're still my boss, but he's organizing everything, and I'm caught in a power struggle between the two of you. Well. That makes me feel important."

Morissa grinned at her and raised her glass. "Now, that would be a completely pitiful situation for all three of us."

Alison toasted, then drank. "Couldn't agree more." She went to talk to Jackson.

191

He was on a settee, drink in hand. As she approached, he slid aside to make room for her. "Business or pleasure?"

She gave a wry grin. "Always a pleasure, but it's business."

"Ah. Our visitor."

"How do you want me to handle it?"

He frowned. "Nothing specific. You're the person to give him the grand tour, because you're the taxi driver who knows more about everything than…well, anybody. On top of your diplomatic skills."

"But…"

"I'm sure you know. He's going to be important, and we want to strike the right note with him. We also want to figure out what he wants and how he's likely to try to get it. Forewarned is forearmed."

"And what is the right note? I wouldn't want to get off-key at the very start."

He shrugged. "I'm sure you know. What Morissa was saying a moment ago about setting up good habits."

"Prime. I was listening. I'll play it by ear, depending on what kind of person I'm dealing with."

"Couldn't ask for more." He laid a hand over hers and squeezed gently. "I'm glad you're here for a lot of reasons."

She grinned. "Are we about to experience one of the more personal ones?"

"An old Space Arm lesson. Take what you can get when you can get it."

"Let's do that."

They rose and slipped out.

* * *

Two hours later, as they lay entwined on his bed, Alison sighed. "I wonder how often we're going to be able to do this."

A shadow crossed his face. "I suppose it will all depend on how the hearing on the bombing turns out."

"Hearing?" Her good mood faded. "I suppose there will be one, won't there?"

192

"Has to be. You made the right decision, but it might not have been the proper one."

"But I had to!"

He took her wrists in his hands and kissed each fist. "You don't have to tell me, my love. It's all about how Space Arm sees it."

"You mean I could have saved the lives of our survey crew and two hundred barwolves, and still get punished for the way I made the decision?"

He nodded, his face miserable. "The involvement of your father makes it dicey. Favouritism, nepotism, conflict of interest; they might take that approach. I don't think that's going to happen, but there has to be a hearing."

"When is it likely to happen?"

"I have no idea, but looking at the practicalities, do you note that there is a Planetary Administrator — namely, me — who sooner or later will need transport back to the embassy for talks with my superior. If the wheels are spinning as they usually are, the taxi driver will be you."

She forced a smile. "That might be a pleasant trip." Then another thought hit her. "Unless we have company. You know how much privacy there is in a Harrier."

"Hmm. Yeah. I'll have to see what I can arrange."

"Prime. I'll just get myself prepared for more serious taxi driving tomorrow."

She curled up in his arms.

20. TAXI SERVICE WITH A SMILE

Alison was in the cockpit early the next morning, because the immigrant ship was set on the time zone of the Human Continent rather than that of Barwolf Base, and she wanted to get the job done while the new man was at his best. So she was out of the atmosphere by ten hundred hours and chased down the gigantic space ship/station in its orbit two hours later. When she disembarked at the dock a reception committee of one man was waiting. He seemed surprised as he introduced himself as Bob Brown, Representative of the Citizen's Committee.

"Pleased to meet you, Mr. Brown. I'm Major Alison Rowell, Squadron Leader of the Planetary Defence Forces." She regarded him. "Is something wrong?"

"Oh, no. No, ma'am. I just wasn't expecting…" He smiled. "I'm very pleased to be the one to greet you. Will you come this way?"

As they strode down the long, curving hallway, she decided not to question who he had been expecting. "What's the gravity here? It seems reasonable."

"Point seven Earth norm, ma'am."

"And you've been at that the whole way?"

"During acceleration we got point eight." He pointed to the white lines in the decking. "We wore the painted line off the running track three times with everyone trying to stay in shape."

"Good for you. Since I've been stationed downplanet, I find I'm staying in much better condition. It will take you a few months."

He grinned. "Looking forward to it. I'm not a spaceship kind of guy."

"I think you'll be happy with Arborea, then. Wide-open spaces and close to Earth-norm gravity."

They entered a large office with furniture showing the evidence of long use. A heavy, red-haired man sat at the largest desk, speaking on a com set. He waved them to wait and continued his conversation.

Alison watched him, interested to see what she could pick up. It wasn't reassuring. He seemed to be pushing the person on the other end of the line, his voice rising as he went on. Finally he stopped, nodded, and his shoulders relaxed. Then he put down the com set and turned his attention to her. "This my ride downplanet?"

"That's right, Dusty. Major Alison Rowell."

The Chairman raised his eyebrows. "A major no less. I'm getting the red carpet treatment, am I?"

She gave him her diplomatic smile. "That could very well be, sir. Of course, we only have six Harriers, so there wasn't much choice."

"Well, something's come up. Give me half an hour, and I'll be with you." He was already turning away.

"As you wish." She glanced at her guide.

"Oh…yes. I'm sorry you have to wait. Would you like a drink? We've been growing our own coffee. Tastes pretty good. Of course I haven't had the real thing for several years. Who am I to judge?"

She gave him a real smile. "We have a wide range of coffee varieties out here, and every purveyor says his tastes just like the real thing. But I'm very interested in your ship. Is there any chance of a quick tour?"

"You can't see much of her in half an hour, but I'll do my best. Right this way, ma'am."

They strolled the perimeter of the torus, viewing the accommodations, recreation facilities, and eating area. The hydroponics section was huge, laid out in regular plots of various garden and orchard plants. There was even a large park full of flowers. Everywhere they walked there were crowds of people going about their business, but they all stopped to look as the stranger went past. Alison took this in stride. "Everything seems well under control. From the look of it, you've had a pleasant journey."

He frowned in thought. "It's hard to think of it as a journey, except for the Otherwhere part, which wasn't so nice. We've been living here for over two years with very little sense of movement. But it hasn't been wasted time. We've all been taking courses in our specialties, as well as studying the flora and fauna of our new home." He glanced at her. "Will we be able to see a barwolf?"

"I'm sure the barwolves are just as interested in meeting you. We don't communicate perfectly, yet, but we have the distinct impression that the local inhabitants are happy that you came."

"Do you see them often?"

"You talk about them as if they're some kind of animal in the wild." Alison smiled. "We have a clan of thirty barwolves living next to our base camp. They visit us whenever they wish. I meet with several of them regularly to discuss things like the legal situation and mining rights. They are keen to learn about us, and we have to be very careful not to infringe on their rights. It's their planet after all."

"Oh." He walked on. "I never thought...I mean..."

She decided that he was a nice young man, so she let him off the hook. "You never thought because nobody gave you any idea what the situation was really like. How could you know?"

A thought struck her. "Do you have an augment?"

"Yes, I'm a Level Three Administrator, so I was given an eight point zero before we left."

"I don't know the civilian equivalents. Is there an organic component?"

"I believe so."

"That's good, because without an organic augment, you can't communicate with the barwolves."

"Not at all?"

"They call normal humans 'deaf-and-dumbs.' Or images to that effect. They don't communicate in words."

The man nodded. "Ah. So that was what the big fuss was about." He stopped and turned to her. "About six months ago the Higher-Ups got a message from the Barnard System, and everything changed. A swath of our medical facility was switched over to development of organic augments, and anyone who didn't have one was given one. I believe they're still working their way down through the ranks."

"So almost everyone who comes downplanet will have an organic augment? That's very good news. I mean, you could function without one. The Human Continent is huge, and you could live your full life and never have to speak to a barwolf. But you'd never understand them, either."

"And it's important to understand them, because we're guests on their planet."

"Give the man a kewpie doll…oh. You've never heard that expression?"

"Not that I can remember."

"You're in the Outback now, kid. You better start learning the lingo."

"Yes, I guess I'd better…" His eyes blanked. "Ah. Mr. Olson is ready to depart. He's peeved that you're not dancing attendance."

She smiled as they picked up their pace. "And I know what that expression means. Is Mr. Olson an impatient man?"

A shrug. "He's a powerful personality. He's not the easiest to work with, but he gets things done. I think he's the man for the job."

"In my experience, versatility and the ability to work with people gets things done in this neck of the woods. We'll see."

Olson was waiting with poorly concealed impatience. "Let's get this show on the road."

"Ready when you are, Mr. Chairman."

He led the way to the landing bay, and she followed, her long legs coping with his pace easily in the light gravity. The moment he was strapped into his accel couch, she applied for departure permission and they were away. Then she came up to the main cabin and sat on the other couch while he removed his safety restraints.

He frowned at her. "Don't you go through pre-flight checks or something like that?"

"Military ArIns are on duty 24/7. Thrifty would never schedule maintenance in the middle of a mission unless something had gone wrong." She crossed one leg over her knee comfortably. "So, do you have any questions I can answer?"

He regarded her suspiciously. "You think you could answer the type of questions I would have?"

She regarded him. "I've been in the Outback for several years. I have a good idea what's going on."

"Prime. Give me an example of something you know that I don't."

So it's going to be a test, is it? "Let's start at the top, Mr. Olson. When you left Sol, you were given the impression that you were going to take over a new planet, and it would be yours."

"More or less." His chin rose. "Why?"

"Because while you were enroute, the situation changed. You're only going to be tenants on a planet that belongs to another species. Didn't they tell you that?"

"What do you mean, tenants?"

"The legalities are being worked out as we speak, but suffice it to say, Arborea is the property of the barwolf species. They are equal members of the Planetary Community, and they own every grain of sand you'll be walking on for the rest of your life. Any human who wants to live here will be welcomed and allowed to lease whatever land required to make a living and provide for the betterment of the Commonwealth. The details of the leases are being worked out. They'll be very long term, but still leases. No outright ownership. You'll have to ask the legal team." She glanced over to see how he was taking it. "Surely you know this. You have been in contact with Mr. Rowell, haven't you?"

"We knew about the barwolves, certainly, but surely our contracts with SolarCorp..."

She faced him directly. "I don't know if anyone has told you this, Mr. Olson, but any agreements you had with SolarCorp were void the day you signed them because they were selling land that didn't belong to them. And when they attacked the planet with a neutron bomb, the corporation became persona non grata in the whole System. The legal battle will take years, but they're out of the picture.

"You and your people are here at the pleasure of the barwolves and the Planetary Cooperative Government. Your best bet is to roll with the punches and try to fit in. Everybody who comes to the Outback makes a similar discovery. Don't worry; you'll find a way to fit in. Everybody does."

His brow drew down. "You may find things don't work out quite like you have planned." He stood over her. "I have ten thousand people at my back, and they won't like this at all."

198

It was difficult, but she kept her smile. "I'm sure they won't be happy. But I've seen the psych profiles SolarCorp used for the selection process. Cooperation and adaptability were high on the list." Alison glanced up at the Committee Chairman. "If I could give you a tip about how we do things in the Outback?"

His head tilted up, and his lip twisted. "You are going to give me a tip, are you?"

"If you like. For example, we are short on people. So everybody has to wear two or three hats."

He shrugged. "You didn't have to tell me that."

"But you have yet to apply it. Who do you think I am?"

He frowned. "You're a Space Arm pilot."

"Which basically means I'm a taxi driver. I'm supposed to shut up and take you to your destination."

He sneered again and returned to sit on his couch. "I could use some of that."

"But what if I'm not?"

"Not a pilot?"

"I'm a pilot all right. But what if I have another assignment as well? I mean, here I am, four hours to spend with a new arrival, nothing else on the agenda, and when we hit dirt there will be no time for the authorities downplanet to find out anything about him before the negotiations start. If you were running the show down there, what would you do?"

"Huh! I'd send a spy to pry into the guy's life."

"That's one way to put it. How about sending someone you trusted to test the guy out."

"Test! Come on…"

"And right now, you're not acing the exam."

He half-rose. "Look, chickie. If you think you're…"

She held up a cautioning finger. "Thrifty, please prepare protocol 35 P-for-pilot S-for-security."

"Already running, ma'am."

She smiled up at the hulking farmer. "If you were to touch me, Mr. Olson, this cabin would be without oxygen in eleven seconds.

199

My suit would automatically deploy, and you'd be out of luck. Please sit down. I'm telling you this to give you a chance. When you get on the ground, do a lot of listening and watching before you start pushing your agenda. Whatever you do, don't try to bully anybody. Especially the women."

"Why the women?"

"Two reasons. First, women are in short supply around here, and there is an extra layer of protection built into the genes of every man on the base. Second, the women you're about to meet don't need any help from anyone." She favoured him with a pleasant smile. "They'll grind you down and use the dust for propulsion mass."

"Huh!"

She leaned back, relaxing. "So, help me do my job. Tell me about yourself."

Once she got him relaxed, it turned out that he was quite happy to talk about his life, his talents and his ambitions, so the rest of their descent went smoothly. Alison didn't want to overuse the word 'brag,' but he certainly had a good opinion of himself. Still, if he got himself elected for an important position it spoke to a certain ability...*unless they gave him the job to keep him out of their hair. Dammit, is every guy in a leadership position some kind of macho-man? Well, there's one I can think of...*

She sat, considering her options, until *Thrifty* gave her the warning call for landing. She returned to her cockpit and her primary duties, handling the operation on manual to keep in practice.

As they left the Harrier, Olson stared around Barwolf Base. "Well, this is a pretty spot."

"It is. You've come to a very pleasant planet, Mr. Olson. The climate is more stable than earth's. There is less seismic activity and less extreme weather. At the moment, there are no biting insects or poisonous creatures..."

"Hey!" He stopped, pointing. "That's a barwolf!"

"Yes, of course. The Base Clan lives just over there."

"But why is the gate open?"

"Because they have decided to allow humans access to their compound. No one is rude enough to enter without an invitation, but the gate is left open. It's symbolic rather than practical." She pointed. "We're headed for the admin building. The Planetary Administrator will be waiting."

We've got a live one here, Jackson. Their lack of knowledge of the situation is stunning, and this guy takes ignorance to a new level. I've softened him up a bit for you, but...

Emotion: humour. I'm sure you did. Bring in the tatters that are left and I'll try to put him back together.

As they entered the room, Alison could feel the man at her side swell, and Jackson, too, stood straighter. She passed him a private eye roll, and he relaxed. Slightly.

"Mr. Jackson, this is Settlement Committee Chairman Mr. Dustin Olson. Mr. Olson, this is Mr. Jackson, the Arborean Planetary Administrator."

Each man stuck out a hand and their fists clasped. The air crackled with tension and their muscles tensed. Then the SolarCorp's agent's eyes widened, and his mouth gradually opened. Jackson kept his grip for a moment, then eased it.

Alison continued as if the incident had not occurred. "Jackson is under the orders of Ambassador Pretoro, who, as you know, answers only to the Planetary Government in Geneva. If you need anything, he's your man. He's also my unofficial partner. If you don't know how the military works, that means were next best thing to be engaged, and are waiting for our assignments to jibe before we set the date." She smiled sweetly at Jackson.

Jackson shot her an amazed glance, then turned to his recent victim. "And if you ever again try to physically intimidate an Arborean employee, you will find yourself on the next ship to the Outer Asteroid Belt, where they're always looking for big, strong miners. Do you follow?"

"Yeah..." He glanced at Alison's stern visage. "I mean, yes, sir."

"Good. Now, Major Rowell, for the moment I relieve you of your duties, which you have accomplished with your usual aplomb. I'm sure you have other willing victims with minds you want to mess up. I'll see you at dinner."

"Thank you, Mr. Jackson. I look forward to our next conversation."

201

"Yes, so do I."

Anything to report?

Nothing you didn't figure out in the first thirty seconds. But the news of our little action last week has not spread. He's still under the impression that his SolarCorp position gives him some clout.

I'll straighten him out on that. See you at supper, love.

Stick to business, honey bunch. We're on duty.

Yes, ma'am, Major Rowell.

As she turned away, Olson was getting the next lesson in local protocol. "Now, I have some people who are willing to meet with you. I'm not saying they're happy that you're here, but they're going to give you the benefit of the doubt..."

* * *

The dinner was a pleasant affair, with Jackson's chef and Nkosenye combining their talents to do Barwolf Base proud. Dusty Olson was somewhat subdued but loosened up after a couple of litres of Jackson's special ale. However, it soon became obvious that culture shock and the higher gravity were wearing on him. Alison made arrangements with him for the tour on the following day, and he went to his room.

The Planetary Administrator returned to the lounge where his Planetary Defence Force Squadron Leader was waiting for him. Together they walked to his quarters.

Once the door was safely closed behind them, they indulged in the kiss they had both been anticipating.

Then Jackson pulled away and gave her his best frown. "And now, my dear lady, you have some explaining to do."

She favoured him with a warm smile. "And why would that be, my dear?"

"Because that was just about the weirdest marriage proposal I've ever heard."

"Heard a few, have you?"

He glowered. "You know what I mean."

"And it wasn't a proposal." She pulled him down beside her on the couch. "You've been playing your usual games, hinting and pushing and making suggestions ever since you showed up here."

"I wasn't playing games."

"I never thought you were. So, that was an acceptance of your proposal."

He sighed. "And, not that I'm complaining, but what brought about this change of heart?"

"It wasn't a change of heart. It was a revised assessment of probabilities."

"That sounds romantic."

"Put it another way. I was brought up assuming that I would marry a man worthy of me. A leader. Someone forceful and likely to be a success. Once again, I have been given the chance to experience a leader. A strong man with a rosy future."

"And...?"

"And all he did was affirm my opinion that I don't like that sort of person at all. Which reminded me that I have a far superior specimen right at my side, and I'd be an idiot not to grab the opportunity. And that was only my practical side speaking."

"I'm anticipating the next part with great...anticipation."

"Goes without saying. I've been in love with you for months."

"You have?"

"Jackson! I do not jump into bed with just anyone. What kind of girl do you think I am?"

"Oh. No. No, of course you don't." He frowned and pushed an index finger against the tip of her nose. "And that was a trick question I have no intention of answering."

"Did I mention you were intelligent as well?"

"Never did me much good in the past. Maybe you're special."

"Maybe? Maybe?"

"Hmm...I'd have to say probably." He gently removed her hand from his throat. "Yes, it is most definitely probable that you are special."

"Omigawd, I'm marrying a diplomat."

"Have we set the date yet?"

She gave him a look of wide-eyed innocence. "I thought that would be a topic for discussion."

"But first we have ten thousand settlers to settle."

"Right. And I have an early morning tomorrow."

"Which means that I don't have much time to remind you of why I'm the superior specimen you've chosen to marry." He slipped his other arm under her legs and rose easily, striding towards the bed.

She put her arms around his neck. "It's early, yet."

* * *

The following day, Alison found it easy to jolly the visitor out of any pout he might want to indulge in. The first item of business was to introduce him to their companion for the tour, who appeared as they were about to board.

Alison noticed that her passenger was staring over her shoulder. She turned. "Brindle! Have you come to meet the new Settlement Committee Chairman?

The barwolf came up for the usual leg-touch/plate scratch greeting.

Emotion: curiosity.

"Yes, of course. Brindle, this is Dusty Olson, Settlement Committee Chairman for your new citizens." *Image: Humans leaving shuttle with farm implements, Olson checking them off on a list.*

Emotion: welcome.

Emotion: hesitant greeting, thanks. Olsen was obviously experienced with his augment but uncertain of the situation. As he should be.

Image: Harrier. Emotion: question?

"We're going to tour the Human Continent and show Mr. Olson the new townsites. Would you like to come along? *VR image: map of Human Continent, zooming in to capital site.*

Emotion: eager thanks.

"Well, come on board and tie in."

The three of them entered, and Brindle settled into the quadruped accel couch the fabrication shop had whipped up for them and installed between the cabin couches. Alison went to her cockpit, leaving the two citizens of Arborea alone together.

She was too busy with the takeoff to follow their conversation, but she got the impression that Brindle was curious about farming, and Olson was learning to communicate. When she returned to the upper deck, they were concentrating fiercely, and she left them to it.

The scenery was beautiful and the weather cooperated. The site for the capital city was a winding estuary at the mouth of the major river with several small islands offshore, and both humans noticed its similarities to Sydney, Australia. Then Alison used the STOL capabilities of the Harrier to set them down in several different agricultural zones, and Olson's instincts took over.

In one spot, out on the plains area, he pulled up a handful of the native grass, clumps of straight stalks with platelet leaves circling them at even intervals. He reached into the hole, wriggling his fingers deep into the earth. Then he stuck his nose into the soil in his other hand. He looked at her and his brow wrinkled. "This is all so…so different. The soil looks right. It's loose and dark. I assume that's fertile organic matter, because of the plants growing in it. But I have no idea what it's supposed to smell like."

He looked out across the prairie and nodded. "I'm beginning to see, now, what they were talking about." He tossed the plant aside. "This Arborean soil, not earth. It has no earth-based bacteria or organics. We're basically hydroponic farming, even if we're planting in the soil. After a few years, the Earth-style organics will build up, and soon we'll have real fields."

Then he stared around. "But we have to keep those fields isolated from the local plants, for fear one of the earth species escapes and takes over." He shook his head again. "They tell you and they tell you, but until your boots are on the ground, you just don't get it."

She smiled. "It happens to everyone out here. Dr. Goodall calls it Comprehensive Culture Shock. I have to say, you've had your moment very early. A good sign."

Brindle had strolled over to investigate the divot and began to dig. In a short time one had penetrated half a metre, leaving a flat cross-section of the soil at one side of the hole.

Olson looked on with interest. *Emotion: thanks.* He investigated the strata closely, several times asking Brindle questions that Alison couldn't comprehend. Finally he stood. "Yes, that would follow. This is an older planet, and there's less volcanic activity and less geo-forming air and water movement, so the soil builds slower than on Earth. Closer and denser strata. Combined with the need for earth-type organics, that will mean more active cultivation for deep-rooted crops. I wonder why nobody ever thought about that?"

She chuckled. "Because they don't live here."

He dusted his hands. "But we soon will." He turned to look down at the barwolf. "And the sooner we figure these things out, the sooner we'll become self-supporting. *Emotion: thanks.*

They finished their tour with a higher-speed sweep of the whole continent at the request of Brindle, who seemed to have a vague knowledge of the geography, although Alison couldn't decide if it was racial memory or seepage from human interaction.

When they returned to the base, Olson once again thanked the barwolf, then got on his augment and hunted Jackson down, demanding an immediate meeting.

When Alison ushered him into the administrative office, he strode right up to the Administrator's desk.

"This is awful. No, I mean, it was a good tour, but it showed me how much needs to be done before we get plows in the soil. We have to connect with these barwolves. They're an invaluable resource. They know what's under the sod. Invaluable." He glanced at Alison. "And cooperative! Never met a stranger with so few reservations. Just dug in and started work. Are they all like that?"

"Well, Brindle's sort of special. One is what we'd call a coordinator, and one has a great deal of experience with humans. Brindle is an example of what the barwolf/human interface could become."

"Fair enough. Say, what's this 'one' stuff? 'One' this and 'one' that. Is this Brindle a transgen or something?"

She smiled. "More like the 'or something.' Just another example of the amount of learning you have ahead of you, Mr. Olson."

"Prime. Cultural differences we can deal with. But Mr. Jackson, we've been going about this all wrong."

Jackson glanced at Alison, but she sent him an augment version of a shrug.

Olson must have noticed. "No, I don't mean this is wrong," he swept his hand to indicate the planet around them. "But we don't know zilch about what we're getting into, here. I though SolarCorp had this end all figured out, but I'm learning that's not the case."

Jackson indicated a chair, and they sat. "Get used to that, Mr. Olson. SolarCorp hadn't thought past dumping you on the planet and letting you figure it all out for yourselves. All the knowledge and progress we have made has happened while you were enroute. So don't feel bad if you don't know anything. We're only baby steps ahead of you."

He glanced at Alison. "Once you've returned Mr. Olson to the Habitat, we need a meeting with Morissa and the rest of the barwolf team. This has brought up all sorts of potential action that we need to discuss."

Olson nodded. "Yes, you do that. I'll go back upstairs and do the same. We'll conference tomorrow. Suitable?"

As they were walking to the Harrier, the farmer stopped. "Is that Brindle coming along? I wouldn't mind a bit more time talking to it…to one."

She nodded. "'One' is correct. I'll ask."

Soon the three of them were accelerating back into space, Olson and Brindle in serious augment conversation. Again, she left them alone.

When the Settlement Chairman was disembarking he chuckled as he thanked her for the ride. "Yeah. Just the taxi driver, hey?"

She smiled. "I did warn you."

"About a lot of things, and I should have listened. Hey, are all the women out here like you?"

She shuddered. "I should hope not. We have all kinds, but remember my warning."

"Oh, yeah. Yeah, I get that. And it applies all over, doesn't it?"

"It's not just the women. If any of the old hands tells you, 'this is how we do it out here,' I suggest you listen up. Oh, some will try to take advantage, but the Outbackers have the same cooperative nature as the barwolves. Any help they give you will be to the advantage of all. There's still not enough of us to make this a commercial enterprise. As long as we're taking handouts from the Planetary Government, we're not free."

His hand rose as if to slap her shoulder, then he recollected himself. "Spoken like a true free-enterpriser."

She laughed. "Just remember that on Arborea we're dealing with the biggest, tightest commune that's ever existed. It can't help but affect how humans comport themselves."

"Yeah. Yeah, I can see that." He nodded. "Well, thanks again for the ride. Next time I'm coming downplanet, try and see that you're the taxi driver. The ride was just as informative as the tour." He turned to look at Brindle. *Emotion: thanks.*

Emotion: eagerness to please.

Emotion: agreement.

Without prompting, they did the leg touch/plate scratch ritual.

Alison shook his hand in the human manner, and the two Arboreans returned to the Harrier. Once they were on course for home, Alison came up to the main cabin.

Emotion: pleasant cooperation.

Emotion: agreement

Question: Olson jumping up and down and shouting at Alison.

Image: barwolf cub jumping up and down. Barwolf adult calming cub.

Alison stared at Brindle. "You did that? You calmed him?"

Image: Brindle and Olson talking seriously. Emotion: satisfaction.

* * *

The meeting of the Barwolf Team was less relaxed. The moment Alison entered, Morissa dove in. "Major, what's going on? I thought you and Olson were doing so well, and now he wants to turn everything upside down!"

Alison took a moment to digest this, glancing to Jackson for support.

He didn't disappoint her. "No, Morissa, that's not what I said. Alison just gave Olson his big 'Oh, my God' moment a little earlier than usual. And a good thing, too. It would have made it much more difficult if he'd waited until he had a couple of thousand immigrants running around in circles before he figured out he didn't know what he was doing."

Morissa sighed. "Right. I'm sorry. It's just that we've done all this planning..." She straightened. "Fine. Alison, why don't you give it to us straight. Where are we, and what direction are we going?"

Alison nodded. "The first thing nobody realized was the information gap. These settlers may have been well chosen, but they were sent out here with SolarCorp's usual disregard for factual knowledge. Plus they left earth and easy communication before we had gained most of the knowledge we have. So they're completely ignorant in two areas."

She ticked off a finger. "First is their legal situation. SolarCorp was playing Wild West. Free land for the taking. It's a big blow to find out they're going to be tenants forever."

She ticked off another finger. "The second is more understandable, and we could have thought of it if we'd been on the ball. The depth of their ignorance about the planet is about as profound as the exploratory team data we had five years ago. General geography, mineral deposits, weather and climate patterns, and not much more."

She turned to Morissa. "Brindle set us off on a new tack in that department. One and Olson connected completely on the discussion of soils. Turns out the barwolf knowledge goes far deeper, if you'll pardon the joke, than just digging dens. I didn't follow much. Brindle, maybe you'd like to fill us in on that aspect of it."

Image: barwolf and human digging and peering at soil samples. Emotion: satisfaction.

"There was also some conversation about overgrazing and site reclamation that I think might send you in a different direction on the topic of mooseyculture and the relationship the barwolves have with their food source, Morissa."

The scientist's eyes widened. "I'll get right on it." Then her face fell. "If I have any time. What else are you going to drop on us?"

"I had a brief conversation with one of the immigrants, a Bob Brown. If his attitudes are typical, they view the barwolves as similar to wolves. Wild animals in their habitat, which a person might get a glimpse of if one is lucky. They have no concept of the barwolves as partners in the enterprise of developing their planet."

"What's your solution?"

Alison held up defensive hands. "I only provide the problems. Solutions are what committees are for. I can only tell you exactly how Olson reacted. If those immigrants come flooding in here with the expectations and lack of information they have right now, there's going to be mayhem."

There was no response. Finally, Jackson cleared his throat. "Well, Major, I suppose we should thank you for tossing us into a minor tizzy now instead of full havoc later. I'll sit down with their lawyers and look at the contracts they signed. I'm sure they're all void, but it will give us an idea of their expectations, and some thoughts about how not to meet them."

Alison winced. "I let that cat out of the bag already, so they'll be expecting contact."

"Nzinga and I are interested in their reaction to barwolves." Toni glanced at Morissa. "It's not unexpected, considering what we knew two years ago. What are we going to do about that?"

"That's easy in principal. Habituation." The scientist shrugged. "We already had it planned. We just advance the schedule."

"Do we want to take some reps up to the Habitat?" Alison frowned. "If they were another group of humans, we'd have already thought of that."

Jackson nodded. "Easy to organize. Which barwolves?"

Toni's eyes brightened. "I've been thinking about the twenty barwolves we isolated. Now we know they've been communicating all along with the group here and have probably done whatever therapy the group does to heal them. I bet they'd be glad to do it. They've already experienced space travel."

Morissa grinned. "Colonial thinking, Toni."

The Commando snorted. "Dammit. Sorry. Brindle, who should we take to the Habitat?"

Image: twenty barwolves lounging on islands. Shuttles bringing food. No hunting. No other interaction. Intense boredom.

Jackson chuckled. "That was easily settled. I'll contact Olson tomorrow and make the arrangements." He glanced at Morissa. "May I assume we are allowed to choose the escorts?"

She glared at him. "Don't overdo the smarm, diplomat. It wears thin really fast."

Toni held up a hand to stop. "Wait a minute. We have to think this through. If all the humans up there have augments, even if they're not practised with them, we have a potential for trouble. What if the barwolves go into their frenzy?" She looked around the table. "I don't want to be pessimistic, but what if the barwolves induce a frenzy in the human population? This is all new, and we have to be careful."

Andrew nodded. "We'll take it slow. It shouldn't be a problem, but we'll keep the numbers small and make sure that *Diablo* and I are in gestalt with them while they're there. Say two triads?"

Morissa gave an open-handed shrug. "Brindle, can you contact them and make arrangements?"

Image: humans talking on com. Emotion: idea/question? Barwolves in close connection.

"Fine. You get into gestalt and prep them, and we'll let you know in the next couple of days. I don't see anything happening too fast." Morissa regarded them. "Folks, we're no longer dealing with a forty-person base, where you can snap your fingers and everybody's onside and working. This is a town of ten thousand people with a bureaucracy to match."

Jackson sniffed. "I may have just been insulted, but I have no defence, so I'll let it drop. That's a third can of worms. We have our government organized, but they have a bureaucracy of their own. Getting any kind of a merge is going to be tricky. Alison, what was it that Olson said to you?"

"He made the mistake of playing his trump card early. 'I have ten thousand people behind me, and they won't like it.' I straightened him out on that one."

Morissa frowned in thought. "For the sake of scientific curiosity, what did you say?"

She grinned. "I reminded him that those people were specially selected for cooperation and cohesiveness, and probably most of them would opt for the easy way. I left it up to my more diplomatic colleague to mention the mining jobs in the Outer Belt."

Toni perked up. "Jackson, did you really say that?"

"Sorry. Failure of diplomacy. He tried to hand-squeeze me. I guess he'd been in low grav too long. It didn't work." His face grew serious. "Joking aside, that guy is a tough cookie. He's tried to steamroller both Alison and myself at the first opportunity. We've got him off balance at the moment, but we have to keep an eye on him. He tries anything, I want to know." He turned a puzzled frown to Alison. "He sounded much more cooperative when he came back from the tour. What kind of magic did you ply him with?"

She pointed a thumb towards Brindle.

Image: barwolf adult calming rambunctious cub.

Morissa raised her eyebrows. "One can do that?"

"One apparently did."

Emotion: placid agreement.

Jackson shook his head. "I must say, I'm looking forward to working with some plain old fractious humans again."

"You are?"

"Yes. Between Freighty and the barwolves, every alien we meet can manipulate us, and we have to be constantly on our guard."

"Don't complain." Alison flicked her fingernails against his shoulder. "When the fractious humans start getting on your nerves, we'll send you a barwolf to calm things down."

* * *

212

It took three days of meetings, but in the end, there was no problem with the contracts. True to form, SolarCorp had stretched the rules so far that even the immigrants' lawyers allowed that the agreements were worthless. Matteo gave them a copy of the Land Use document and passed them on to Jackson for instructions on the registration process.

Alison regarded the lawyer, who wasn't his usual cheerful self. "You're being uncharacteristically quiet. Something bothering you?"

"I was just thinking."

"All right."

"Am I finished here? I mean, what further use do you have for a lawyer? Jackson has a specifically trained ArIn that knows as much about real estate law as I do."

"We can turn you loose. What did you have in mind?"

"Going home, I guess."

"Is that what you want?"

"Have you got a better idea?"

"Much better. You need to go to the embassy to have your organics installed. I was thinking it would be to your advantage to hang around there a while and pick up some experience and contacts. We'll keep you on a retainer, you can handle any barwolf business that comes up and the rest of the time you can freelance. The Embassy has a big population, so there are always legal matters coming up: marriages, contracts, divorces, minor criminal charges."

Immediately he brightened. "I could do that?"

"I'll clear it with Morissa. There's personnel carriers going back and forth almost every day. Jackson can line you up with accommodation."

"That would be great, Alison. Thanks."

"Just keeping our assets under control. You never know when we might need a lawyer again."

As she walked away, the cold thought slipped into her head. *I just might need one myself.*

21. PRE-HEARING

Matteo departed, life settled down, and for a month or more the bombing incident seemed forgotten to everyone except Alison. The concept of a hearing into her actions hung a grey pall over her enjoyment of the time she had to spend with Jackson. Although truth be known, they were both too busy to get together much.

Until one day when she was coming in from patrol, and she got a distinct feeling. Not a contact, not a request, but she knew that Jackson wanted her company. She redirected her steps and stuck her head into his office. "Yes?"

He looked up from where he was working at his desk, papers strewn around. "Much as I enjoy the distraction, I didn't ask for a visit."

She nodded. "You don't have to. I got the feeling."

He waved a hand at the viewscreen. "That's probably why. I have my orders, and I assume you'll be soon getting yours."

As she sat, she caught a glimpse of the ambassador's image on the screen. "What's the scoop?"

"I'm going back to the embassy for meetings. *NightHawk* is passing near, and it seemed an opportune time. You'll get your orders soon…"

She grinned. "Just like we planned, but a more comfortable ride."

He didn't smile. "…with an escort of two Marines…"

"What!"

"…who are due for checkups on their new augments."

"Oh." Her fists relaxed. "Dare I hope it's Kirstina and Campbell?"

"You dare."

She frowned. "But they are designated as my escorts? Should I be worried?"

He shrugged. "You're asking the wrong guy about Space Arm protocol."

"No, I'm asking the only person I know with contacts outside Space Arm."

"You wouldn't be asking me to make some subtle enquiries in a certain elevated office?"

"I wouldn't dream of it."

"Of course not. You'll just depend on my curious nature."

She grinned. "I always knew you had a curious nature. I just didn't know that you were curious by nature."

He closed his eyes and shook his head. "And now, may I go back to work, which, by comparison to this conversation, I suddenly realize is not that complicated at all."

Her augment alerted her. "And I have an incoming message from Admiral Mira. I wonder what it could be about?"

He looked to the heavens and wiggled his fingers. "I predict that you are going on a long journey with a dark, handsome stranger."

"Who is not so strange. No, I take that back." She blew him a kiss and spun out the door before he had a chance to answer.

* * *

It was good to spend time with the *NightHawk* crew, but Captain O'Rourke couldn't give her anything new on the topic of inquiries, except that she had been through a couple herself, and it was no fun, but part of the job.

"Will you be attending this one?"

Natalia leaned back in her chartroom office chair. "Much though I'd like to show the flag, you don't need me, and I have a few small details that need my attention."

"No, no, I didn't want you to show up on my behalf." She regarded the captain. "Tell me about one of your inquiries."

O'Rourke put her feet up on her desk. "Well, I was in a fight with a pirate battle cruiser that an alien ArIn stuffed into a miniature black hole."

"Of course. The *Clyde*. What was the inquiry about?"

"In the first place, all hands aboard were lost. About four hundred souls. That had to be straightened out. Then there was the fact that Freighty had committed the actual destruction. Believe me,

215

there was a lot of discussion about the morals, ethics, and practical considerations of that aspect. I was on the stand for five days straight."

"But no one questioned your part in the battle."

"Everyone questioned everything. There are factions layered upon factions back in the Planetary Community and in Space Arm Headquarters, and all of them wanted to grind their axes on that particular stone. Believe me, I'm happy to be out here in Barnard System, where if I have a problem with anyone, I shoot them, and if there's political permutations, I toss them over to Alfino, and he takes care of them."

"But Jackson says there will be political considerations to my case, and Alfino is staying completely out of it."

The captain smiled. "But his former aide and number-one trouble shooter has been 'called back for consultation.' On the same ship you're riding in. What a coincidence." She sat straighter. "Don't worry too much, Alison. All the right people know what happened, and what you did was exactly what they wanted."

"Is that official?"

"Heavens, no! What good is the word of a mere Scout Ship Captain?"

Alison slumped. "Yes, I know. I just have to shut up and put up with it. It's a part of my training to be an officer."

Natalia grinned. "That's the attitude. Now practise that until you can say it as if you mean it. Maybe you'll start to believe it yourself."

Alison rose. "Thanks, Natalia. I don't feel a whole lot better about it, but at least I know I'm following where many good Space Arm officers have led in the past."

"And the ones that survived ended up with even higher rank."

The side of her mouth twisted. "Thanks. I needed that."

Natalia laughed, and Alison dredged up a sort-of smile as she left.

* * *

The two Marines fitted in well with their Commando counterparts, with a whole lot of good-natured jibing and competition. Their combined antics managed to keep her relaxed to some degree during the trip, but her concern kept rising.

Then she was standing in front of Admiral Mira's desk, trying desperately to look at ease.

His stern look didn't help. "Major Rowell."

"Yes, sir."

He glanced at a screen on his desk. "Hmm…yes." He looked up at her. "This is a rather unusual situation."

"Yes, sir."

"We have to be very careful that everything we do is by the book."

Her heart sank.

"Because everything else in the Barnard System is not by the book."

I wonder what he means by that?

"So, it is necessary that we investigate the incident in the standard manner."

Whatever that is. "Of course, sir."

"You were briefed on this earlier in your career, but nobody ever thinks it will happen to them, so they never listen. Here's the way it goes. Our Advocate General's Department controls the proceedings. They have hired Andreas Napoca to do an Administrative Investigation of the event. If he finds enough evidence to concern him that impropriety may have occurred, he will advise me, and I will order an Administrative Hearing."

"I see…"

"Which takes a similar format to a trial, but is not a trial, because there is no discussion of guilt or innocence, and no specific charge. It is a hearing to make everyone aware of what happened in the event. Should some crime be discovered, then a court martial would ensue."

"But if there was no crime?"

The admiral turned his palms up. "Then all is proceeding as it should in the universe."

"I see." Her mind was whirling with possibilities, not all of them happy. "and if I might ask, sir, who is Andreas Napoca?"

"A legal expert from the Mars judiciary who decided to make a name for himself in a new arena. I suspect he, like a lot of people out here, has dreams of a higher position than he was likely to achieve back in the Sol System. So he has set up shop here, and I have retained him to assist the Space Arm Advocate General's Department to investigate the matter."

"Pardon my saying it, sir, but it sounds like you're lining up some big guns against me."

"It isn't against you, Major. This is not a trial. This event has diplomatic and political implications, and we want to handle it with the best minds we can assemble."

"And what minds will I be allowed to contribute to the investigation?"

"You will be provided with a military advocate."

"Dare I ask for the second-best man you have?"

"I am thinking an up-and-comer with a sharp and open mind might serve you better."

"Thank you. But I don't have to use him if I don't want to?"

"I strongly suggest you do. Military ways are not civilian ways, and a defence attorney unfamiliar with our protocols could find himself rapidly at sea. And you would be sinking along with him."

"But you hired Andreas Napoca, who is not a Space Arm lawyer, because you said that this case has diplomatic and political significance."

"Exactly."

"So you wouldn't be surprised if I did the same."

The admiral seemed to be hiding a smile. "No, I would not."

"Sir, I hope you don't mind my asking a question that might be out of line."

"I will allow a certain latitude, given the difficulty of your position."

"Then if you can, will you please tell me what you obviously know and I don't."

Now he did smile. "It won't do you any good, but of course I can. There's only one lawyer in the whole system that you're likely to turn to, and that's Matteo Regia. He's made quite a splash at the embassy, causing all sorts of trouble for everyone in his polite and unassuming way. I'm sure there are several department heads in the military and civilian areas that would thank us for taking him out of their hair for a week or so."

"But you don't like him, much."

"I find him a worthy opponent, and I would like our relationship to be less combative. I'm not sure that objective would be fulfilled by this hearing, but there are other considerations. Mainly, that he and Faruq Durum, the Space Arm advocate I have in mind for you, have crossed swords a few times and each has developed a healthy respect for the other."

She shook her head. "Again, not wanting to seem forward, but you have everything well planned out, There is nothing for me to disagree with. If it turns out you're setting me up for a fall, I don't see there's anything I can do about it."

He frowned and sat straighter. "This is Space Arm. It is not a democracy. As admiral, I have all sorts of powers, but using them to set one of my officers up for failure is not something I enjoy being accused of."

She slid to attention. "I did not intend to make an accusation, sir. I said, 'If you are.' No disrespect was intended, sir."

"And no offence was taken. These proceedings will all be done as fairly as I can possibly manage. The process is now underway. Mr. Napoca is already reviewing the reports. I expect to hear his initial findings late today or tomorrow. I will keep you and your team in the loop." He lowered his head and looked up at her. "Don't be under any misapprehension that this will all get swept under the rug. Given the nature of the situation, there must be an Administrative Hearing."

"I assumed, so, sir."

"Good. And lest I seem to be managing the situation too closely, I will leave it up to you to contact your advocates. My secretary will give you Mr. Durum's particulars."

She was about to salute when he spoke again. "Major Rowell, I won't tell you not to worry, because you should. But this is an experience every officer goes through. Consider it part of your training. It creates more cautious officers in the long run."

"I can already see that, sir."

He rose. "We will not meet again until the hearing. It would not be appropriate. You are dismissed, Major."

They exchanged salutes, and she did a sharp about face and marched out.

Walking down the corridor later, her head was still abuzz. *Dammit, there are questions I should have asked, if I could only think of them. Well, I suppose that's what my legal team is for. I guess I better contact this Durum person. At least Matteo's going to be happy. Another feather in his cap. All he has to do is win a case against the best Space Arm has to offer.*

She gave herself a mental shake. *At least he has one advantage. His client is innocent.*

* * *

Faruq Durum was a tall, slim Ethiopian with the erect posture and fine features of his people. He gracefully ushered them into his tiny office and crowded in an extra chair for Matteo. For a moment, the three of them stared at each other in silence.

Alison decided it would be best if she take charge. "So, Mr. Durum. I don't want to seem rude, but what qualifications or qualities do you have to make you the counsel I need?

The lawyer gave a gentle smile. "Do you know what 'Faruq' means in Ethiopia?"

"Not likely."

Matteo chuckled. "It means, 'Justice.' That good enough for you?"

Faruq stared at Matteo. "Did you look me up?"

"Of course I did. Before that hearing about the shoplifting midshipman."

"Which, you will note, I won handily."

"Because, you will note, my client was caught with the goods tucked in his shirt."

Alison slapped the table. "If the mutual admiration society could take a break…"

They both looked at her.

"Thank you. Now, I have never been in court before," she raised a hand to stop them, "and everyone keeps telling me this is not a court case. Matteo has little experience with a Space Arm hearing, so we'll be depending on you, Faruq, to keep us in line. However, your knowledge of Space Arm proceedings isn't going to help you cope with the Outback political nature of this case."

The Ethiopian frowned. "Can you explain that?"

"The admiral assured me that there was a political aspect to the situation. I assume that was a hint. Of what, I've been trying to figure out."

Regia nodded. "We're dealing with mining law, here, and mining law in this system is not the same as on Earth, Mars or in Sol's Asteroid Belt. Also, we want to keep it that way as much as possible. Any time those two sets of regulations disagree, we have a point of conflict. I have little idea how that's going to play out in our case, but we have to be aware of it."

"And that's only the local side of it. There's a higher level political angle as well."

Now both lawyers looked puzzled.

"I have a close contact in the Office of the Ambassador — Matteo, wipe that smile off your face — and Alfino is watching this very closely. I'm not exactly sure why, but if we can figure that angle out, we might use it."

Faruq frowned. "Do you usually refer to the ambassador by his first name?"

"Social etiquette lesson number one. Outbackers are much less formal with names. Answer to your question? Only in private conversation."

He nodded. "I'm beginning to get the picture. This is more complex than it seems."

"That's right. You two are in charge of your respective legal systems, but there will be times when my knowledge comes in handy. Everyone okay with that?"

Durum glanced at his fellow lawyer. "At least at the start, right?"

Matteo grinned. "We'll let it run for now."

She frowned at the two of them. "And what does that mean?"

The Space Arm advocate met her eyes. "Most clients think they're going to run their defence team because they know all about the case. After their first brush with the legalities, they usually scamper to hide behind Mother's apron, and are quite happy to let us take over."

She gave them an icy glare. "Well, then we'll let it run for now, shall we?"

Matteo glanced at his compatriot. "Um...if you haven't seen her at the controls of a space fighter with an enemy in her sights, you might think she's a pushover."

Faruq grinned. "Respect for the client is the first thing they taught us in law school."

"Glad we've got that straight. So, my intelligent and well-trained friends, what is our defence going to look like?"

The hearing would take place in what used to be the wardroom of the carrier. It was a low, well-furnished space which could have been the dining room of any decent hotel, except for the conduit lining the ceiling, the rims on the edges of the serving surfaces, and the many threaded holes in the floor to allow for various furniture configurations to be bolted down. For the purposes of the hearing, one long table for the three presiding officers was flanked by smaller tables for technicians and secretaries. Similar tables for the opposing sides sat across a small space of empty floor. A semicircle of chairs behind those accommodated a dozen or so select audience, most of them in Space Arm uniform.

When Alison entered with her team, the Advocate General was already at his table. It seemed he was handling the case on his own. He immediately rose and approached them.

Andreas Napoca was a slight, dapper man with swarthy skin. He greeted her gravely in a mild Slavic accent. "I am pleased to make your acquaintance, Major. I have had the opportunity to meet with your father on a project a few years ago."

"Oh…"

"Yes. I was acting for a client of his in a…" he made a graceful sweep of his hand, "matter of business."

"I see." *Matteo, how am I supposed to treat this guy?"*

This isn't a trial, and he's not a prosecutor. Any way you like.

Thanks. She clicked into "polite conversation" mode, and after a moment the lawyer returned to his desk. Alison glanced at Matteo. "I didn't get much from that."

"You wouldn't. He's rather shy."

"Shy?"

"All right. Reserved. Or would you prefer standoffish?"

"I'll take shy. It sounds more human."

"Don't make that mistake. He has a very sharp mind, and he's not afraid to use it."

"Warning received." She twisted in her chair to scan the observers. Her father was on her four, giving her a nod and a supportive smile. On her eight three sturdy figures constituted the rest of her cadre. Jim and Kirstina looked overawed by the serious nature of the situation, but Jackson reassured her with a head tilt, a wink, and his usual smile. Who the other observers were, she hadn't a clue. Most were in uniform.

At that moment Admiral Mira and two other captains strode in, and everyone took their places. There was little ceremony. A midshipman read off the case name and number, with a brief description of the events, and then Mira invited the two legal teams to make their opening presentations.

Napoca stood, glanced at her, then turned to the panel. "Gentlepersons, first we should get some simple facts established. There is no argument that SolCorporation was stopped from executing an illegal invasion of Arborea. It is also possible that they planned an illegal and unjustified attack on the citizens of a quarantined planet. Evidence collected at the scene of the explosion indicates that they set off a neutron fission bomb in the upper atmosphere. These facts have been established to the satisfaction of my investigators. How they affect the deliberations of this panel is a matter for this hearing to decide.

"To turn to the matter at hand. In the process of dealing with this incursion and in other actions, Major Alison Rowell has left the question open as to her attitude and commitment to the precepts and aims of Space Arm. Her close connection to a high-level official in SolarCorporation, namely her father, and his role in the incursion and its aftermath raises the possibility that Major Rowell is acting under the influence of her father and his masters, and that her objectives are concerned with furthering the objectives of their business, even to the point of using her position in Space Arm in a treasonous manner. It is my intention to expose Major Rowell's recent actions to the scrutiny of this panel, in order to allow you to judge her motivation and commitment to Space Arm. Thank you."

He sat, staring straight ahead.

Augment conversation was fast and furious between her two lawyers while the Space Arm advocate spoke. She stayed out of it. Hearing the charges against her, even knowing that they weren't

224

really charges, put her mind in such a turmoil that she would be no use to them.

Matteo rose. "Gentlemen, I'm glad my learned colleague has established the facts of the recent attack on Arborea. What he neglected to mention was that it was solely due to the actions of Major Rowell, aided by her father, that the attempted atrocity did not take place. We plan to show the court that Major Rowell is a talented officer, cognizant of her position in Space Arm and enthusiastic in the achievement of her duties. Furthermore, we plan to demonstrate that her adoption of the new skills required to function in this alien environment has allowed her to achieve considerably better results than would be expected had she stuck closer to general Space Arm procedures."

He glanced at Alison, then turned back to the three officers on the board. "In general terms, gentlemen, it is our contention that regular Space Arm procedures were created back in the Sol System for civilized interactions. Out here in Barnard's System, circumstances are often quite different, and require a more creative approach from the officers who function where the ordnance is live. Thank you."

"Thank you both. Mr. Napoca, I see you have a question."

"I do, sir." The lawyer stood. "I would like to ask my young colleague where he gets the evidence to suggest that Major Rowell's actions were what averted the catastrophe."

Matteo rose as well. "I think perhaps it would be of more use to ask my elder colleague if he has any evidence to the contrary."

When the lawyer failed to respond immediately, Regia turned to the admiral. "It seems to me, sir, that in his role during the Administrative Investigation Mr. Napoca has used the evidence he discovered to set the scene for this hearing in ways that will work to his advantage. I merely wish to balance the books somewhat by establishing one simple fact that has a great deal of bearing on the outcome of the proceedings."

The admiral took a moment. "I feel I should remind you that this is not a trial, and Mr. Napoca is not in a position of prosecuting anyone. He should have no reason to take advantage of anything. However, I think it is a fair question."

He turned to the other lawyer. "Mr. Napoca, in your investigation, did you find any evidence that the actions of any other party influenced the outcome of the attack, or did you find any evidence to counter the contention that Major Rowell's actions did, in fact, save the lives of a large number of sentient beings from the explosion of the bomb?"

"No, sir, I did not."

"Thank you. The hearing will accept as fact that Major Rowell's actions, aided by George Rowell, did save a considerable number of lives." He looked up from where he was making a note on his tablet. "Now, if that is all…? Then Mr. Napoca, will you call your first witness."

Matteo sat facing forward, but there was a curl to his lip. *Score one for us. You've been officially declared a hero before the first witness was called.*

She glanced at Faruq, who nodded.

Makes it easier for us.

Trying not to get her hopes up, she focused on Napoca's first witness, a Space Arm communication specialist whose duty was to blend the recording of the radio communications from Barwolf Base and the various ships during the incident and verify their origin and purity. It involved a lot of technical talk that she tried to follow but couldn't.

She made eye contact with both her lawyers, who just shrugged and kept listening.

When the witness was finished, Regia had no questions for him, and the man stepped down.

If he's playing any games with the veracity of the feed, I have no idea what they are.

She glanced at Faruq. "What about that redacted material?"

"It's usually something that deals with Space Arm security issues or higher level clearances."

"I should ask about that." Matteo faced Faruq. "What's the procedure?"

"Challenge the redactions."

"Admiral Mira, I have a challenge."

"You have that right. What do you challenge?"

"I would like to know the reason for the redactions."

"Those were made on my orders. There are security concerns involved."

"Am I allowed to know what was redacted, without going through my version of the record and comparing the two?"

"Without moving into information dealing with that very security issue, it would be hard to answer you. Suffice it to say, it is not the purvey of this hearing to deal with any issues concerning the denizens of the planet, except to grant that a considerable number of their lives were at risk."

Faruq shipped a quick warning. *Don't mention barwolves again.*

Easy for you to say. Matteo nodded. "Thank you, sir. If at any time in future I wish to enter any of that evidence, I will run it past you first."

"I would appreciate that. I would also like to remind Major Rowell that Mr. Regia only has basic security clearance on this topic."

"I'll be careful what I reveal, sir, though it does put me in a bit of a bind."

"In what way?"

"I may find a piece of evidence crucial to my case and discover that I can't even tell my lawyer what it is."

The admiral stared at her for a moment. "If that happens, we will convene an in-camera session with individuals who have the appropriate clearance."

"Thank you, sir. Also I should remind everyone here that Mr. Regia has been working in person with the aboriginals on their land use legislation, so probably has more knowledge of them than people with far higher clearances, including everyone in this room."

The admiral nodded. "A good point. But we are only talking in possibilities. Let's not borrow trouble."

He looked to his fellow captains. "This session has brought up some questions we all want to mull over. Let us reconvene at fourteen hundred hours." The three officers rose, and a hum of conversation filled the room as everyone filed out.

When the hearing convened after what had been a rather nervous lunch for Alison, Napoca opened with the suggestion that for the purposes of clarity, an audio version of the incident, as recorded by the *Tyrol,* would be useful.

"Our technician has edited it for brevity and security issues. Does anyone have any objection?"

Alison huddled with her team. "Anything against it?"

"We have nothing to hide. Faruq?"

The Space Arm lawyer considered. "Listen very carefully. If anything strikes you as problematic, mention it immediately and get it cleared up. Once it has been put into the record, it's very difficult to get it removed."

Matteo raised his head. "No objections, sir."

Alison obeyed the order to listen, although she had gone over *Diablo's* version several times in preparation for the hearing. As the recording progressed, she became increasingly concerned.

Matteo, there's a lot missing.

Yeah, it's like Brindle wasn't even there. Faruq, how do we deal with this without mentioning barwolves?

No idea. Better to ask.

When the recording was finished, Napoca professed himself satisfied.

Matteo rose to his feet. "Mr. Napoca, I find it difficult to believe that you expect this case to be solved on the basis of so incomplete a recounting. There are huge gaps in the narrative. We both know why, but I assume that for security purposes it is not possible to mention the presence of a participant whose actions played an appreciable part in the action. Surely the mere mention of a being who wanders comfortably around Barwolf Base in plain sight is no security breach."

The older lawyer shook his head. "It is obvious that you are unversed in the complexities of Space Arm security issues. Do you think that just because you have observed an individual being going about its daily life, you can therefore freely discuss it with all and sundry? I suggest that we accept this record as complete to the degree that Space Arm security allows and leave it at that. What is your objection? What legal precedents do you bring to our attention to support your claim? What bearing does it have on this creature and its place in the System? I suggest that you follow proper courtroom procedure, and do not try to throw this hearing off its normal course."

Matteo turned to the admiral. "Your Honour, my esteemed colleague has addressed several questions to me directly, and I think, for the edification of the court, I should answer them. It has bearing on the actions of the people involved in the incident in question."

"That seems fair to me."

The young lawyer paced to the front of his opponent's desk. "Mr. Napoca, I am what is known in the outback as a First Waver. I was born on a sub-light mining transport fifteen years after it left Mars orbit, and sixteen years before it reached the Barnard System. My people came here when there was nothing, and we have been eking out a living and building a society in this system ever since.

"Since Otherwhere travel was discovered, we have been inundated with two more waves of immigrants, each more naïve and inexperienced than the last: first, the officially sanctioned population, and now the unofficial mess that followed. The Fourth Wave is hitting the atmo of Arborea as we speak. It has been a great trial for us to make these new folk welcome and try desperately to teach them what they need to know to survive. In many cases we have not been successful, and we feel guilty for our lack. So when I try to explain to you how things work out here, and you sneer and tell me that's not how it works in the real world, I have a great urge to tip my hat and usher you to the nearest airlock, because that would save all of us a lot of bother. But I don't do that, because one thing the Barnard teaches us is patience."

He turned to the admiral. "This may be irregular, sir, but if I may give a couple of examples, it may enlighten many as to the actions and motivation of my client."

"You are proposing to take on the role of outside expert? Friend of the court?"

"That would explain it, sir." He grinned. "And since this is not a trial…"

The admiral nodded. "I think we may take a certain latitude in these matters. It seems to be the way things are done, here in the Outback."

The young lawyer shot a glance at the admiral, but the officer kept a straight face.

"Thank you, sir. You actually bring up my first point. We are very short on personnel here because of our small population. As a result, everyone wears several hats. A young miner's son may be a lawyer, but also an expert witness on sociological matters."

"Precisely. Please go on."

"The second derives from that and deals with family and friends. I note that while you, as Admiral of the Fleet, are heading this board of enquiry, two of your captains are here to support you, and two others are witnesses for the defense. No one else."

"That's right." He indicated the officer on either side of him. "These are the most senior officers who have not had direct dealings with Major Rowell."

"My point exactly. And it's the same all over the Outback. It is virtually impossible to turn around without running into someone who is the brother, second cousin, or best friend of someone you know. The fact that Alison Rowell happened to be in charge of air and space defence of Arborea at the same time as her father seemed to be head of her SolarCorp antagonists might look like suspicious circumstance back in the Sol System. Here, it's an everyday occurrence."

"Have you made your point?"

"For my client, yes." The young lawyer smiled. "But speaking as an old-timer attempting to put the young whipper-snappers in the picture, I think everyone in this hearing needs to understand that here in the Outback, conflict of interest is a concept we tiptoe around very softly. Members of boards and organizations are very quick to recuse themselves from discussions where they might be perceived to get a benefit from the outcome. The concept is often discussed, and there must be a great deal of consensus among us as to exactly how it must be applied in order to prevent unnecessary strife."

"And how does that apply to the present proceedings?"

"The whole Outback is watching this with great interest. We are all waiting to see what kind of rules Space Arm applies to a case which we all agree is open and shut. The security measures my colleague is so anxious to protect are common knowledge to everyone in the system. The experts with boots on the ground of Arborea tell me that everyone there wants to be very certain that the beings involved are given full credit for the responsibility they have taken on, and the actions they participated in. We are all interested to see how Space Arm deals with it."

"Are you telling me that you are here to judge me?"

"I will be reporting to my clients and my people, sir. It's rather unavoidable."

Admiral Mira interlaced his fingers and stared at Alison over them. "Major Rowell, were you aware that your lawyer came to these proceedings with a political agenda?"

"It is the Outback, sir."

The admiral gave a small grin. "Walked into that one, didn't I?" He turned to Matteo, "Are you willing to return to your original task, now, councillor?"

"Of course, sir. Oh, just one more thing. A matter of cultural sensitivity."

"I can't wait."

"Without going into details I am not allowed to know about for security reasons, my client asks this hearing not to refer to members of the indigenous population on Arborea as 'it.' The proper pronoun is 'one.' As in, 'Please ask that individual if one would answer a question for us."

"Since your client is of appropriate security level and has the experience, I will try to follow her directive. What bearing might that have on this hearing?"

"Because my client is suggesting that she might want to ask an individual of that species for one's testimony in this matter."

"An outcome I consider highly unlikely, but the matter has already been dealt with. Does the prospect of an in camera discussion if needed not suit you, Major?"

"Of course, sir. Thank you." *Let's try not to antagonize the admiral quite so early in the proceedings, please, Matteo."*

Emotion: Oops!

"Then if we are finished with the social niceties will you call your first witness, please, Mr. Regia."

"As I mentioned in my original deposition, I would like to ask your indulgence to discuss another incident that speaks to Major Rowell's ability and attitude."

"I was aware of this. You may do so."

"I will call Captain Jones of the *Devonshire,* sir. He is waiting on the com."

"Go ahead, Captain Jones."

The viewscreen lit up with the scene of a destroyer's chart room, considerably larger and better furnished than Natalia's little cubby on *NightHawk.* The Captain's long, craggy face appeared. "Jones reporting, Admiral."

"Mr. Regia, please proceed."

"Thank you, sir. Captain, I gather your destroyer, the *Devonshire,* was involved in the incident last year when the group of barwolves was kidnapped, and Major Rowell brought them back. Could you describe Major Rowell's actions and your analysis of them?"

Only a brief time lag ensued. The *Devonshire* must be somewhere nearby.

"Certainly. The barwolves had been kidnapped by what was purported to be a SolarCorp agent, although that connection was never proven. That agent was known to Rowell, I gather. She was a Lieutenant at the time. When she discovered that he had committed the crime, she immediately informed the Commando leader in charge of barwolf security, then-Lieutenant Toni Jacobs, and the two went in pursuit in Rowell's Harrier."

"And how did the operation proceed?"

"Rowell put Jacobs and her auguar aboard the perpetrator and then stood by in her ship. A firefight ensued, during which the barwolves got loose. I don't understand the mechanism, but they went into some kind of frenzy and killed all the crew of the ship that had captured them. I gather the auguar…"

Mira raised a finger and the image froze. "If I might interrupt, Captain, I think you're getting into classified material, here."

The image moved again. "Probably, sir. In any case, once they had control of the ship, they got the barwolves calmed down and waited for help to arrive. Then they brought the victims home, and the operation was concluded successfully."

Matteo nodded. "And your analysis of Major Rowell's conduct?"

"I think she was in a difficult situation because of her prior communication with the possible perpetrator. Two things stand out. First, she informed the proper authority the moment she discovered the crime. Second, I was listening to their battle com during the action. It was clear that Rowell was accepting leadership from the Commando lieutenant despite their similar rank. This was good procedure for two reasons. First, it allowed the officer with the best experience in the situation to lead. Second, if there was any conflict of interest, she was removing herself from exercising her position, a prudent move. In my opinion, she handled a tough situation with conduct becoming a Space Arm officer."

"Thank you, Captain Jones. Mr. Napoca?"

"Captain Jones, you twice mentioned Major Rowell's previous contact with the supposed perpetrator of the kidnapping. Can you expand on that?"

"Not really. My knowledge came from her report, which, I believe, has already been entered as evidence. In my opinion, an admission of a possible conversation with a suspect of unproven guilt is hardly grounds for treason."

The Space Arm lawyer gave a grim smile. "Fortunately we are not here for your opinion, Captain Jones. That will be all."

The admiral stopped Jones's response with a chopping hand and the screen image froze. "Mr. Napoca, that is exactly what we are asking Captain Jones for. His opinion of the Major's conduct relative to the conduct of other officers in his experience. I remind you that this is a military hearing and not a civilian court of law. I also remind you that this is a small community, and if you plan to continue living here, it is not a good idea to gratuitously offend its senior members."

The prosecutor's face reddened. "My apologies, Captain Jones."

The image unfroze, and after a moment the Captain responded. "Accepted."

"Thank you, Captain Jones."

The screen blanked, and the admiral turned to Regio. "And your next witness will testify by deposition, I gather."

"That's right, sir."

The admiral nodded to the technician, and Cortez appeared on the viewscreen.

"Captain Jaime Cortez of the Space Arm Destroyer *Tyrol*, here. I am making this deposition to give my observations as to the comportment of Major Alison Rowell in the action against the intended bombing of the Mother Lode mine."

Cortez gave a wry grin. "Though I must remind the hearing that I do not consider myself or any officer in the whole of Space Arm qualified to make this assessment."

The admiral signalled the technician to stop the playback while he quieted the room.

The deposition continued. "I know that sounds dramatic, but is serves to remind us of the unusual nature of the situation. There has not been an action since the Twentieth Century where a military officer has entered conflict supported by indigenous allies. This pushes Major Rowell's situation to a level outside the norm, and as such, any action she took which resulted in a successful conclusion would be, *de facto,* appropriate."

He paused, then continued. "However, I felt that this was a rather cut-and-dried case. Harm reduction to the civilian population was paramount, and all efforts were first directed to that end. After all official channels were exhausted, Major Rowell took limited military action involving appropriate threat of superior firepower. Subsequent scientific data indicates that there was definitely a neutron bomb involved, thus justifying a far greater use of a military solution than the major indulged in. My crew's subsequent analysis concludes that, had she made good her threat and blown the reactor of the enemy ship, there were no sentient beings within the probable radius of that blast. So her action worked, her backup plan would have worked, and even had she not been successful, her initial efforts would have saved about fifty percent of the indigenous population of the area.

Again he paused, sitting straighter. "In conclusion, I felt that Major Rowell demonstrated all of the qualities we look for in our young officers, and she should be commended for her creativity and cool head in a life-threatening situation."

The screen blanked.

Alison exchanged glances with her team. "Well, that was good."

Faruq nodded to draw their attention to Napoca, who was getting to his feet.

At the admiral's nod, the lawyer stood forward. "A glowing report which basically adds nothing to the needs of this hearing."

"Why so?"

"Because we established at the beginning that Major Rowell's actions were successful. Captain Cortez lauds her for her planning and execution, as do we all. That is not what is at issue here." He sat, not exactly gloating, but not hiding his satisfaction, either.

"Damn, is he good." Matteo glanced at Faruq. "Any point in arguing?"

The other lawyer shook his head. "We could pick that statement apart, but the admiral doesn't like that kind of waste of time. I'd advise we let it stand. It was a great testimonial."

Once again, the admiral called adjournment, and once again, Alison's team huddled.

"What's next, Matteo?"

"The question is whether we put your father on the stand."

"Why is that a question? He knows more than anyone else what was going on. In fact, he's our only chance of getting to the bottom of some of this."

"Do we want to get to the bottom? More important, does he want to get to the bottom?"

"What do you mean by that?"

"What if he's involved more than you think? This would be a good opportunity for him to slant the record in his own favour. He could shift the blame all over the place."

"Are you suggesting my father might sell me out in order to protect himself?"

He held up his hands. "My only knowledge of your father is what I got from you, and quite frankly, it sounds like a possibility."

"Did I ever give you that impression that my father had the ability to sway my opinions?"

"No, the poor sod." Matteo grinned. "He seems to have raised you with the strength of character to stand up to him."

"Something like that."

"Prime. Is your father in any way sneaky or sly? Could he be putting something over on us?"

"Sneaky? Quite the opposite. He's obnoxiously, in-your-face sure of himself, and he'll tell you so constantly. Drives me bonkers."

"That agrees with what I saw. Well, I was counting on the two captains' testimonies, and that hasn't worked so well. So, we put him on the stand. I'll talk to him before we go for lunch."

She waited at her table while Matteo held a brief discussion with the elder Rowell. He returned looking satisfied.

"What is he going to say?"

"The truth."

"As he sees it."

"He says you are completely clear of any wrongdoing, and he's going to make sure everyone knows it."

"While making sure he clears himself at the same time."

"I got the impression that we will hear the story of a fractious father and daughter putting their differences aside in order to allow justice and truth to prevail. Do you think he can swing it?"

"My father has a talent for rewriting history to make sure it leads to the point at which he wants us all to find ourselves."

* * *

At the beginning of the afternoon session, Regia expressed the desire to have George Rowell testify.

Once he had been sworn in, the lawyer made it simple. "Mr. Rowell, could you please tell us in your own words what happened,

236

why it happened, and how Major Rowell's behaviour fitted in with the successful conclusion of the mission?"

"Certainly." Rowell turned to the admiral. "Your Honour, I need to go a fair way back in order to put the tribunal into the total picture. At the time of the Rebellion, I knew there were commercial opportunities developing in this system. Any power vacuum finds ways to fill itself. At that time I had no relationship with SolarCorp at all, but I was intrigued by my daughter's descriptions of the SC1 asteroid project. I did not feel she was breaking any regulations in what she told me, because she had never actually been to SC1. Her information came from Board members of the Factory 4-80 Fabrication Consortium, and as such were public knowledge. Her communications were cleared by Space Arm censors at the time, and have been entered as evidence, should you choose to peruse them."

The admiral nodded. "We will certainly do that."

Alison sent a private augment message to Matteo. *He never told us about this.*

They were included in our pre-hearing evidence package. I saw them. Faruq saw them. They're boring.

Emotion: skepticism.

Emotion: reassurance.

"So, I contacted Factory 4-80 with a proposition. As you can see from the look on Major Rowell's face, she was unaware of this, and probably does not approve. However, that's what I did."

Image: Alison rubbing George's face in puddle of radioactive lubricating oil.

Emotion: approval. Keep it up. That's exactly the way he wants you to react.

Emotion: disgust.

"I suggested to the factory ArIn that Asteroid SC1 was a forward-looking project with great potential, but the group of Outbackers who had taken over the controlling interest from SolarCorp would be underfunded and underexperienced for organizing the broader applications, especially once the project became operational. Freighty agreed and offered to match any amount of funds I was willing to invest. I was able to buy a 16% share in the new corporation, and find like-minded people willing to invest another 14%. Freighty put up 30% to match."

The admiral nodded. "At which time you stopped looking, because you wanted to be in charge of your bloc of votes."

Rowell smiled. "You don't spend all your time chasing claim jumpers, do you, sir? That's exactly what I did." He sobered and glanced at Alison. "Now, here's a point where some of you may not approve, but this kind of thing happens in business all the time. Freighty and I had approached the SC1 corporation separately, not revealing our connection. The Outbackers were desperate for a cash infusion and, thinking they had a balanced power structure, took both offers."

"So, unknown to the Outbackers, you and the factory 4-80 owned 60% of the project."

"Correct. My other backers had all been SolarCorp executives who were hedging their bets against a possible event such as the outcome of the Rebellion. This group understood the potential of the Barnard System, but they were concerned with SolarCorp's methods. They were trying to diversify just in case.

"When it all went south for SolarCorp at the end of the rebellion, they joined with me, and we pooled our resources to continue the SC1 project. With a bit of normal business skullduggery, they used their position in the corporation as leverage and had me installed as SolarCorp's Manager of Operations in the Barnard System."

The prosecuting attorney indicated that he wished to speak. At a nod from the admiral, he stood. "So, Mr. Rowell, you are saying that your dealings with SC1 were private."

"Yes, although I was still employed by SolarCorp."

"Which does nothing to distance you from that corporation's criminal activities. How is this going to help your daughter escape her responsibility for helping you?"

"Thank you, sir, for refocusing on that very topic. I'm sure everyone here is acutely aware of the time lag between communications and actions in the Sol System and here in the Outback. When I took on the position, both the legitimate colony ship and the completely illegal and ill-advised claim jumping operation had already left Sol System. I was not even aware of the mining plan.

"It was necessary that I know about the immigrants, and once I was told, I came to the same conclusion that your ambassador did later on. It was a very clever ploy, it wasn't illegal, and in the end, it would be to the benefit of everyone. If SolarCorp's executives hadn't fallen back on their shady ways with the mining stunt, they would be well-placed in the Barnard System right now. So, I set about doing my appointed tasks, easing the way for the colony ship when it arrived. There is nothing wrong with anything I did in that respect, and most relevant to this hearing, my relationship with my daughter played no part in it. We only met twice during that time, and our conversations were strictly on private matters.

"I continued to do my best for my employers, despite their ignorance. I based my decisions on my daughter's reliance on, and respect for, the people involved in the Barwolf Project. You can't put a muzzle on personal beliefs. It doesn't happen very often in this complicated universe, but if someone you know and trust indicates in many ways that they trust a third party, and if your own observations bear out the veracity of that party's findings, it is possible to act with certainty.

"Once the barwolf information started rolling in, I had no need of Major Rowell. All I had to do was gather the data that Dr. Goodall was releasing. It was easy to see that she was heading for a verdict of intelligent species. That got me worried, because it spelled problems for my job of settling my people on their planet."

He paused and glanced at Alison. "And then a strange thing happened. I doubt if any of you noticed, but I detected a definite shift in the subtext of Dr. Goodall's messages. At first, I assumed it was a deliberate attempt by Space Arm or the embassy to slant the information released to the public, but once I started digging, I realized it was genuine. The researchers at Barwolf Base were changing their minds. Instead of rabid protectionism, they were beginning to look for ways humans and barwolves could interact. For example, the term "Barwolf Continent" started appearing. Where did that idea come from? Who was the other continent meant for? I dared to hope.

"And then, just when things were rolling my way, I caught a whiff of this stupid mining stunt." Rowell sighed and shifted in his chair. "This project, you understand, was conceived a year ago, based on faulty information collected six to eight months before that time by agents in this system with their own agendas. Even on that basis, it was highly problematic, because SolarCorporation Head Office has never had any idea what it's like out here. I was surprised, myself, when I arrived and I had to scramble to adapt. They continued to play the same commercial ploys they have always used, assuming they could get away with them as they often have.

"Fortunately, I had a position in the company where I was able to twist arms and gain full information. The neutron bomb was the final straw. I realized that no matter what SolarCorp's attitude and reputation was back home, in the Barnard System I was working with a bunch of vicious criminals, and I would be tarred with the same brush. It wasn't going to be enough to distance myself from them. I had to stop them before they committed this atrocity against an intelligent species. But how could I do that?"

"And here's the place I admit I used my influence. There was only one person in the whole of Space Arm who had both a chance of believing me and the power to take action quickly enough. I didn't want to involve her, but I knew that if this dragged me down, she would forever be dogged by suspicion anyway. I admit it was a tough sell. She had every right to believe it was some sort of trick, and my past history didn't help me."

He glanced over at Alison and smiled. "Now, you might suspect that she made the same calculations I did and realized she was in it up to her neck already. But I'd like to think that she had enough feelings for the Old Man to believe him when the chips are down. And she and her team came up aces." He stared at the Advocate General. "I understand that a lot of hay has been made on the fact that I was together with her during the action. Sounds nefarious, doesn't it? Well, the truth was, she dragged me out to ground zero to make sure I suffered the consequences of my actions.

"And that's about it, sir."

"Mr. Napoca, do you have any questions?"

The prosecutor stood, a tablet in his hand. "I have records of some interesting movement recently on the Barnard Stock Trading Pool."

240

"I suppose you are referring to certain stock in the SC1 Asteroid Corporation?"

"I am."

"Consisting of about 14% of the total shares?"

"A suspicious number."

"Not if you consider a bunch of former SolarCorp executives trying to put as much distance as they can between themselves and any SolarCorp projects. They wanted nothing to do with Barnard System. I wanted to liquidate my holdings in Sol System. Win/win."

"So you admit to buying this stock."

"I do. I liquidated all my assets on the Sol exchange to pay for it." He turned to the panel. "What that means, gentlemen, is that I have now divested myself of all holdings in the Solar economic system in order to make a place for myself here. Please don't screw this up, or I'm in trouble."

The admiral gave a tight grin. "I assure you, we have no intention of screwing anything up, and your commercial success or failure has little to do with our motivation..." he held up a cautioning hand "...until we consider you the spokesman for a 30% share in one of our major local enterprises, in which case that may not be true, either."

Alison, what is he doing?

You're seeing my father at his best. He has just swung Space Arm into his camp. Look at the prosecutor.

Napoca was not a happy man. "But you admit to influencing your daughter to intercept the mining machine."

"Of course. I had certain knowledge that a catastrophe was about to take place, but because of my position, logic was against me, and I was unable to do anything about it. I submit to you that most officers would have been too suspicious to act with the speed and determination that saved the day. The evidence shows that we arrived on the scene twenty-seven minutes before the bomber did. Only Alison's knowledge of me allowed her to disregard the evidence and make the right choice in time. You can't argue with success."

241

Matteo nudged Alison with his augment. *That was a bad question. He set your father off again. Watch. He won't ask any more.*

"I have no more questions, your honour."

"Mr. Durum? Mr. Regia?"

They both declined.

"In that case I would like to thank the witness for his rather lengthy testimony. While much of it was not germane to the case at hand, it was a bit of an education for all of us, I suspect."

"A pleasure, sir." Rowell nodded to the prosecutor, then Regia, and with a wink to Alison, went back to his seat in the audience.

The admiral glanced at his two cohorts. "Well, that was a long enough session. We have been sent down several paths we must research, so we will adjourn until ten hundred tomorrow, when we will hear the last witness and the final arguments."

Everyone rose, and the captains departed.

Jackson was chuckling as he took her arm.

"What's so funny?"

"I'd like to get your father and Kirstina Zuyeva on opposite sides of an argument."

She frowned. "Kirstina? Why?"

"They both have an amazing talent for organizing the facts so they come to a preordained conclusion."

"Oh. Yes, I suppose. And do you think he did that today?"

"I guess we'll find out tomorrow."

A chill ran through her. "I suppose we will."

* * *

Her own testimony the next day was less difficult than she thought, but did nothing to reassure her of her chances. Napoca took her through her report of the incident, keeping her very strictly to the incidents as written, and only allowing her to explain in places where he thought he had reason to suspect her loyalty. Since her loyalty was never in question in her own mind, she found it

242

relatively easy to answer. How it appeared to the panel, she had no idea.

Then he paused and regarded her with a look that spelled trouble. "Major Rowell, did you recently make a statement in the presence of other Space Arm Officers to the tune of 'to hell with promotion, ambition and all that other crap'?"

A chill ran down her spine. *Who sold me out?* She was so busy with her feeling of betrayal that she did not answer immediately.

"Come on, Major. It wasn't that long ago. Surely you would remember such a blanket statement of disregard for the ideals that Space Arm tries to inculcate in its officers. Did you or did you not call ambition 'crap'?"

She looked at the panel. "Admiral Mira, I don't know how to answer this question. How can a random comment to a group of peers in a bar have application to this trial?"

The admiral regarded her. "This is not a trial, Major Rowell. It is an investigation into your state of mind and your attitude during a difficult time. I would be interested in your opinion."

"Then yes, I did say it. I was talking to a group of ambitious, upwardly-mobile officers, and I was trying to get them to see that there are other things in life besides the blind pursuit of winning."

The prosecutor allowed a smirk of triumph to cross his face. "And did you also say something to the effect that you had good prospects in the commercial world once your term in Space Arm was up?"

She sighed. "Yes, I did say that. I suppose you will use that as evidence that I am not wholeheartedly committed to my career in Space Arm."

"You said it, not me. No more questions, your Honour."

Mira glanced at Regia. "Would you like to redirect?"

The young lawyer sprang to his feet, trying to look enthused. "I am sure my client would like to explain more fully her reaction to a quote taken completely out of context."

All eyes in the room returned to her.

"Yes, I would. The last statement came during a discussion about future possibilities. The point I was making was that advancement in Space Arm wouldn't do me much good in the commercial world if I hadn't also gained some leadership experience. A pilot who spends ten years of his life as a Space Arm junior officer only has experience to allow him to be taxi driver in what some of us would like to call the 'real world.'" Out of the corner of her eye, she could see her father shaking his head, and her anger boiled.

"And my comment about ambition. Drive to win over others is a good thing when held in check by other, better objectives, like loyalty to your unit, determination to do your duty and respect for other officers and their opinions. Unbridled ambition, of the sort that would sell out a friend in the hope of taking her position, has no place in Space Arm Officer Corps. I'm sorry if I offend anyone by saying it, but if the outcome of this hearing means I'm stuck as a major for the rest of my career, so be it, but by the time I'm finished I'll be the best damned major Space Arm has ever seen."

There was silence in the room. Matteo looked around, glanced once more at Alison. "No further questions, sir."

Admiral Mira made one final note on his tablet, then snapped the lid shut. "In that case, we will hear final arguments this afternoon. Then we will adjourn until tomorrow morning. I see no reason to expect a lengthy debate?" He received nods from the two other captains. "Until thirteen hundred hours, then." The panel rose, and the rest of the occupants of the room began to trickle towards the doors.

Alison sat, her heart heavy.

A hand descended on her shoulder. She looked up into her father's face.

He gave a sad smile. "Well, it was a risky gambit. We'll see how it works."

"Gambit?"

"Yes. The 'honest emotion' bit. A good ploy in the civilian courts. I've seen it work time and time again, especially for a female defendant. Not sure how the military will take it, but we can hope."

"It wasn't a gambit, Father. It's how I feel."

"There is a time for honesty as well."

She frowned at him. "I'm glad to hear you say that."

He raised open hands in defence, smiled and turned away.

The final arguments that afternoon were a complete letdown and left her with no further idea what the verdict would be. Each lawyer made basically the same statements he made at the beginning of the hearing, pointing out the evidence that supported his case.

Napoca outlined her main actions, stressing her frame of mind with regards to the interplanetaries in general and SolarCorp in particular. "It is possible she is a tool of the interplanetaries, completely concerned with furthering the projects of her family business, even to the point of using her position in Space Arm in a treasonous manner."

Alison felt a pang of terror. She had to allow that in two different conflicts, she had made previous contact with the perpetrators. *I've been sailing too close to the wind in that respect. Something to remember in the future. If I have one.*

Matteo summarized their main points, ending the same way he began. "My client is a talented and experienced officer, making the best decisions possible, taking into account all the factors involved, and using superior human resources skills and Outback ingenuity to save the day. I hope your panel does not put too much credence in events that did not connect with the incident in question."

Mira nodded. "Thank you, counselor. I might remind you that one of the incidents you brought to our attention yourself, and the other incidents have bearing on her attitude. Should a court martial result, these factors will be key."

With no further ceremony, the hearing adjourned for the day.

She sat staring at her lawyers. "Well. That didn't go as planned."

Faruq frowned. "I don't like the way he rebutted one of the points in a final argument. That's not normal procedure. Do you think he was sending us a message?"

Regia looked miserable. "I guess I shouldn't have brought the kidnap incident into it. But we needed Captain Jones's testimony."

Alison squared her shoulders. "Don't worry about it, lads. We did our best, and win or lose, it will be all over tomorrow."

They mumbled agreement and rose, leaving her to agonize until the verdict was returned the following morning.

She curled up in the protection of Jackson's arms that night, taking what solace she could. "I'm sure glad I don't have any decisions to make right now."

He smoothed her hair. "Why is that?"

"This experience has been so draining. I'm not sure of what the verdict should be anymore, and I'm not sure I care a whole lot. I just want it to be over."

"Then don't go making any decisions, and tomorrow it will be over, you'll be a hero, and everything will be happy again."

"At which point I'd better not make any decisions because of my delirium."

"Precisely. Aren't you glad you have Space Arm and me to take care of you?"

She frowned. "That's what I'm worried about. How is Space Arm going to take care of me? Dump me on the scrap heap?"

He ran his fingers lightly up her arm. "Don't take this the wrong way, but if they do, I hear you have pretty good prospects for a cushy job in the private sector."

She snapped her head around, snatching his thumb between her teeth.

"Now, now. Don't talk with your mouth full. It's not polite."

She laughed and turned the bite into a kiss. "I hope you're enjoying yourself."

"Maybe a little bit, why?"

"Because there's a good chance that's why I'm marrying you. The rest of our life together is going to go like this. I get into trouble, and you provide staunch support while I wiggle my way out of it."

He rested his chin on the top of her head. "Actually, I sort of had it planned that you would go on to do wonderful things while I provided moral support and basked in reflected glory."

"Hmm. Same scenario, different point of view."

"Right." He squirmed his arm underneath her and encircled her waist, holding her firmly. "and tomorrow's going to be one of the glory times. I've been listening and watching. Regia's doing a good job. Mira's on your side; can't you tell? And Napoca just doesn't have that much to go on. There's no jury to be swayed by politics or emotions. These are Space Arm captains, used to taking action like you did. I'm not worried."

She squirmed around to look up at his face. "You're truly not?"

"Definitely." He shrugged. "But then you're smarter than I am. Maybe I'm wrong."

"I don't know if that's funny or not."

Alison entered the courtroom at oh nine forty-five, dressed her sharpest, her back straight, her eyes clear. Jackson strode beside her, comfortable as usual. He glanced down at her. "You look marvellous."

"We'll see what I look like in half an hour."

"Stunningly triumphant, of course."

"I wish I had your confidence."

"You do. You have all my confidence."

"I don't think this is a time for humour, Jackson."

"Of course it is." He stood by while she seated herself between Regia and Faruq, then went to his usual spot in on her eight where she could see him from the corner of her eye. When she glanced back, Captain O'Rourke was beside him, giving her a serious nod.

Soon the three members of the panel entered and sat. She watched them, trying to read their expressions, their body language.

Matteo leaned in closer. "I don't know these guys. Do they look a bit relaxed to you?"

"That's what I thought, but I don't want to read too much into it."

Admiral Mira tapped his gavel on the table, and the room went silent. "Ladies and gentlemen, I have often been chided for my lack of dramatic sense, and I see no reason to change at this time. My co-panelists and I have come to a unanimous decision on all points we have been considering.

She glanced at Matteo *Is that good?*

No idea.

"There are several parts to our ruling, but I will not draw out the suspense." The admiral glanced at his enterpad.

So don't. Tell us!

"Since there were no charges involved, there is no 'guilty or not guilty' verdict. This panel's first and most important task is to state that in the circumstances of the bombing attack on Arborea, we find that Major Alison Rowel acted in accordance with Space Arm regulations and requirements."

Alison reached out and grasped Matteo's hand. He grinned at her.

"However joyful some of you may feel about this, there are several other points I would ask your indulgence to listen to before you celebrate."

Alison's elation disappeared. She stared at Matteo in panic. *What does that mean?*

He shook his head, helpless.

The admiral continued. "In addition to our findings, we feel it important to make several points about Major Rowell's actions and opinions as stated to this board. First, we congratulate Major Rowell on handling a delicate situation with a deft combination of Space Arm policy and Outback common sense. In doing so you have saved the lives of several humans and a large number of other sentient beings.

"Furthermore, although there was never a charge laid against you, as much as it is in our power to do so we absolve you of any responsibility in the deaths of the two SolarCorp pilots. It is the opinion of the board that their own company had most probably decided to remove them as potential witnesses, and your preventing them from committing their crime had no effect on their fates."

Then the admiral turned his stare on George Rowell. "And our panel has another recommendation. While we have no jurisdiction over the civilian legal situation, we feel it important to note that Mr. George Rowell acted in a way that saved sentient lives in accordance with Space Arm objectives, and, if no new information arises, we recommend no charges be brought against him in civilian court."

Alison turned to find her father. He caught her eye, made a brow-wiping gesture, and smiled. She returned the smile and faced front again.

"However, Mr. Rowell, we would like to remind you that the Space Arm protects its own. No one here has any doubt that your daughter's cool and intelligent action in protecting those beings saved your reputation in the process. We assume that you plan to continue your life in this system. We recommend that you take no action in the coming years to endanger the future of one of our best officers, no matter how advantageous it might seem to your commercial interests at the time."

Rowell stood. "Admiral Mira, I think it's quite obvious from the content of this hearing that my days of trying to influence my daughter's behaviour are long over. I will be quite happy to trail behind her from now on, basking in reflected glory."

Alison kept her best straight face. *He's at it again, already.*

Matteo grinned. *Doesn't waste much time, does he?*

Yeah. Be nice to him. He'll be looking for a good lawyer, soon. It always happens.

Do I want to work for him?

Sure. He pays well and on time. But pick and choose your cases. If you go on a retainer, it's a slippery slope.

To riches and sleepless nights.

Give the lad a kewpie doll.

The admiral cleared his throat, and the buzz of conversation stopped. "It is our further intent to comment on a certain portion of Major Rowell's testimony."

Alison glanced at Matteo, who held up an open hand and shook his head.

Mira raised his voice. "This has to do with the usefulness of ambition in Space Arm officers. Major Rowell has reached the stage of her career where she realizes that there are other qualities necessary to good leadership over and above the ability to gain power. Once you have reached where your ambition drives you, there is the small matter of how you fill the rank you have earned. If a young officer has spent so much time and thought on how to climb the promotion ladder that he thinks telling tales on a fellow officer demonstrates leadership, most of us can see where that officer's career is headed. Or not headed."

The admiral closed his tablet and looked straight at the official record camera. "And now, since the record of these proceedings will be made available to the press, let me state categorically that Barnard System is firmly under the control of its citizens and the Planetary Community. There is no place for Wild West tactics such as those attempted by members of the SolarCorporation. While we take no part in commercial regulation, Space Arm will assess with a fine-toothed comb any further action by the SolarCorporation in this system. Thank you all for your time in this important matter."

Dinner that night was at Emilio's, the best restaurant on the plaza, and Jackson intimated that his expense account would stretch to cover the cost. After a brief congratulation, Ambassador Pretoro declined to join them, as did Alison's two Marine "escorts," who said they didn't want to intrude. Noting the glances that passed between them, she suspected they had other ways to enjoy civilization before heading back to work on Arborea in two days.

Jackson and Alison showed up early. She looked around as the human waiter brought them in. Dim lighting, real art work on the walls, secluded tables and quiet music. But a table for six with no one else there. "What's going on?"

He grinned. "I told them all to come later. Wanted you to myself for a moment."

She sat down and ran a hand along his leg. "Any special reason?"

"Yeah. I've been working on my imaging. What do you think of this?"

A passable VR image of the arctic regions of the planet seemed to appear on the table before them. The colours were pale, but the details sharp.

"Not bad. A geography lesson as part of our celebration?"

"Do you appreciate the geological and meteorological significance of this region?"

She frowned. "Not in my skill set, I'm afraid. Enlighten me."

"We have mountains. We have cold. We have no change of seasons."

"A lousy place to live, in my books. What does it mean to you?"

"Ski season all year round. Hockey, curling, sleigh rides behind teams of mooseys. Maybe the barwolves would pull people on sleds, just for the fun of it. Can you imagine being in a sled race where you were in gestalt with your team?"

"You're talking a resort project."

"This is the only planet in the whole system where people can access the open air. The Arctic Islands are designated a human/barwolf interface area. It's perfect."

She placed a finger across his lips. "And you're looking for an excuse to lose a couple more teeth."

"Oh, no. Now that I'm a diplomat, I must be concerned with my image. I'll wear a face shield and a mouth guard. But I will play hockey again!"

"Hmm. Did you know I was a passable figure skater until I grew too tall?"

"You were? Why didn't you tell me?"

"What, and give you another weapon in your campaign to overwhelm me with our affinities?"

He turned to look at her and frowned. "Why am I getting the feeling that all along you were letting me chase you until you caught me?"

She gave him a sweet smile. "Whatever gave you that impression?"

"I dunno. I've been learning about that Occam guy you talk about so much."

"In any case, I am suspicious of your reason for this lesson at such an inappropriate time."

"Well, I was just running some ideas of a place to go for our honeymoon…"

"I see. Now that I've set my criminal past behind me, you consider me an appropriate wife for a budding diplomat?"

He smiled. "You could put it that way."

"I prefer not to. I'd sooner have romantic declarations of love and undying devotion. But I suppose that's a little over the top. I'll take the approval. It's likely to be worth more in the long run."

"Now who's being unbearable?"

"You'll get used to the burden. You've got years."

A voice sounded behind them. "Are we intruding?"

Alison turned, "Ah! The triumphant lawyers. No, come have a seat."

"Thanks." Matteo grinned as the two bumped fists around the table and sat. "Well! That was really something, wasn't it? I can't believe we took a case in front of a Space Arm Administrative Hearing and actually won!"

"I'm rather glad you did, too."

"Oh, I'm sorry you had to go through that, but..." he stumbled. "I don't want you to feel I took advantage..."

She laid a hand on his sleeve. "It's all right, Matteo. I was joking. There had to be a hearing. I'm glad my lawyer was you." She turned to Faruq. "And you were right about the Space Arm angle. Every time."

Their smiles returned, and they got down to ordering the meal. While they were having an appetizer, another intruder appeared. "May I sit a moment?"

Alison kept from frowning. "Mr. Napoca. Of course."

He gave a polite smile as he pulled out a chair. "I just had to congratulate the winning lawyers." He stretched out a hand.

Somewhat flustered, Matteo shook. "Oh. Well...thank you."

The older man nodded. "We will meet again, I'm sure. Perhaps you won't be so lucky next time."

The young lawyer sat straighter. "Are you insinuating that luck had anything to do with it?"

"Of course it did. You were lucky enough to have an innocent client."

"You knew she was innocent?"

"I thought she probably was. You know how it goes."

"Of course. You had to do your best to make sure the law and the people were served."

"And in this case, the objectives of the Space Arm."

Alison twisted to face him directly. "And what objectives were those?"

Now the lawyer's smile widened. "Perhaps the necessity of clearing you of charges, so the admiral could enter into the record all those nice things he said about you."

She put on a frown. "...and now the part I'm not going to like?"

"Space Arm had a message to send to the citizens of Barnard System."

Matteo tilted his head. "What message was that?"

Now Napoca burst out laughing. "The one you gave them, of course."

"Oh, that."

Alison grabbed her lawyer's wrist. "Just what's going on, here?"

The lad sighed. "I suppose you had to know. The Co-op Board held a meeting before I decided to take the case. Everyone agreed that there was something going on. There had to be an investigation, to make sure everything went down as it seemed. But why ask for a miner lawyer? It didn't add up."

"But I asked for you. I wanted you because what I did was based on the Outback way of doing things. I knew you would understand, and hoped you could interpret it in legal terms for Space Arm. We're at a delicate balance, here, between the old ways and…"

Matteo put his hand on her arm. "And that's exactly what Space Arm needed. A venue to broadcast to every Outbacker that they were listening and adapting. Which is why I gave that speech. Couldn't you tell how happy Admiral Mira was? Letting the defence lawyer testify as a friend of the court!" He turned to Napoca. "If you want to appeal the verdict, there's your first cause right there, and I'll give you that for free."

"Because you know I won't. I took a hit for the team, and I have no complaints."

"You mean you never really wanted to convict me?"

"I did if you were guilty, but I figured you weren't. No, Major, that was the show trial of the decade for the Barnard System, and you'll go down in the history books as the hero of the little people."

She sat straighter. "I don't mind going down in history as saving a bunch of sentient beings. I don't want to be known for a bunch of political hype."

"Who says it's hype? If I had been prosecuting you in a Sol System court, I guarantee you'd have had a much tougher time. Count your blessings, cash in your chips and chalk it up to good luck." Their meals were arriving, so he rose. "And once again, congratulations to all three of you. It was a tough experience, and you played your roles well." He smiled and strolled off.

She stared at Matteo. "Why didn't you tell me?"

His mouth turned down. "I couldn't, really. You were on trial and I was trying to save you. That was the main thing. I don't care about the politics. I just wanted you to be all right."

She smiled and patted his hand. "And I am. You did a great job of my defence, as well. Let others judge the success of the politics."

His smile returned and he addressed his meal. "Say, this is a real rack of lamb. Bones and all!"

She sighed. "And the champagne is courtesy of my father. He's happy I won, but didn't want to intrude. How am I going to deal with that man?"

They continued with the meal, but Matteo and Faruq, aware that they were excess baggage, soon left the two alone together, saying they had a few friends to look up and brag at.

She rubbed Jackson's hand where it lay on the table. "You haven't said much."

"Nothing to say. It was pretty frustrating, not being able to do anything. Except report to Alfino, of course."

"He was keeping track of it, wasn't he?"

"Couldn't be seen interfering, but he was right on top of it. He wanted it to go well, too, you know."

"For political reasons."

"For your sake as well. For some reason he likes you. Can't think why."

"Probably because I keep you out of his hair." She glanced at him. "And speaking of the political angle, do we have any idea what's going to happen to SolarCorp?"

He shook his head. "We're small potatoes in that stew. SolarCorp dumped all its assets into the Arborea plots. They basically don't exist in the Sol System anymore. If the Planetary Community follows its past practice, the assets of the perpetrators will be directed towards the good of the victims.

"The barwolves and the colonists."

"Exactly. As I understand it, the tractor ship was under contract, so it will turn around and find a cargo going back to Sol. If Dr. Pretoro has anything to say about it, the mining equipment will be turned over to the Barwolf Collective."

"That would be appropriate. What about the habitat module?"

Jackson grinned. "Now, there he's being really sly. He wants the government to assign it to the Arborean Collective."

"There's no such animal."

"There isn't, yet."

"Aha. But sooner or later the human and barwolf populations will have to create some kind of cooperative government. He's just forcing the timeline."

"Exactly. And Alfino has plenty of support in high places."

"When is this all going to happen?"

He shrugged. "As I said, the court case is a big deal. A major corporation accused of an act of terrorism? It's likely to swing the government-interplanetary balance. Best guess is several years."

Alison grinned. "Then we don't have to solve it all in the next ten minutes. Are we finished, here?"

He regarded the mayhem on the table. "Done all the damage we can."

"Then let's go to your rooms. I've appreciated the cuddling this week, but now that it's all over..."

He rose with alacrity, holding out his hand. "Let's not waste valuable time."

25. PARENTAL ADVICE

She only had two days left at the embassy, and she wanted to spend as much time as she could with Jackson, because the moment they hit dirt in Arborea, they were both back to work. However, he had meetings, and she had some unavoidable responsibilities.

As she was straightening his tie the second morning, she kissed his cheek and gave him a twisted grin. "Wish me luck."

He ran a finger over her lips. "You rarely need luck, but whatever. What's going on?"

"I'm meeting with my father this morning."

"And this requires luck because...?"

"Because he's waited just about long enough after the hearing to let me get settled. Now he'll be moving on to his next project."

"Hmm. Which you don't want to have anything to do with."

"Damn right I don't. I was listening to what the admiral said in his verdict. That was directed at me, too. My best plan is to focus on my Space Arm duties to the exclusion of everything else."

"No argument, here." He slipped an arm around her waist. "As long as you have time for a life."

"As much time as I can manage."

They stopped in the doorway. "Time for a decent kiss."

She grinned. "Or indecent, as the case may be."

A considerable time later they straightened their clothing and left his apartment.

Her inner glow faded as she watched his bulky figure retreat down the corridor. Then she straightened her shoulders and headed for the Wolf's Den.

The place was almost empty, as might be expected at this time of the morning, but her father was already there, a colourful fruit drink in his hand. He looked up as she approached. "Hello, dear. Have a seat. Drink?"

"Coffee sounds good."

He paused to contact the service robot, then put his elbows on the table and regard her over folded hands. "Well, we got out of that one nicely."

She raised her eyebrows and waited.

"All right. You got us out of that one beautifully. The admiral is a big fan of yours, isn't he?"

"The only reason an admiral knows a mere major is because I could have caused him some trouble but I didn't. He'll now file me somewhere with the other ten thousand spacers under his command and go about his business."

"Until he needs someone with your skills again. Then he'll remember."

"I'm not counting on it. You heard what he said. My best career move right now is to keep my head down and my nose clean. Which is what I'm going to do."

He took a sip of his drink, watching her over the rim of the glass. "Quite right. But that doesn't stop you from having a life of your own."

"Having a life and a Space Arm career are sometimes mutually exclusive activities."

"But surely you'll have time for a few small projects?"

She sighed and put down her coffee cup without getting a sip. "Father, both of us know you mean a few small projects of yours, and I'm telling you flat out that the answer is, no. Getting involved in another of your schemes right now would be career suicide."

"I don't mean involvement. Couldn't you just advise me from time to time?"

There's no way I'm getting out of this until I let him make his pitch. She sat back in her most uncompromising pose. "What did you have in mind, Father?"

"It's this way. If I was about to launch a project and I needed some advance knowledge about how Space Arm was going to react to that project, I wonder if there was some unofficial route I could take…?" He tilted his head to one side, gazing at her.

"…without actually breaking the law."

"Of course I don't want to break the law. I just want to find a small weak spot I can peek through. Can you think of one?"

"Hmm…that would be an interesting question."

Her father regarded her with his usual superior look. "That doesn't sound like the razor-sharp mind I trained."

She set down her cup. "Father, you didn't train me to have a razor-sharp mind." She rode over his protest. "You trained me to see every situation from a single point of view: the same one you have. You trained me to start with, "What's in it for me?" and then to interpret all the data through that filter, ignoring anything else. And you know what? It worked."

"Of course it did."

"That's right. It got me to be one of the youngest, greenest, and least prepared squadron leaders in the whole Space Arm."

"What?"

"Look, in case you weren't listening to my testimony, this is how it goes down in the military. If you play the promotion game and excel at everything they ask, you top out at about Lieutenant or Major grade. You're a robot that follows orders. But no initiative, no ability to improvise outside the usual political games. You're basically a bureaucrat. No leadership skills above a certain level, and unless you have friends in high places, that's where you stay."

"That's probably true in many cases."

She regarded him. "Do you know who Toni Jacobs is?"

"She helped you on the barwolf rescue. Is there a reason why I should?"

"No, there isn't. She's a nobody. When I met her, she was a Commando, a lieutenant just like me. From no family, with no background, no fancy education."

"And why do you bring her into this conversation?"

"Because for the last two years we have been working together, and every time an emergency arises, she's the one who leads. She comes up with the best solution faster than anyone else. She thinks outside the box. She listens to her crew. She takes into account both short-term and long-term consequences. She intuitively puts the right people into the right places to get the job done."

"So, she's a genius."

"She isn't. By any test you want to use, I'm smarter than she is. But she's a leader. She never thinks of the effect of any action on herself. She thinks about the team. And I follow along, because it works. You know something? I got promoted to Major six months before she did, and I still looked to her before I made a decision, just in case she had another idea. It only happened one time; I followed her suggestion, and it saved three lives. That's the kind of person I want to be."

Her father shrugged. "It sounds like an honourable objective."

She regarded him, frowning. "You make honourable sound like a dirty word."

"Beyond the usual expectations of polite society, I never found it to be much use to me."

She nodded. "And that's why whatever it is that you want me to do, I won't." She gave a wry smile. "In fact, I'm going to follow your precepts for once. I'm looking out for myself. I watched your face as Admiral Mira was reading you the riot act. You didn't believe a word of it. So you look into my eyes right now and believe what you are hearing. You and your edge-of-the-law buddies think about what happened to the last bunch that tried to turn me into a puppet."

"I've been meaning to talk to you about that…"

"But you're not going to. We have already dealt with it as far as I am willing to go. Space Arm works on a 'need to know' basis, and the last thing I need or want to know is how much my father had to do with the illegal kidnapping and torture of members of a sentient species. Are we clear on that?"

"But…"

She stood and towered over him. "Are we clear?"

He turned aside and twirled his drink, looking up at her. "Certainly. I'll never mention it again. That suits me, in fact."

"I'm sure it does. Now, is this meeting over?"

He stared a moment. "I didn't consider this anything official. Just getting together with my daughter for a chat."

"Well, we've had our get-together and reorganized our relationship in a satisfactory manner. Now, unless you had anything else to tell me, I have a busy schedule. There's some changes coming, and whether they affect Barwolf Base or not, there's a lot to arrange."

"Oh? What is it this time?"

"Need to know, Father. You don't." She turned and strode out of the room, not looking back. As she walked her emotions calmed, and a feeling of satisfaction eased through her. *That went rather well.*

Yes, it certainly did.

She stopped in her tracks. *Captain O'Rourke?*

Sorry for listening in. Been having trouble with your new organics again?

I thought I had them pretty well under control. It's been several months, but they are far more powerful than I'm used to. Did I slip?

You were broadcasting rather loudly. And usefully as it happens.

Usefully? What's going on?

Why don't you drop around to NightHawk? We're on docking ring B. No reason we can't be comfortable.

Be there in a moment.

She turned down the next corridor, picking up her pace. *Not sure I'm in a hurry to hear this, but it doesn't do to keep a superior officer waiting.*

When she entered the ship's chartroom, Natalia waved her to a seat. "Pull up a chair. This won't take long."

She sat, regarding O'Rourke.

The other woman didn't seem upset or worried. She steepled her fingers and stared at them. "Admiral Mira asked me to have a chat with you before you went back on duty."

Alison's heart sank. "What about?"

"Just the usual ramble about your career, your progress, your ambitions."

"Oh." She regarded the captain's demeanour. "Has something new come up?"

"Not especially. It is the opinion of the Higher-Ups that you are making reasonable, steady progress."

"May I assume that's good?"

"In my opinion, yes. I'm always hesitant about shooting stars. Sometimes it happens because of a lucky coincidence of talent, attitude and opportunity. More often it's a careful application of system manipulation skills."

"What do you mean?"

"What you were doing that got you the assignment to Barnard's System. Climbing the ladder."

"I was?"

"Of course you were. All young officers do that. It's expected." She grinned. "Demonstrates ambition."

"Oh." Natalia seemed to be waiting, so she thought that over. "You watched the hearing...?"

"I scanned through the testimony. You made some good points. Some officers can never see past the ladder. Ironically, those are the ones that find themselves stalled on it, because ambition is all they have. We have to watch that sort, because if they don't become resigned to their lot, they start looking around for other ways to progress. Some of those ways are not good for either their careers or the objectives of the Space Arm."

"That sounds logical."

"You are remembering that I caught a certain amount of your rather heated exchange with your father a moment ago."

"Where I demonstrated how I felt on the subject." She thought back to the conversation. "And gave out a lot of other details."

"Which we were already aware of because of your testimony at the hearing. You've made up your mind."

"I was lucky, you know."

The Captain tilted her head. "In what way?"

"The bait was dangled in front of me at exactly the wrong time. I didn't know my career was in danger of stalling, and I was just beginning to make some serious steps forward in leadership skills, applying my abilities to the betterment of my squadron and the wider group I was involved with. The experience of leading a team to success is heady brew. Solo achievement is sort of hollow by comparison."

Natalia rubbed her hands together, then reached into a drawer and withdrew a bottle and two glasses. "And that pretty much sums it up."

"It does?"

The captain grinned and poured. "When you walked in, I already knew you were on the path. You told Admiral Mira at the hearing and you just told me over again."

"The path to where?"

O'Rourke raised her glass, and they drank. "Who knows? You have the right skills, the right attitude, and are in the right theatre of operations. Probably your own command of a larger vessel, relatively soon. Above that, only time will tell." She sipped again and regarded the pilot over the rim of her glass. "Admiral Rowell sound good to you?"

Alison frowned. "I suppose." Then she met the other woman's eyes. "You know, if you'd asked me that two years ago my answer would have been instant and enthusiastic. Now, I'm not so sure. Who knows if I'd make a good admiral? Even now, I have little idea of the skill set, and no idea of how many of those abilities I have or might acquire." She sat back. "No, I have no problem working towards a proper command. After that, I'm willing to wait and see."

THE END

If you enjoyed this book, please do the author and other readers a favour. Go to Amazon or another online retailer and give it a review. Even a star rating would be nice.

Brought up in a logging camp with no electricity, Gordon Long learned his storytelling in the traditional way: at his father's knee. He now spends his time editing, publishing, travelling, blogging and writing Fantasy, Sci-Fi and Social Commentary, although sometimes the boundaries blur.

Gordon lives in Tsawwassen, British Columbia, with his wife, Linda, and their Nova Scotia Duck Tolling Retriever, Josh. When he is not writing and publishing, he works on projects with the Surrey Seniors' Planning Table and is a staff writer for <indiesunlimited.com>

MORE FROM GORDON A. LONG

Available at Online Retailers

"Factory 4-80" Freighty Novels 1
"Outback Rebellion" Freighty Novels 2
"Asimov's Laws" Freighty Novels 3

"Ocean of Grass" Petrellan Saga 1
"Waves of Stone" Petrellan Saga 2
"Path of Water" Petrellan Saga 3
"Zoysana's Choice" Petrellan Saga 4
"The Innkeeper's Husband" Petrellan Saga 5
"Mercenary's Dream" Petrellan Saga 6

"Out of Mischief" World of Change Book 1
"Into Trouble" World of Change Book 2
"Mountains of Mischief" World of Change Book 3
"The Trouble with Tents" World of Change Book 4
"Queen of Mischief" World of Change Book 5

"A Sword Called...Kitten?" Romantic Comedy with an Edge
"The Cat with Many Claws" Sword Called Kitten Book 2
"Cloud Cat" a Sword Called Kitten Book
"Why Are People So Stupid?" Social Humour with a Point

Look for Gordon's books, selected reviews, poetry and short
stories at <airbornpress.ca>
Gordon's opinions on humanity are at the
"Are People Stupid?" blog
Find his weekly reviews and his ideas on writing at
"Renaissance Writer"

www.ingramcontent.com/pod-product-compliance
Lightning Source LLC
Chambersburg PA
CBHW060623260626
47161CB00008B/2791